REGENTS OF THE DEEP

Book One

The Beginning

Patrick James Blair

REGENTS OF THE DEEP

Book One

The Beginning

A catalogue record of this book is available from the National Library of New Zealand. First published 2012.

Design and layout: www.driftwooddesign.co.nz

ISBN: 978-0-473-28585-2

www.patrickjamesblair.com

About the Author

This former pilot, soldier, rancher and hotelier has journeyed from his rural place of birth and harsh upbringing, to cramped cockpits in the skies over South East Asia, flying over the tropical killing fields of Vietnam, frequenting tawdry bars and meeting intriguing characters while experiencing the wild side of life in the South Pacific.

Now, living in a peaceful villa located in the isolated South Island of New Zealand, Patrick James Blair allows an imagination honed sharp by years of living on the edge come alive.

Contents

REGENTS OF THE DEEP

Book One

The Beginning

Prologue

The Great God Poseidon called his beloved Regents of the Deep to gather. As he moved amongst them, he revealed the future and told of the many tasks he would undertake. He spoke of how and why Atlantis was to be no more, and gave hint of a great journey the Regents would embark upon…

It was with a sorrow laden voice that Poseidon spoke: "I am to destroy this place you have called home for all of known time; for those who dwell therein have turned against me. But be not afraid, for I, your only God, will help you find the new world that is to be your new home."

With those words to his Regents of the Deep, Poseidon turned to the heavens and raising his hands towards his heavenly home, he did move the stars into a zodiac of thirteen houses.

Once this task was completed, he turned back to his beloved ones and spoke again… "Prepare to depart from this place; you must go within the time it takes the light of day to pass three times. In this allotted time, let the wisest ones of you study the new heavens, for what I have written and prophesied therein this day will guide you and all those who follow on from you for a time that knows no end."

Before this loving God sent his Regents from their place of tranquillity he did gather up the very youngest and did hold them to his breast; so they were blessed. Thus began an odyssey that started in the calm waters of the Bay of Shallows and, as time would dictate, did embrace both the known and unknown worlds.

And so, in time, it came to pass that this heavenly divinity kept his word, and Atlantis fell to the promised deeds of this mighty God.

The Main Characters

Zen, the grandson of the King, a lovable scout who rises quickly through the ranks, then when the Assembly faces its greatest challenges, he is thrust to the fore. He will need the wisdom of the ages, for every decision the Great Assembly expects of him will have a hidden crown of thorns.

Hur, only son of widowed **Dy**, always has something more important to do than learn the lessons the teachers scan in each day – "I will catch up, I promise" – his words at times have a hollow ring to them.

The beautiful **Lute** with her flirtatious body and flashing black eyes, but those eyes are for her one and only great love.

The absent-minded **Time Weaver**, always forgetting who he is or even where he is. His scantily clad **Nymph** always has to remind him that he is the Time Weaver, and a Master Time Weaver at that.

The **Master War Lord**, whose fists are fired by fury… "his first strike ripped open the porcelain white face of Ming Lee sending blood cascading down in a river of red."

Mio who refused to let the cancer that riddled her body distract her from the teachings of the creed.

The **Sand People,** and many more… as the Weaver of Time weaves time.

The Assembly

1

Uninterrupted, the meeting of the Great Council of Elders had been in progress for some two days. The slowly circulating steel-grey- and white-bodied group rose en masse to break the ocean's surface, and in so doing, cast themselves into full view of the heavens. Then, just as quickly, they vanished into the deeps beneath the tasselled blue waters of the zephyr-lashed sea.

This Great Council of Elders, comprised of fifty of the wisest and most honoured of their time, had been called to serve by the greater community. As was demanded, these chosen ones had each shown an inner strength and fortitude that had endured the hard rigours of time. These few had been further gifted with a level of intelligence to undertake the training that had elevated them to the fifth order of their creed.

The governing body of this most enlightened and gifted Great Council of Elders was divided into five councils. From each of these councils, two members unanimously selected by their fellow members undertook the further training in the higher levels of their doctrine that encompassed the sixth order, and so were promoted to the rank of Council Master. From this select group, when time decreed, those so chosen and prepared were further elevated to the ruling body of the Inner Sanctum.

The ten members who made up the Inner Sanctum, having completed training to the seventh order, had bestowed upon them the prestigious rank of Senator.

Then, according to the time-honoured mandate, through a process of rituals and heavenly readings, one of these Senators was endorsed by his fellows, and thus became the Great Leader and appropriately named The Most Wise One of the eighth order. The premier office of The Most Wise One, with its accompanying honours, was treated with high reverence by all those of the Great Assembly, and regarded as their direct link to those of the heavenly dwellings.

This creed and its developmental process that dated back to the dawning of all time had been taught by degrees through many passes to all those who dwelt in the Assembly. And it had been so written in the creed that only those few who possessed the abilities to obtain the higher levels of learning were allowed to progress on to the highest of rank, thereby ensuring only the intellectually strongest of the strong had access to the keys of knowledge that unlocked the intellect to the distinguished and final degree – and the very pinnacle of leadership.

Out a distance of four sigmar from the Great Council's place of meeting, fifteen of the Assembly's finest scouts led by Scout Leader Mio, daughter of Senator Ku, circled the Great Council. The task bestowed upon her and her scouts was to intercept and escort the departure of all but those with the appropriate credentials. There was no tolerance for any strays that breached the ultrasonic protection barrier the scouts had placed around the Great Council of Elders.

The rapid rise of Mio to the position of Scout Leader of the Second Order had surprised many. The Great Council of Elders recognised her abilities – her dedication to learning and devotion to the creed had enhanced her reputation. Having reached the first order quickly, her promotion to a position of leadership in the second order was most welcomed by all in the Assembly, for it was most unwise to ever question the wisdom of a Senate endorsement. Scout Leader Mio, whose sharp wit, sympathetic ear, and strong disposition were beyond her tender age, encouraged many of the younger generation to solicit her counsel. The distinction of being promoted, and then appointed Scout Leader, Protector to the Great Council of Elders for this very prodigious occasion, was a fitting tribute, and a tiara of distinction.

Three sigmar to the east, under the watchful eyes of The Learned Ones, the teachers in the Assembly went about their duties of enlightening their pupils with the knowledge and awareness that had been given unto them by The Learned Ones. Those of the Assembly known as The Learned Ones were the holders of the great storehouse of knowledge and the chronicles of history. They passed on what they had received from The Learned Ones that had gone before them. So it was that the creed was taught and remembered.

Tai, third son of Senator Ark, had been trained to the fourth order and demonstrated that being blind from birth was no hindrance. He was now well established into his third duty as teacher. This was a task he relished: quenching the thirst of the many eager young minds that abounded. Tai's small body was more than compensated for by his great passion for teaching the young. This endearing quality placed him in a position of high esteem with The Learned Ones. That group of six, whose intellect held all records, knew of all things from the beginning of time. Their most senior, The Most Learned One, was revered and at times even feared by all. Moving through the Assembly, his foreboding dark features with deeply penetrating eyes ripped bare any outer façade and lay one's inner soul open for his inspection. As spiritual leader of the Assembly, he held the position to the right of The Most Wise One.

Teacher Tai enjoyed his given tasks, scanning the day's lessons into the sponge-like young minds as they swarmed in close – eager minds not wanting to miss a scan. Tai and his pupils were oblivious to the gathering events that would soon unfold and bring with them changes that not even those of great learning could comprehend.

Two sigmar to the west, the nursery was its usual hive of activity. One hundred and thirty-two infants had to be nourished and cared for. Some of the birth mothers who had been given rest from their daily responsibilities swam freely, leaping clear of the surface in aerial acrobatics displays, and then plunging deep into the cold blue waters as they enjoyed their unbridled freedom. While they swam freely, relishing their short-lived liberty, the care-giving matrons and those on assignment duties took charge, moving about in their methodical manner, providing nourishment with their warm rich milk, and tending with affection to all the ones so young.

Dy, widowed mother of Hur, was one of the more specialised matrons. Her skills had been recruited to the confinement area – her responsibility was for the delivery of the newborns: taking them from the mother's birth canal and, with her help, guiding them to the surface for their first breath of life-giving air. Her tasks this day were made more difficult by a nagging concern for her son who was about to depart on his fourth assignment to the long-range patrol under the command of a newly appointed Scout Leader.

Her state of mind did not relate to the new leader's abilities, but to the fact that she felt this should have been the first command of her son, Hur. He should have been the one promoted. Why, she had demanded of the Great Council of Elders, had they not rewarded Hur with this posting? Why had Hur been denied the chance to prove himself? His failure at the second order level should not have been held against him. He had studied hard, but had been unwell on the morning of the exam. Dy mentally pleaded her son's case as she tried in vain to vindicate her wayward son to herself.

Of late – as in the past – the Senate's advice to Dy had fallen on deaf ears. Dy refused to listen to the Council – or for that matter to anyone – where her son was concerned. Dy was convinced that what she had heard as rumour and other whispering was nothing more than unfounded malice, and she condemned those who spread it. Her Hur was not bad-tempered, nor was he hot-headed, and Dy flatly refused to believe her son would rush into a situation without first considering all the consequences of his actions.

It was determined that justification for the Great Council of Elder's recommendations to the Senate need not be explained to Hur or to his mother, Dy. The Most Wise One decided it was in the best interest of all that Hur, at this time, not be given the new command and that he again be passed over for promotion. This decision created a heavy sentiment of disaffection between Dy, the Council of Elders, and The

Most Wise One.

Dy and Hur were called before the Senators the following day to hear an explanation of why Hur's functioning and demeanour was again being challenged. However, this only served to further alienate them from the Senators, and put both mother and son on a collision course with all – a position that was beginning to jeopardise their standing within the Assembly. In itself, this was the onset of a deviation from that fine line of the all-important teachings of the Creed.

Four sigmar to the south, the main body of the two thousand inhabitants in the Assembly went about their daily tasks. Some slept by first shutting down the right side's systems and resting on the surface in a type of alerted sleep, and then after a time, repeating the same process on the left side. Some played, stalking each other over and under the water or chasing branches of kelp that were wrenched from the sea-bed, tossed into the air, and then used for friendly games of tug-of-war. Others studied to enhance their progress up through the higher orders and degrees of their Creed, scanning in and absorbing the brain pattern transmissions of the Teachers.

Those who imparted the knowledge bequeathed their lessons of wisdom, legendary lore, and founding principles of the Creed from its inception in the great zodiac to its development on Earth. The elders of the Assembly amused themselves by reliving memories of long ago with stories and deeds of past Most Wise Ones.

A large number of the juvenile males, those as yet too young to be given daily tasks, or those who had completed the day's learning, grouped together on the outer fringes of the great Assembly needing the unobstructed expanse for the boisterous games they played. They bumped and pushed each other, diving to great depths then turning and leaping high into the air only to crash flat on their sides, trying with great gusto to out-perform each other in the effort to see who could make the greatest splash. They endeavoured to impress the many young females that clustered together, chattering as they watched the young bachelors show off. The females themselves were not above flaunting their flashing eyes and streamlined bodies in flirtatious passes, albeit against all that had been taught to them regarding proper female behaviour and conduct.

Those members of the Assembly assigned to the victuals had to have their numbers increased for this day. All those drafted in had been trained in the higher perfection of scanning, as the ever-widening search for food progressed and took them further away from the Assembly. It was the task of the Food Scouts (as they were known) to seek out the schools of mullet that entered the Bay to feed, and to use their ultrasonic sound waves to drive the fish towards the Assembly. Once in close proximity to the Assembly, these schools of terrified fish were surrounded.

Then, as the Food Scouts' ultrasonic sound bands tightened, the thrashing fish were forced into an ever decreasing circle to a point where the ball of thrashing fish was so dense it extended up from the water in a mass of flashing silver bodies. Then, on signal in a practised order, the Assembly fed. The older, more frail of the Assembly fed first; they were followed by those from the nursery, then by the youngsters, in a learning curve under the guidance of the teachers, followed by the remainder of the Assembly.

Zen, third son of Ira, grandson of Senator Zoa, and great grandson of the Most Wise One, was enjoying some time alone. He was cutting the rolling swells with ease, and as was becoming more the norm, his mind was again preoccupied with Lute.

"Scout Commander Zen! Scout Commander Zen!" The incoming message from a Senate Runner snapped Zen back to reality.

"Yes, runner. How can I help?" Zen asked of the runner as they broke the water in unison.

"The Senator of Security, Senator Ku, has requested that you present yourself before him."

With a nod of acknowledgement, Zen dismissed the Senate Runner and made his way towards the inner sanctum.

"Challenge! Challenge!"

The first challenges went unheard by Zen.

"Challenge!"

The third and sharpest challenge rebuke broke Zen's mental wanderings. Get your mind on the tasks at hand; get your mind off Lute, Zen mentally reprimanded himself. "Challenge acknowledged!" Zen scanned back to the Outer Ring Guard.

"Err… Scout Commander Zen, what brings you to the Senate?"

"Zuke, you old fossil! How be it that you have not been sent to the pod of the aged?" Zen scanned back at the approaching Outer Ring Guard.

Before the old Outer Ring Guard had time to read and respond to Zen's scan, and knowing full well that to get into a conversation with old Zuke was a lot easier than it was to get out of, Zen sent back. "Senator Ku has requested I present myself before him in due haste."

"So it is, so it is. Pass, my young friend." With that the old Outer Ring Guard Zuke turned away, disappointed that his young friend had to move on so quickly.

Hearing the scans of the old guard's muttering, "no one wants to stop and talk – always in a hurry," Zen noted that he really had to take time when next passing to endure a little time with old Zuke.

Zen quickly moved through the outer ring of guards and scanned the Inner Sanctum of Senators looking for his appointment.

"The Senator is here, Scout Commander Zen." The incoming scan from the Senator's runner called Zen to alter course to the furthermost corner of the Inner Sanctum.

"The Senator will see you now." Again the scan of the Senator's runner called to Zen in its monotone drone.

"Scout Commander Zen! It is great to see you again."

"The pleasure is mine, Senator Ku – entirely mine, I assure you." Zen felt the warmth of the Senator, who had always been one of his favourites, as the two Regents of the Deep swam in unison.

"Since I recalled all the scouts some time ago..." the Senator started, then stopped as if in deep thought before he continued, "... the majority of Senators think it most wise that these patrols be resumed at the earliest. And I, for one, who spoke out and stated at the time that it was not in the best interest of our safety that these patrols be halted..." Again the Senator seemed to hesitate as if choosing his words carefully.

Zen kept silent, waiting for the Senator to gather his thoughts.

After a lengthy silence, the Senator continued, "The Senate has, therefore, instructed that the Great Assembly should not be left in the position of having no scouts out on patrol. With their thoughts to the fore, I am here to pass on the Senate's instruction that you, Commander Zen, go and gather together the best available scouts and support and prepare them for the resumption of the long-range patrols."

"Commander? You called me Commander, Senator Ku. Pray, let me correct you; if you please, the rank bestowed on me by the Senate is only that of Scout Commander."

Senator Ku turned to the young Zen. "Let me correct you, Commander Zen. Commander Zen it is."

Zen was somewhat taken aback by the turn of events. "Commander? You did say Commander, Senator?"

"Yes, my friend, The Most Wise One wants you to take the next step." Then, after a brief pause, the Senator, now in his more formal voice, continued. "Do you, Scout Commander Zen, accept this promotion to the rank of Commander Zen?"

"It is surely a great honour, Senator Ku. It is with due reverence and respect that I do accept the rank of Commander that The Most Wise One, in all his wisdom, has seen fit to bestow upon me," a somewhat dumfounded and now humbled Commander Zen replied.

"Well, my newly appointed Commander Zen, you have much to do. So now, take your leave and prepare." With these final words, Senator Ku turned and moved away, and in so doing dismissed the Commander.

"Well, well! We have a new Commander among us. Let me be the first to congratulate you, my young friend." The incoming scan of Outer Ring Guard Zuke brought the rushing thoughts of Zen to some order of normality.

"News travels fast, Zuke, you old fossil."

"When you have been around as long as I have, nothing is secret. Let that be today's bit of wisdom I impart to you – those who remain silent and watch, hear and notice more."

"This time I am going to spend a little time with you, you old fossil," Zen thought as he moved into harmony with the old timer.

With that obligation fulfilled, Zen set about the task of recruiting and briefing his scouts. When he was satisfied with his final selection, he sought solitude. Taking time out alone, Zen mulled over the possibilities of who he would request to accompany his patrol as his second-in-command.

—— Ψ ——

Senator Ku called Commander Zen along with his selected patrol members to a final briefing, and then all that remained was for Commander Zen to verify that each in his command was fully prepared for the long-range patrol. He had been trained and achieved status in the third order of their creed, and now moved among his hand-picked Scouts as they congregated in the departure area, checking each and every one.

—— Ψ ——

Their pre-planned course would take them away from the Assembly for twenty-one days as they travelled to the outer limits of their known realm. Their task was to monitor and report back to Senator Ku any changes or signs of foreign intrusion into their greater living area.

First, they tracked out over that area called The Shallows – an area of shallow water and reefs that gave the bay a natural protection from the heavy, thunderous seas that crashed and rolled in during the last days of each pass. Here, the water never reached a depth of more than ten dikmar. The Shallows was a place that, for as long as all could remember, had been the playground of their youth – those first passes of their life – where the young played, safe from the unknown dangers of the outside. They had ducked and dived in and around the rocks in the warm shallow water – a time of play that had sharpened and honed those skills that would prove invaluable in their later lives.

Once clear of The Shallows, the patrol would turn in the opposite direction to where Hyperion, the Sun God, entered the heavens at the beginning of each day. This track would then be followed for three days to their first place of rest, the vast under-water hot springs that belched their boiling waters into the ocean.

This arena contained an ever-increasing cascade of huge bubbles of water, red molten rock, and rushing underwater air that hissed and roared as it escaped the shaking seabed. Out a safe distance from this place, well clear of the great lumps of rock and streams of hot mud that were constantly being thrown from the gaping bowels of Mother Earth, was where the patrol would take its next course heading. The patrol would then follow the hot water current as it took its path out over the sea's barren desert, crossing a long, rolling plain depleted and bereft of all life, to the great subterranean mountains that reared from the seabed and reached hundreds of sigmar in height. Then, the patrol would turn into the valley of the Petrified Forest that marked the narrow winding pass which dissected the mountain range, and then follow it to the point where the underwater fresh water river oozed

15

from the mountains and, by its density, precipitated down into a dark murky ravine.

After a short period of rest, the patrol would then follow this vast ravine to the third volcano and lock onto the magnetic field that bordered the outer limits of the unknown across to the cave of Amphitrite. Finally, they would set a course that would take them back across the barren sea desert to the jagged reefs at the perimeter of The Shallows, then eventually into the Bay, and then home.

After their final farewells, and under command of newly appointed Commander Zen of the Third Order, the patrol moved out across The Shallows. They were all consciously aware that one of the seven great Gods, the distinguished Poseidon, God of the Sea, had called the Great Council of Elders to an urgent meeting that at this very time was being convened.

The Arrival

2

For all but the very oldest of those left in the Assembly, it was the first time they had felt the reverberations that were soon to herald the presence of the exalted Divinity. So, it came to pass, that on the three hundredth day of the tenth pass, in the time of the Most Wise One, Irk, the meeting of the Great Council of Elders was summoned to order in the fifth decree. The fifth decree of a Creed that had its very foundations at the birth of all time when only the Great Gods ruled and walked the heavens and Mother Earth, Gaia, lay bare. This call together was so ordered by The Most Wise One on the direct instructions of the Supreme God of the Sea, Poseidon.

"Guard Protector Mio, daughter of Senator Ku, Protector of this Great Council Meeting, present yourself before me and my Senators of this, The Great Assembly," The Most Wise One called to the youthful Mio.

"As ordered, Most Wise One, so I obey," replied the somewhat nervous Mio.

"Guard Protector Mio, daughter of Senator Ku, Protector of this Great Council Meeting – can you vouch that all present are allegiant and disciplined to the fifth decree?" The Most Wise One issued the first charge to the young Guard Protector.

In a time-honoured ritual, Guard Protector Mio circled the gathered, scanned a challenge to each and every member, and in turn, acknowledged their response.

"As so inquired, Most Wise One, as so I can confirm," Mio replied.

"Guard Protector Mio, daughter of Senator Ku, Protector of this Great Council Meeting, how can you warrant that all conceivable has been addressed to safeguard that all here gathered are protected?"

The Most Wise One issued a further charge.

"By way of fifteen of the finest scouts in due formation, I warrant the full protection of all here assembled, Most Wise One," responded Mio to the second challenge.

"Guard Protector Mio, daughter of Senator Ku, Protector of this Great Council Meeting, I order you to take your leave and commence your obligation," The Most Wise One replied.

"As so instructed, Most Wise One, as so I comply."

Then in a dictated ritual, Mio slowly circled the Great Council of Elders three times, stopping momentarily each time before the grouping of the esteemed Inner Sanctum Senators, and so departed to take up her command.

"Most Learned One, Keeper of the Creed and all things sacred to the Assembly, present yourself before the Great Council of Elders," The Most Wise One ordered.

The Most Learned One rose to the surface then circled the body of the Inner Sanctum members, coming to a stop in front of the Most Wise One.

"As so instructed, Most Wise One, as so I comply," the Most Learned One countered.

"Most Learned One, Keeper of the Creed and all things sacred to the Assembly, remind all here congregated of our beginnings." The Most Wise One issued his second challenge.

"As so directed, Most Wise One, as so I answer. In the beginning, the universe was ruled by two Gods: Apsu, God of the fresh water, and

Tiamat, Goddess of the Sea. From them came first Chaos, then Gaia, or broad-breasted Earth, then Tartarus who lives under the earth, and then Love who was fairest of all the new Gods and who alone inspired creation.

"From Chaos, Erebus was born – God of the Darkness and the Night. And from Night were born Day and Ether.

"Gaia (Mother Earth) first bore her consort Uranus, and then the starry heaven to cover her, and the mountains and the nymphs who dwelled there-in; and she bore Pontus who would father the unharvested sea. All were borne by Gaia herself; but then she lived with Heaven, and bore the Titans – the elder Gods.

"First came Ocean, the great waters that encircle the world. Then Gaia bore Hyperion – the sun that travels the heaven; Japetus, father of Themis, God of Justice; and Mnemosyne, God of Memory, who was mother of Phoebe, the moon.

"Last of all, Gaia bore Cronus – the son destined to inherit the Kingdom. Cronus had three sons who, on his demise, drew lots for their inheritance: Zeus first taking the broad heaven and the upper air; Poseidon, the sea and all things therein; and Hades, the underworld."

The Most Learned One paused, as if having momentarily lost his way.

"Continue, my Most Learned Friend," ordered the Most Wise One.

"When Poseidon was looking for the dark-eyed Aphrodite to make her his bride, it was we – who were nothing but lost souls of sailors thrown to the sea by Dionysus the God of wine and frenzy – he called upon to seek her out, and it was we who found her hiding in a cavern deep in the sea. For our labours, Poseidon bestowed upon us the three highest honours of all. Firstly, he gave us intellect; secondly, he made in us an image of his hands; and thirdly, Poseidon moved the stars into a constellation of the zodiac and named it in our honour – the Constellation of The Dolphin. And it was so that we had our beginning."

"As so inquired, Most Wise One, as so I have answered."

"Most Learned One, Keeper of the Creed and all things sacred to the Assembly, how many foundation principles constitute the Creed?" The Most Wise One asked.

"As so inquired, Most Wise One, as so I answer. There are six foundation principles that constitute the Creed," replied the Most Learned One.

"Most Learned One, Keeper of the Creed and all things sacred to the Assembly, I call on you to now recite these six founding principles of the Creed to all of those here assembled."

The honoured ritual that had spanned all time continued.

"As so inquired, Most Wise One, as so I answer," The Most Learned One replied. "The first principle is to pledge to the order that all shall respond to the call, regardless of all peril, distance, and difficulties – to support, protect, or defend, and never to reject the call to unite to form a column of defiance against all adversaries and things of evil.

"The second principle is to adhere to and practice the twin virtues: Charity, suffice it to say, has the acceptance of both heaven and earth; and like its sister, Mercy, is twice-blessed – it blesses the one that gives, and blessed is the one that receives.

"The third principle is to promote the adoption and the application of a higher evolution by precept and example, and to propagate the knowledge of all things of the mystic.

"The fourth principle is to perceive that we are all chiselled from the same stone, and are participants in the same cosmos and sharers of the same aspirations. And although distinction among all is necessary to perpetuate subordination and to reward worthiness, no prominence of position should make us forget we are all equal.

"For even those who are ranked on the lowest and most insignificant plane of life's fortunes may be able to attain a higher consideration, and rank with those of the most distinguished and eminent stations. As a time will come – and even the wisest of us knows not the time – when all distinctions save those of honesty and virtue shall cease, and death, the greatest of all levellers, shall reduce us all to the same status.

"The fifth principle is to observe a due balance between avarice and profusion – to hold the balance of truth and sincerity with equality; to moderate emotion and intolerance; and in all pursuits to always have eternity in view.

"The sixth and final principle is to agree to hold in reverence the original Rulers and Gods of this Universe, our Assembly, and all further successors supreme and subordinate according to their rank, and to yield to the accords and proclamations as decreed by the Gods or their Supreme Council.

"As so inquired, Most Wise One, as so I have answered," The Most Learned One concluded.

"Most Learned One, Keeper of the Creed and all things sacred to the Assembly, I summon you to take up your position on my right," the Most Wise One ordered.

"As so instructed, Most Wise One, as so I comply."

Then again, in a ritual that spanned the time of all grace, The Most Learned One slowly circled the Great Council of Elders, stopping momentarily in front of The Most Wise One before taking up his position on the right.

The Most Wise One called out to the heavens as he breached the surface. "Oh, Great Poseidon, God of the Sea and God of all things herein – I, The Most Wise One, Irk, leader of the Great Assembly, here with all fifty of the Great Council of Elders whom you this day summoned to gather before you in due ritual, now await your arrival."

The sky grew dark and day hurried from view. The clouds swirled about with a threatening ferocity and it seemed as if time had stopped, causing the seas to grow cold.

"Oh, Great Poseidon, God of the Sea and God of all things herein! I, The Most Wise One, Irk, leader of the Great Assembly, here with all fifty of the Great Council of Elders whom you have this day summoned to gather before you in due ritual, now await and beg your arrival." The Most Wise One again called to their God Poseidon in the heavens.

The skies grew even darker as day departed the heavens and cowered from sight; then turbulence and fear crept into the very heart of the Great Council of Elders.

Suddenly, from the dark threatening heavens, the King of all Gods, Zeus, appeared in all his heavenly splendour and delivered down a fork of lightning that was chaperoned by thunderbolts, and these shook the earth.

The water of the oceans boiled as they were cast aside in a great eruption of defiance that issued a challenge to the mortality of all living things. As the ocean in torment was held at bay, a second bolt of lightning from the hand of Zeus banished night from the sky and called day to account.

All in the Great Assembly trembled with trepidation as the great God of all Gods, Zeus, flaunted his might for all those in the earthly

22

domain of insignificant transients to observe. Again and again, Zeus hurled thunder and lightning bolts from the skies at the oceans below; and then from the bowels of the great abyss of turbulent waters of this God-made hell arose the God Poseidon.

In a defiant gesture to his brother Zeus, Poseidon swept a heavenly arc with his trident and called to the raging waters to quell their anger and be still. The ocean waters fell to calm, and the Sea God Poseidon was heralded on his arrival.

The Great Monarchs of the deep did then rise up to meet their God Poseidon, who this day they had called before them, and they carried him before them in reverence and adoration, and the love of Poseidon reached out and encompassed all in the greater Assembly. And so it was that the God Poseidon moved with and spoke to his Regents of the Deep, and he did disclose to those of the highest learning – the undiscloseable.

He told of floating flowers that turned golden waters to red and brought the rain that turned to fire. The God Poseidon warned of the unwarnable, and he told of the untellable and he cast these tellings and disclosures as thirteen writings.

These thirteen writings he then cast into the thirteen houses of the zodiac of the heavens, to be deciphered and studied, and to be as deeds that the Great Council of Elders could do naught but allow to come to pass; for so it was told to them: "So shall be the will of the God of all Gods, Zeus."

Poseidon spoke of his past great losses, sadnesses, and joys – of the future he had to bring to be, and the rewards to reap. And so it was that the scholarly ones and those of great intellect did take heed and perceive these strange events their God said would come to pass.

23

Poseidon warned of a great turbulence that would shortly befall Atlantis: that island in the bay that was surrounded by the sea and protected from the storms by The Shallows – an island that was larger than the two known lands put together.

He told of the time he had received Atlantis as part of his inheritance, and how he had fortified it and made it abundant in all good things. How he had brought forth and caused hot and cold springs to flow through its streets, and how he had gifted it with precious metals and they were all in abundance. All manner of plants grew there at his command, and many animals including elephants roamed through the forests. The young herds of goats feared not to lay down with the lions and tigers, for all animals were at peace with each other.

On this island, he told of how he had allowed a couple – born of Earth – to live, and they had a daughter Clito. Poseidon told of how he had also lain with her and sired five pairs of male twins whom he made into the Kings of this place he named Atlantis after the first of these boys, Atlas – and he spoke of having divided the island for them.

These ten Kings made laws for their subjects that were written on stone tablets and placed for all to see and follow, which the people did to honour the Kings. To please them, they all made sacrifices to the Gods.

The country had become wealthy and powerful, especially as the Kings of Atlantis never fought against each other. The Great Council listened as they were told of how the Kings and the people had eventually become corrupted by their good fortune. How they then planned to make conquests of the friendly countries that were close by, and how the Gods were saddened by their desire to dominate and feared this very action would threaten the whole world. Poseidon told of how these Kings and their people no longer kept the laws as written, but instead, now sought power over each other.

In thunderous tones, Poseidon then pronounced: "The great God of all Gods, Zeus, has thus given direction that he desires the downfall of these people. The time will soon come to pass that I shall strike the ground with my trident and a great earthquake shall cause the sea to swallow up the land of Atlantis. All those there shall perish, and the seas shall cast all traces of the city and the Atlanteans far and wide, and they shall be no more. As this comes to pass, I, Poseidon, will also settle a long-standing score with the Phaeacians who, being such skilful navigators, have always escaped from the storms and towering seas I have thrown at them. I will wait, and when they make their way home from Ithaca, I will transform their sailing ship into a rock. Then, I will again strike the ground with my trident and summon the mountains to move and block their port. No sacrifices or prayers from their Kings will move me to undo this deed that I now must do."

Poseidon told of these most grave times that were to come to pass, and told his most faithful Regents of the Deep that the time was nigh when they must leave this place in which they had so long dwelt without fear.

"You must prepare a course that will take you all into the New World – beyond where Gods have gone before. There, you must seek out a place where the mountains rule both the seas and the land, and these mountains do stretch forth in a straight line. The people who share these new lands are of a different skin and will look upon you as I do, and you will be endeared to them."

The God Poseidon looked at The Most Wise One, Irk.

"Oh my Most Wise One, in you I place the very future of these, my

25

beloved children."

The Most Wise One rose briefly to the surface.

"This journey you say we must undertake – will our God Poseidon guide us to this new place of dwelling?" The Most Wise One asked.

"No, my old friend, I have been given many other tasks I must undertake in this world – tasks that will take as many passes as there are stars in the heavens to complete."

The Most Wise One sensed sadness in the reply of the God Poseidon.

"This place we seek, is it far?" the Most Wise One asked of his God Poseidon.

"A great time and distance will flow beneath you, and many dangers will unfold their wings before you find that place you seek."

"This place we seek, how will we know it?" The Most Wise One asked of Poseidon.

"A great peace will surround you, and when this comes to pass, this place you seek shall be nigh, and you will live in harmony with those of a different stock." Poseidon answered to the Council of Elders.

As the grey- and white-bodied mass continued to circle, slowly rising and falling beneath the cold waters, a feeling of great sadness begin to overwhelm the Assembly. Many felt their noble God who had brought them out from the wilderness of lost souls would shortly depart for a time of which they knew not the end. The God Poseidon continued in the most sombre terms.

"A time will come when you will live in harmony; but beware, this is a false harmony."

The Great Assembly listened, spellbound by the things of which the great Poseidon spoke.

"Beware! Be vigilant! For it is at this time of false peace and harmony that an invisible enemy shall surround you. This unseen adversary shall not steal in at night's darkest, but will come to you portion by portion, and each portion shall then unite, and shall grow and become strong. Just as the people of Atlantis were led into temptation, so you must keep vigil. For at your darkest, there will come forth a shining dog that will appear in many places, and he shall cast off his fleece and this invisible foe shall be smitten before you. So it is that this shall be my twelfth writing, and all shall come to pass."

"Oh Great God, Poseidon, you spoke of thirteen prophesies, yet you yield up only these few hints to us when we seek answers to all those as cast up; can you not tell us more?" The Most Wise One inquired.

Poseidon looked across at his friend of old. "As so inquired old one, as so I reply. Of those first twelve, only time will reveal; of the thirteenth, I will now speak. As it shall be so that the end will now become the beginning, then it shall also be that the beginning will now herald the end, and those of you who can see, will."

"What will those ones see? What will they see?"

The interruption of The Most Wise One was ignored, and thus the thirteenth prophesy was hidden in the thirteenth house of the zodiac of the heavens. With these sagacious words, the God Poseidon rose through the waters and was suspended atop the quelled oceans.

"Most Wise One, your friendship and loyalty to me and to all those Gods who dwell in the heavens and on Earth over many passes must be rewarded. So it has been decreed by the mightiest of Gods, the great exalted Zeus, and all we Gods concur. Now, my dear friend, I call on you to arise and be anointed." The warmth of the great God Poseidon reached out and embraced all of those gathered before him.

The Most Wise One rose and presented himself at the feet of Poseidon, and that God, so loved by these Regents of the Deep, swept his trident in a high arc bringing it down to rest on the head of The Most Wise One as he proclaimed:

"From this time forward, you shall be known throughout the heavens and Earth as Epiphanes, The Magnificent One, King of all Dolphins."

And then, in a final departing gesture of Godspeed, Poseidon swept his trident over the Great Council of Elders and invoked the blessings of all Gods upon these his friends, knowing full well that many passes would cover Mother Earth before he would once again be reunited in harmony with those from the deep.

"Go now, my Regents of the Deep, go now onward from this place." With these last words, the God Poseidon lifted to the heavens and was seen no more.

And so it came to pass that on the three hundredth day of the tenth pass in the time of the Epiphanes, The Magnificent One, the God Poseidon, departed from the realms of the earthly beings for a time not knowing an end.

The Patrol

3

The first day of the twenty-one day patrol went as planned, with the group moving on rapidly in eager anticipation out over The Shallows towards the open water. Commander Zen, relishing his first command, was well pleased with his decision to take his request to the higher order and have Lute approved as his Second. It was an added bonus to have his close confidant and friend along to help alleviate the decision-making. In unison, Commander Zen and Second, Lute, with the other scout members, fanned out in vee formation, and sped through the breaking waters of the outer reaches of the bay. Soon their sleek bodies would be slicing through the long rolling ocean swells as they headed into their patrol proper.

Scout Leader Lute, newly trained and promoted to the Third Order, was fourth daughter of teacher Jason, and had known Zen for what seemed forever. They had been born within two days of each other in the eighth pass in the time of the Most Wise One, Irk. In adolescence, along with Mio and Hur, they had grown up exploring The Shallows, playing the games as had been played by the many generations of the past. Diving deep then turning sharply to race at their fastest to soar into the air, or chasing feathers that had fallen from some seabird onto the still waters of the bay they all called home. With the other youngsters they had ventured out over the rocks that protected The Shallows to chase the turtles that flourished in their multitudes, feeding on the abundance of food that proliferated in and around the bay.

Lute was never afraid when Zen was close by. Lute, Mio, and Zen had received instruction from the teachers, and together all had progressed through the first foundation orders of the Creed. Having passed the examination to the First Order on the same day, all three, one pass later, were given important promotions: Zen to Scout Leader attached to the long range patrols, Mio to Scout Guard attached to the Great Council meetings, and Lute, with abilities at the scan, also to Scout Leader. All three had come to the attention of The Most Wise One, and on his instructions were marked for the higher training that would further develop their skills.

Hur was unsighted, that day of celebrations. Lute and the rest of the First Order qualifiers were consciously aware of his absence. The three friends had tried to help Hur to keep up. They had tried to help him with his studies, doing all they could: from giving up their time at play to asking the teachers how best they could help their wayward friend. But, as always, Hur was forever engrossed somewhere else – immersed in doing what he called more important things, and many gaps started to appear in his schooling.

"I will catch up, I promise. Just give me time." Hur's promises had a hollow ring to them, and it followed that while Zen, Lute, and Mio progressed with speed, Hur fell by the wayside, and in so doing, he came more and more to the attention of the teachers and, in turn, to The Learned Ones.

Zen felt the affectionate quivers from Lute that communicated her warm feelings toward him as they continued their patrol, passing over the outer edges of The Shallows and on into a now calm sea. The ocean had taken on a deep green colour, giving indication of its growing depth.

Three days into the patrol, with The Shallows now far behind them, they skirted around the stark, barren seabed that rolled out before them in a never-ending carpet of grey, undulating dunes. The bare ocean floor was occasionally interrupted by dead coral or sea trees frozen in position by the sands of time that had been piled up around their bases by the constantly moving currents that gently caressed the seabed in a never-ending serenade of surges and counter surges.

Zen had called the patrol to slow down and close formation in an effort to conserve energy, for as the seabed was devoid of all life, it was, therefore, devoid of all food.

The day was in the zenith of its fifth since leaving the protection of The Shallows when directly ahead of the patrol, Lute picked up a dark shadowy movement on her image rectifier. Lute's caution broke through Zen's rest period and brought him immediately to her side.

"What is it, Lute?"

"Scan up forward. I am sensing a body of movement fifteen sigmar out in front of us, as yet at too great a distance to identify. Be quick! It's fast disappearing from my scan."

The cold shiver of the unknown disappeared as Zen broke the water next to her. Zen scanned out an arc, carefully deciphering the impulses as they bounced back in return. His first sweep revealed nothing. Again, he swept across the area directly in front, this time taking in a wider arc in a slower scan. Two locks in, he faintly imaged momentarily the outline of a fast fading shadow of an object – then it was gone, completely vanished from view.

"What do you think it was, Zen?" Lute asked, turning to Zen, as he made one final scan of the area ahead.

"We are close to the hot water springs, which sometimes can cause shadows to appear on our scanners," Zen answered in an effort to quell any fears in his troop. "We are also on a course that takes us closer to the outer boundary of the unknown than anywhere else on this patrol, so it may be that something from out there has ventured into the area," Zen continued.

The very thought of the unknown sent another cold shiver through Lute's body as she remembered the stories some of the older members of the Assembly had told. Stories of great black and white sea monsters that were turned loose by their masters to roam the Outer Unknown in packs – feasting on the fresh flesh torn from any form of life they could catch. Zen signalled all members of his patrol to close up in pack, and then briefed them on what Lute's scan had gathered in.

"From this point on, I want all members to scan in the alert pattern," Commander Zen ordered. "Hur, you take up position at the right rear, scanning that side to the Outer Unknown and behind. Lido, you will take up position at his side and slightly to his rear, scanning that side to the barren seabed and behind.

Lute and I will scan ahead. Jason and Deva, take up the centre and rest. You will be called to relieve on a changing day."

"How long do you expect us to continue with the scan?" Hur asked.

"Until such time as I believe any danger or threat to our patrol has passed," Zen answered, slightly annoyed at his orders being questioned.

And so it was that Zen, in his first command, ordered his patrol onto alert. For the next three days, the patrol kept in close formation, each scout taking their turn in rotation to rest, and then to take up a position to scan. Zen and his second-in-command alternated in leading as front runners.

On the tenth day into the patrol, Zen sensed the water temperature had raised a number of points; the rolling barrenness of the seabed was now giving way to isolated patches of kelp. Ahead, Zen could scan the changes from the bleak sand to what he knew was a multi-coloured assortment of weed-covered rocks. So, with the patrol on course and with no further alerts called, or any sightings of unidentified images, Zen led the patrol into the Hot Water Springs.

Lute let the drifting movement of the sea carry her along over the white sands as she watched the schools of silver and red fish that filled the shallow waters beneath her dart to and fro. The warm waters of the springs offered soothing comfort to her tired body. The long eleven-day non-stop trip from the Bay had taken its toll on her. Commander Zen had ordered a full day's rest before the patrol would again be on the move, so Lute was determined to make the most of the recuperative powers offered by the warm waters of the springs. Their massaging, tempered waters induced a state of drowsiness, and as she dozed, her thoughts turned – as they often did – to Zen. What was the matter with her, for heaven's sake? She was no longer a child; she had met many fine young males from the Assembly as she was growing up, but none of them had affected her as Zen did. As a youngster, she had trusted him and loved him with an innocence and inexperience. Now, she was growing weary of trying to ignore the obvious physical reaction of her feelings toward him as her senses relayed to her the total of his maleness, the faintly arousing body movements whenever he came close to her, and the devilish ease with which her mind provided her with an image of him whenever he was not around.

"Alert, alert, alert!"

The incoming signals jolted Lute from her daydreaming. The other scouts had tracked a school of mullet and were herding them towards her. Hur was rapidly scanning signals to her with a request to indicate her position.

This was a time Lute loved: the thrill of the chase, as the group hunted in a pack, and the speed with which scans were sent out, received, and then incorporated into the master plan. Lute read Hur's signals. Turn them at the reef edge – Lido would block any move to the right. Lute moved quickly forward, her scans picking up the block of terrified fish as they raced towards her. With her heart rate increased and adrenaline now screaming through her body, Lute consolidated the hunt, putting aside her tender thoughts.

Two days from the Hot Water Springs and three asmar from the narrow winding pass that would take the patrol through the Valley of the Petrified Forest to the other side of the mountains, Lute carried out a routine scan of the area directly in front of them, and once again picked up the weak shadowy impulse of an unknown moving image. The unidentified image's location, now at one asmar out and two dikmar below their elevation, was still too distant to positively recognise.

Lute's mental caution instantly alerted her five companions. Commander Zen surfaced at her side to confirm her outer scan, and then mentally ordered the others in his scout unit to shut down their sonars and close in to form a line abreast on the leader's right. This would give him and his second-in-command an unimpeded scan of the objects that were slowly moving towards them. Nine sigmar, then eight sigmar, and still the unidentified objects continued, ever so slowly, to close.

Lute overlaid Commander Zen's scan. For the second time in the last seven days, the silhouetted outline of large moving objects had caused him concern which was instantly relayed on, compelling the scouts to automatically go into a higher state of alert and come up in closed formation. Then, for the second time, the approaching objects turned away and slowly faded from the patrol's image rectifiers.

Zen signalled to all but Lute to drift back and spread out in the stand-down mode. This, their last sweep up the boundary of the mountains, was nearing an end. In two more days, they would reach the volcano which marked mid-way.

Once there, they would rest before embarking on the predetermined heading that would take them home. Zen, like the rest of his scouts, was eager to start that second and final leg of the patrol.

The Destruction

4

A ripple of anticipation swept over the Assembly, invoking a feeling of great excitement among the youngsters who dashed between members of the gathering, seeking out those who could answer the many questions generated by their inquiring minds. Teacher Tia tried to calm his pupils as they crowded in close, pushing and jostling as they scanned in their questions much faster than he could answer.

"When are we leaving?"

"Will we be excused from The Learned One's teaching?"

"What is beyond The Shallows? Will we be safe?"

"The New World! What is that? Where is it?"

Teacher Tia called for silence. "In three days, King Epiphanes will speak of these things. Until then, like all the rest of us, you will have to show a little patience and wait."

Teacher Tia's answer failed to dampen the relentless pursuit of response to the constant flow of questions.

The sudden appearance of two of The Learned Ones finally brought some relief and sanity to the place of learning.

"Teacher Tia! Present yourself," called The Learned One, Alto. "Teacher Tia, did you not hear me?"

The Learned One's second call sent a chill down the spine of the blind teacher. There was something the teacher could not quite get his mind around, but something nevertheless just did not feel right with this Learned One.

"Teacher Tia!" The raised voice seemed, to the blind teacher, more like a rebuke then a call to notice.

"Yes Learned One," Teacher Tia responded as he quickly moved in to take up the position formality decreed, directly in front of The Learned One.

"Teacher Tia, before I scan in the day's lessons, I want it noted that during the King's speech, those in this school of learning are to continue with the day's lessons."

Teacher Tia acknowledged the directive.

"Now, prepare to receive the day's lessons, Teacher Tia."

And so, as it had been done for all remembered time, the day's lessons were scanned in for the teachers to pass on.

King Epiphanes, flanked by the Senators who were followed closely by the Great Council of Elders, moved towards those members of the Assembly gathered to hear the King's address.

"Guard Commander Mio! Present yourself before the Senators," King Epiphanes, called.

"As so ordered, as so I obey," responded Mio.

"Guard Commander Mio! How has all been prepared for my address?" King Epiphanes asked of the young Guard Commander.

"By way of positioning fifteen of the finest scouts throughout the assembly to relay your message: so it has been prepared," the Guard Commander responded.

So it was that the rituals of calling together the Assembly began, continued, and in due course, were completed.

"Most Learned One, present yourself before the here gathered Assembly," King Epiphanes ordered.

"As so ordered, as so I obey," The Most Learned One replied as he moved from his place at the right of King Epiphanes to the front of the Inner Sanctum members.

"Most Learned One, I call on you to bring down the blessings of our God, the Great God Poseidon, upon those here gathered," ordered King Epiphanes.

"As so ordered, as so I obey."

"Oh Great God Poseidon, ruler of the seas and all things therein, brother of the King of all Gods, the Great God Zeus – we are gathered here at the summons of King Epiphanes to receive your blessing and guidance as was delivered to our leaders at the Bay of Shallows when you blessed us with your appearance. Grant to our King Epiphanes, this day, the strength and wisdom to lead us safely along the path of life, that we may not deviate from this your course that has been plotted and cast to the thirteen heavenly houses of the zodiac."

Then again, as another time-honoured ritual dictated, The Most Learned One circled the Inner Sanctum Senators twice before he resumed his place on the right of King Epiphanes. With the blessings of Poseidon now bestowed upon those of the Great Assembly, King Epiphanes proceeded to scan out the proclamations.

"As it is the command of our great God Poseidon, we are to take our leave from this bay of our dwelling. Our God Poseidon has given forewarning of a great tragedy that will shortly befall those that inhabit the Island of Atlantis, for they shall be smitten by the trident of death.

At this happening, Poseidon will call upon all the waters that surround this place of pending doom to rise up and swallow all Atlanteans.

"Then it shall come to pass that this Island of Atlantis shall vanish beneath the seas, and all the dwellers therein shall be cast to the four God Winds: Boreas, Zephyrus, Notus, and Eurus. They will sweep the seas, and all remnants of this place and its people shall be cast far and wide, and hence, lost forever."

King Epiphanes hesitated as he broke the surface of the water, and an eerie calm descended over the Assembly as they waited for the King to continue with these words of grave tidings. King Epiphanes hesitated, and then continued.

"The Learned Ones have deciphered the positions of the thirteen houses of the zodiac, and consulted the heavenly bodies, and so it is proclaimed that the time of departure from this place will come to pass fourteen days from now."

Again, King Epiphanes paused before continuing. "Our God Poseidon has disclosed that a great time and distance will flow past us, and many dangers will unfold before we find that place he called the New World. As dictated, we must be well prepared for these coming times; so, it is decreed that the Council of Elders will convene, and in due course instruction will be given regarding the preparations for our leave-taking."

With these last words, King Epiphanes bowed to his Assembly, and then turned and bowed to his Senators to signal an end had come to these proceedings.

As King Epiphanes accompanied by the Senators and The Great Council of Elders left the arena of the Assembly, a growing chatter of anticipation filled the air.

Many days had come and gone since Poseidon departed his earthly realm, but there inevitably came the time when, on the instructions of Poseidon, Hyperion the Sun God pushed night from the heavens and sent forth the dawn to streak across the skies in an ominous warning that the time to leave Atlantis had arrived. Then, as was deciphered in the heavenly bodies by The Learned Ones, the final gathering together of the Great Assembly began in earnest as the time for the destruction of Atlantis was nigh.

Hyperion, the Sun God, took his rest at the zenith of the fourteenth day; without warning, he was struck from the sky and a gloom descended upon those in the earthly domain as Erebus, God of the Darkness and Night took on the rule of the heavens, and Hades, God of the Underworld stalked the domain of Mother Earth.

— Ψ —

Senator Zoa summoned Commander Zen and Guard Commander Mio to his presence.

"King Epiphanes has signalled we must begin our journey. Is all prepared?" the Senator queried of the Commanders.

"Two of the forward party's escorting scouts who left in the day ten times passed have since returned; they report that at this time the forward party have prepared a place at the cave of Amphitrite. It is at this place that King Epiphanes will be safe." Commander Zen reported.

"Guard Commander Mio, has all been undertaken to protect King

Epiphanes on this journey as was ordered by The Great Council?" the Senator further enquired of the two.

"By thirty scouts, fifteen of whom are presently on patrol and will return later today; they will be aided by another fifteen who will encircle King Epiphanes and all seven Senators. All scouts, at that time, will be under the command of Scout Leader Lido, whom I must add leads that patrol due in today. As no alerts have been called, I expect he will be fully fit for the tasks we have assigned the Scout Leader," responded Mio.

"It is so that I will inform King Epiphanes of these things." And with that, the Senator silently dismissed Zen and Mio.

The excitement had grown with great speed and intensity in the Assembly as they milled around The Shallows, awaiting the signal that would announce their departure. Since the dawn, the youngsters had pestered the Teachers with their never-ending questions and impatience – even to the point where Teacher Tia threatened some with extra lessons in an effort to get a little peace. Then, as the dawn was kept at bay by blackened clouds, King Epiphanes signalled that for the final time the Assembly would depart from this, their only known home.

——Ψ——

And so it came to pass that on the four hundredth and sixty-fifth day of the tenth pass in the time of King Epiphanes, the Great

Assembly left forever the Bay of Atlantis.

In the darkness of that same day, the turbulent clouds swirled in anger, and forks of lightning lit up the oceans as they reared in turmoil and thrashed the shores of Atlantis.

From a gaping wound slashed in a terror-inducing sky swept the God Poseidon. In fury, he hurled down his trident of foretold doom, and its terrible destructive force was felt throughout the Island of Atlantis. The land then did tremble as if in living fear and the very mountains of this once beloved island did explode.

From its very bowels spewed forth rocks that soared into the skies. These burning rocks then fell back onto Atlantis, and brought havoc to the buildings that housed those who had offended their Gods. Again and again, fire was sent belching from the bowels of Mother Earth so that no living Atlantean could escape from this God-made hell.

And as the great God Poseidon had foretold to his most beloved Regents of the Deep, so the oceans in great turbulence did continue to soar up in anger until they had covered and swallowed up the Island Atlantis. Then it was the turn of the nymphs and demons sent by the God Hades, and they did descend on those hapless Atlanteans who had escaped the inferno, tearing at their flesh and crushing their bones as their screams of anguish echoed out over The Shallows.

Even at a distance, every member of the Great Assembly did feel the reverberations of their God's anger.

Once the nymphs and demons had completed their grisly task, it was the turn of the falcons of the God Horus. These birds of prey then did swoop down, and in their talons of steel did carry up to the heavens and deliver to the four God Winds – Boreas, Zephyrus, Notus, and Eurus – the remnants of these people who had dared to turn away from their known God,

So it did come to pass that all traces of this, the Island Atlantis and all things that dwelt therein were cast to the God Winds to be spread throughout all known places of the world as a warning to all living things. Only then was the wild fury of the God Poseidon spent, and he did then bring the raging waters back to calm.

The fires that had roared and burnt unimpeded were quelled, and their embers extinguished by a watery covering that turned embers to floating ash. And so it was, as the God Poseidon had ordained, that peace and tranquillity did return to the Bay, the oceans did cower in retreat, the Island of Atlantis was no more, and the ocean surface was devoid of all things. So it came to pass that a great peace did then descend and cover the silent oceans with tranquillity, and all the Gods that dwelt in the heavens did concur that their deeds were done.

The Cave

5

ach tenth day, as Hyperion the Sun God entered the heavens and dark withdrew from the skies, the eight Senators congregated to address those matters that influenced the smooth running of the Great Assembly. The Assembly had only moved once from the time of leaving The Shallows. That first move was to escape the destruction of the Island of Atlantis, and had taken the Assembly no further than to the most revered of all landmarks, the Cave of Amphitrite. Here, the Assembly again learned of the time, long since passed, when their forbearers had captured the Goddess Amphitrite, and had delivered her to the God Poseidon.

As the King Epiphanes, escorted by The Most Learned One, moved through this cave, the memories of that time long past were further revisited, and thereby cemented into the great storehouse of knowledge they carried.

"We shall not dwell in this place for many more days," King Epiphanes informed the Most Learned One. "The waters of this place are far too deep to sustain our people for much longer. Which Senator has the responsibility of scouts and guards, Most Learned One?"

"Senator Ove has that duty, King Epiphanes."

"Have Senator Ove present himself to me before this day has passed, Most Learned One."

"As so instructed, King Epiphanes." The Most Learned One confirmed the instruction received, then took his leave.

"King Epiphanes!" Guard Commander Mio signalled from behind them.

"King Epiphanes! I, Senator Ove, as so you ordered, do present myself here before you," the incoming Senator scanned as he approached The King.

"Thank you for your attendance this day, Senator," King Epiphanes scanned back to the advancing Senator. Then, with a little hesitation, he spoke again. "Advise me of the progress that is being made in the search for food."

Senator Ove rose to the surface of the ocean, breathing deeply of the fresh air. "My scouts are ranging many asmar in all directions from this place of our dwelling, and they all report only deep waters that house but few schools of fish."

"Those scouts who plot the oceans farthest from here – what do they report?" King Epiphanes further queried of his Senator.

"King Epiphanes, it has been made evident that the waters six hundred and forty nine asmar to the north of this place grow shallow. It is the opinion of these scouts that land's edge may be close to that point."

"Pray, tell me Senator Ove, how it is that scouts feel land's edge is close when all they report is that the oceans become shallow?"

"King Epiphanes, Commander Zen, the Assembly's finest scout and his second, Scout Leader Lute, have only just now returned to the assembly and reported of these things."

The Senator and The King rode the rolling swell with ease as they spoke of these matters.

"Continue on, Senator Ove," King Epiphanes ordered.

"From this first report, King Epiphanes, the sensors of the

Commander have indicated the presence of fresh water which has mixed with the oceans; also, signs of life by way of a single feather were found."

"Then, we must prepare to move from here to this place of which you speak. Have all Senators present themselves before me at the dawn of the next day, and I will convey to them what I have decided. Will you do that for me Senator?"

"Your wish is my command, my King."

As the Senator moved to take his leave, the King continued: "Before you go Senator, and on the subject of Scout Leader Lute, I arrmm…, arr… The King seemed to somehow have momentarily lost his train of thought.

"About Scout Leader Lute," the Senator prompted, hoping it would stir the Kings thinking.

"Ah yes! Scout Leader Lute. I want you to have it posted that after due deliberation with her teachers, and her success at the fourth order of the Creed, and of course I cannot forget discussion with and input from the Most Learned One… Excuse my rambling Senator – the mind is just not as sharp as it once was. Now, my Senator, where was I?"

"Scout Leader Lute, my King. You were about to say something about Scout Leader Lute."

"Yes, yes you are quite correct, Senator. Quite correct!" Again, the King seemed lost as what to say next. The Senator and the King, in unison and silence, rode the swells.

"Senator, did I tell you I wish to have Scout Leader Lute promoted to Scout Commander?"

"No, my King, you didn't tell me. Shall I have it posted?" The Senator was a little worried about his King, who was now just ever so slightly showing the signs of that old adversary – age.

"Yes, Senator! Please have it posted as so I this day order."

With that, King Epiphanes dismissed the Senator and returned to the Cave of Amphitrite.

As he entered the cave, he called to The Most Learned One to join him. Then, as they had long done, the two most honoured of the Assembly did confer as The Most Learned One sought to access the advice of the Most Wise Ones who had long since passed to the heavens, and to read their thoughts now held in the great storehouse of knowledge.

These two of the highest decrees could decipher the spiritual writings as they read what floated with the heavenly bodies. For as the great God Poseidon had foretold, so it was confirmed that the onset of the great migration was signalled.

As the new day took up next dawning, the eight Senators joined The Most Learned One in positions at the entrance to the Cave of Amphitrite as they awaited the pleasure of their revered King Epiphanes.

As King Epiphanes slowly emerged from his solitude, those of the inner sanctum then joined together, and so it was that the King relayed to his Senators the decision he had reached.

"Senators!" King Epiphanes started his address as he moved among them. "Our scouts, having the last day past returned from distant patrol, have told of a place some two hundred and forty-nine asmar to the north of this Cave of Amphitrite. At this place, the oceans have grown shallow, and these scouts further report that traces of fresh waters have been detected. The Most Learned One has read of those writings in the heavens, and I have called upon those Wise Ones who have gone before us. All signs, as having been read, dictate that the time is now upon us to venture beyond this charter place we have always known. This journey we have held in nervous anticipation must now come to pass.

"From the time of crossing The Shallows, we have spoken often of how we are to take our leave from this place of charted knowledge and go beyond into that which is unknown to us." King Epiphanes signalled a response from those of the Seventh Order gathered before him.

Senator Ove sought the permission of The King to speak.

"So as requested, as so you may speak."

"As Senator for scouts and guards, I have advised you, my King; those scouts who seek out the schools of fish that give us our nourishment report they are forced to travel many asmar, crossing over the boundary of the unknown to fill the quota needed to sustain those of the Assembly. Many of the Assembly now have become restless, and complain of this lack of sustenance. I believe the time has come when we must leave this place; so I concur with you; it is time we left to follow the words of our God."

Having said his piece, Senator Ove, in tradition, bowed to the King Epiphanes and returned to his designated berth.

"Senator Inca, you are Senator of discipline and wellbeing. I understand there has been a matter of discontent that has been brought to your attention." The sharpness of The King's tone took those assembled by complete surprise.

"Oh, King, arr…, yes, yes!" The sudden call to account by the King had startled Senator Inca.

"Well! Come on! Out with it! What is all this discontent about Senator?"

"My King, it is my grave burden to give account of that of which you have spoken, and yes, there is much substance to it, I fear"

"From whence does this disharmony come, Senator Inca?" The sharp interruption of King Epiphanes again cut through the water.

Senator Inca smarted at the sharp rebuke.

"Well Senator! I am waiting – I want the truth, and by the look of my Senators, we are all waiting and wanting to know the source of this disharmony."

"My King," the Senator began, "and fellow Senators! The source of the disharmony, much to my sorrow…"

"Sorrow! I don't want know about your sorrow. I want to know where the root cause of this so-called disharmony hides." Again the Senator was cut short by the once mellow King's sharp interruption.

"My King," the Senator started again, "the problem had its beginnings with Dy, widowed mother of Hur, who has voiced her concerns in the loudest possible way to all those who would listen – about the lack of food available for those of the nursery."

"The shortage of food? But this should not arouse discontent. Does any other Senator have knowledge of why Dy, widowed mother of Hur, has this resentment?" The King asked as he moved among the Senators, seeking their comments.

Senator Ira spoke first. "King Epiphanes! Dy, mother of Hur, still refuses to accept in her heart the failure of her son in his attempts to reach the second Order. It is her belief that it is the teachers who are at fault. It is my humble opinion that Dy, widowed mother of Hur, is using the shortage of food to heap scorn indirectly upon the Senators.

She is doing this in a devious way by continually criticising those very hard-working food scouts who, my King, work so tirelessly as they search the great oceans for nourishment."

"And what say you, Most Learned One, of these claims?" King Epiphanes asked, turning back to the head of the gathering.

The Most Learned One waited until their leader had resumed his position before he replied. "Hur has been judged, as we have all been judged, and this judgement has been lodged in our storehouse of all things. It is so recorded that Hur is of those ways that cause his failings."

"I have studied the register of progress that Hur has made, and it pleases me not that this discontent – that grows like a cancer in his mother – has its roots in his failings. Before a final decision is reached on the path I must choose to guide his future, I need to dwell further on this matter." With this statement from King Epiphanes, those of the inner sanctum knew there would be no further discussion on this subject.

The King then turned his attention to Senator Opek. "Senator! You are charged with the responsibility of ensuring that this great journey is well planned. What do you have to report on this matter?"

"King Epiphanes, as so I have been charged, so it has been that each detail of our pending parting has been scrutinized in the very smallest of detail. A number of Senators contributed, and were actively involved in the various stages of the planning, and all that is left now is for you and the remaining Senators to review this planning and, if you see fit, grant it your endorsement."

The King nodded his approval.

Senator Opek continued. "The next step that is proposed is to proceed with the formality of calling together and informing those in the greater Assembly. This must be given the highest priority."

King Epiphanes nodded again in approval, and asked Senator Opek to continue.

"My King, that is all I have to report."

"Thank you Senator. Now, present these plans to all those Senators gathered so that it may be finally ratified, and the Blessing of the God Poseidon may be invoked upon them."

So it was that, as instructed, Senator Opek scanned out the following plans to his fellow Senators.

"As Hyperion the Sun God enters the heavens from the same place each day and follows a path that varies by just a very few locks, then so it is that we should follow this path, knowing full well we are then assured of two things that will always come to pass. Firstly, we will be given a course to follow. Secondly, this course will keep the Assembly out of the reach of the underworld denizens that rule all places of permanent darkness." Senator looked across at the King, as if waiting for some sign of approval.

"Continue, Senator Opek," was the only response he got.

"It is the advice of the Senators, that the Assembly be divided into four sections, with each section having its appointed scouts to ensure its continuing protection. The first of these sections shall embrace all teachers and their students and those of great age, along with those mothers with suckling offspring. The rationale behind this is that the young and very old can set the pace of travel and not be left to drift out behind."

"Your planning is good to this point. Continue on!" The input from The King momentarily silenced the Senator.

"The second group, My King, shall then comprise the food scouts and those young ones not yet in training or creed learning,

"And your reason for this, may I ask, Senator?"

"But of course, my King. This group having the food scouts within will follow closely behind the lead group, and the Food Scouts should have the task of ensuring the very young are first receivers of nourishment when the Food Scouts return each day."

"And how have you placed the rest of us, Senator?" The King inquired

"The remaining two groups shall have the balance of Leaned Ones and those scouts on rest. Add to them the unwell and their care givers. The last group will include yourself and those in your support, my King."

"That's all very well, Senator, but what about the many in the Assembly? What becomes of them?"

The Senator turned to the King. "I have taken care of that. Those who have families will be assigned to another group, and all remaining members will be assigned to a sixth group."

Before the King could interrupt again the Senator quickly went on.

"Each group shall have two Senators attached to it, and as of now, these Senators have made their choices as to which groups they will be joining." Senator Opek waited for a response from the King, but with none coming, continued.

"As well as each section having two Senators, these groups will be further reinforced with two Guard Commanders and two Scout Leaders, and as many guards and Scouts as are available at the time attached to them on a rotating basis. Each section shall be further enhanced by the addition of members from the Great Council of Elders."

The pause in the Senator's address gave the King time to again add his thoughts.

"You seem to have planned well, Senator Opek, but there one matter that I think you may have overlooked."

"And what might that be, my King?"

"Scouts! Do we have enough scouts to cover all the groups, as well as having long range patrols out there in what is the unknown?"

The Senator waited to see if the King had anything further to add before he commented on what the King had said.

"My King, I agree we have a major shortage in the field of trained scouts and guards, and I have discussed this matter with Senator Ova, who I have no doubt you are aware is Senator directly responsible for Scouts and Guards."

Again, the pause in the Senator's briefing gave The King the opportunity to interrupt. "Well! What did you and Senator Ova come up with to address this shortage?"

Before the Senator answered, he made a mental note not to pause, to give the King no room to continue with his interjections. Then, on second thought, he replied. "My King, I will let Senator Ova, speak on this matter."

As the spotlight moved off Senator Opek, he began to wonder about the state of mind of The King, but then promptly dismissed those thoughts, putting them down to the pressures of the great changes that were taking place.

"Senator Ova, what have you to say on this matter of this scout and guard shortages?"

Moving to the front of The King, Senator Ova replied. "My King, as our Assembly is divided into six, thus it is that all the remaining scouts and guards will be united under one legion banner. The tasks will therefore be allotted to them so they will be better accomplished. It is my, as well as the opinion of Senator Opek, that those so consolidated scouts and guards should be increased by another fifty."

"Do you think that will prove to be a sufficient number?"

"Yes, my King. At these unsure times, we believe that in the short-term, this number will overcome any shortages we may face."

"Then continue, Senator."

"That is all I have to report, my King." The Senator again fell to silence, awaiting any further comments or direction from the King.

"Senator Opek, you have done well, and I must congratulate you and Senator Ova for your efforts."

With that Senator Opek took his leave.

As the swell of the oceans grew with the winds, King Epiphanes ordered the assembled Senators to go fourth and continue with all preparations, and to do so with great haste as the tides of change were beginning to sweep across them all.

"Proceed, Senator Ira – let not the wrath of the God Wind Boreas hinder you. Announce that we are to be ready to leave at the very earliest of the day following," King Epiphanes instructed, as they, the two of the oldest Assembly members surged through the now heavy, rolling, wind-chilled swells.

So it came to pass that the Great Assembly – which since a time long past, had lived as Regents of the Deep protected by the God Poseidon – did gather into their respective groups in great anticipation of the journey that now lay before them. As decreed by The King, the newly combined legions of guards and scouts under the watchful command of Commander Zen who was now trained to the Fourth Order of the Creed, were briefed by the Senator of planning, Senator Opek, and the Senator of Guards and Scouts, Senator Ova.

Now, that the great odyssey as ordained by the great God Poseidon was upon them, Commander Zen moved out and ordered his scouts to take up their positions.

And so, under the vigilant eyes of a newly promoted Commander Mio and twenty scouts, the first of the Great Assembly to depart the Cave of Amphitrite took their leave before the Sun God Hyperion had graced the skies with his presence. Mio kept her nervous anticipation in check. While not happy with being lumbered with a second-in-command like Scout Leader Hur, she reluctantly accepted those things over which she had no control. She and her scouts were assigned the task to keep some two asmar to the fore of the first group and to scout a safe path that the others would soon follow. With each member spaced two sigmar apart, the scouts were sent skipping over the oceans on track, following the path of the Sun God, Hyperion, towards where the unknown worlds awaited them.

As so preordained by the God Poseidon and sanctified by King Epiphanes, the four sections passed from the Cave of Amphitrite – the last known mark. An eerie calm settled over the zephyr-swept oceans, as if issuing a departing gesture of respect. Commander Zen and Guard Commander Lute made one final scan of the area that surrounded the Cave of Amphitrite, and bid farewell to the known. Then, in unison, they turned and set out after the wake of the departed Great Assembly.

For the next thirty-seven days, the oceans were alive with a multitude of flashing bodies as the Assembly surged through the waters, their steel-grey and white bodies slicing the white caps of the blue oceans. For ten asmar in all directions the waters boiled with their masses. By the dawn of the thirty-eighth day, the Assembly had reached and passed all recorded marks. Ahead lay the true unknown, where waters grew dark with depth.

So it was that the Great Assembly moved on, always following the Sun God Hyperion. Those in their learning curve did take the lessons, the new-born were cared for, and life as they all had known it did progress with little change.

The feeding scouts left as usual at daybreak, seeking to herd in the shoals of fish that now filled the oceans in abundance. Commander Zen was fully occupied with those under his command that were kept the most active of all factions. There were the long-range patrols that departed at ten-day intervals to meet briefly at five days out with the incoming patrol as they returned. Then they would continue on, keeping up the constant vigil, and taking care of the progress of those scouts promoted to the new position of leader scouts in the third decree. Scout Leader Hur, whom King Epiphanes ordered to be promoted in an effort to stem his waywardness, and in an attempt to appease the widowed mother, was causing the most concern to Zen.

As each day rolled into the next, time marched on ever so slowly. Zen sought the companionship of Lute to snatch precious time from the drudgery of his responsibilities. Together they pursued solitude beyond the outer ring of the Assembly guards, riding the long low swells that seemed to be never-ending, and marvelling at the new phenomenon of mountains of frozen water that had appeared with some abundance over the last ten days. The melting water from these drifting mountains merged with the oceans, adding to the clarity of the surrounds that enhanced and sharpened the senses. Skies of cloudless beauty blended with the oceans, creating a serenity of tranquillity and peace that descended over all in the Great Assembly.

— Ψ —

On the four hundredth and thirty-ninth day since crossing over The Shallows, it was the calling together of The Great Council of Elders that was the order of the time. Each Senator took up their designated position, with The Most Learned One on the right of The King.

"Most Learned One, present yourself before those gathering here," ordered King Epiphanes.

"As ordered, as so I must obey," replied The Most Learned One as he moved from the side of The King, and positioned himself in front of the eight Senators

"I call on you to bring down the blessing of the great God Poseidon on those gathered here," ordered The King.

"As so ordered, as so I must obey," countered The Most Learned One.

"Oh Great God, Poseidon, ruler of the seas and all things therein, now a dweller in the heavens, we thank you for leading us away from the souls of the lost, for having led us safely through many unseen dangers, and having kept struggles and entanglements thus far at bay. We call on you now for continued guidance in our search for the New World. So, let it come to pass."

57

"So, let it come to pass," the Senators replied en masse.

With the call for guidance to the God Poseidon complete, The Most Learned One resumed his rightful place on the right of King Epiphanes. The Great Council of Elders waited while The King gathered his thoughts. Age, as the great leveller, was unmistakably becoming more obvious in the Assembly's older statesman.

Senator Zoa moved in a little closer to his father, King Epiphanes.

As he broke the surface of the water, the King spoke to his son. "What brings you in close Zoa?"

"Senator Ku, father of Scout Commander Lute, this day seeks his leave to address this gathering, my father and My King."

"So be it, so be it, my son." The King's voice was now only a shadow of its former self.

"Senator Ku, present yourself to those here gathered," The King ordered.

"As so ordered, as so I obey," replied the Senator as he moved to the fore of the gathered.

The Senator, having taken up his place, awaited The Kings approval.

"You may proceed, Senator Ku." The King's voice was now a little more laboured.

"King Epiphanes, Most Learned One, Senators, Council of Elders – I, Senator Ku, bring unto the Assembly glad tidings." The speed and excitement in the voice of the Senator's delivery took all by surprise.

"Slow down Senator! We do have time. By the sound of it, you do have good news to impart; so tell it to us a little slower if you please." The gentleness of The King's voice had returned.

"I am sorry, My King. The excitement of my news overwhelmed my better judgement."

"Continue, Senator. We understand." The King's words put the Senator at ease.

The Senator continued. "At last day's darkest, Commander Zen, son of Senator Ira, sought from me my approval for a union with my first-born daughter, Lute."

"Does Senator Ira know of these things?" The King interrupted.

Turning to Senator Ira, The King ordered his presence to the front of the Assembly.

"Do you know of these happenings of which Senator Ku speaks?" The King asked the approaching Senator.

"Yes, King. It is the truth that Senator Ku speaks."

"Do you agree with this proposed union, Senator Ira?" The King queried.

"I do agree, my King. From the beginning of their time together, it has been my wish that this union would come to pass."

The two Senators now side by side awaited The King's pleasure. The King looked across at the two Senators.

"This will be a good union; so let it be decreed that four days forward, both of those who seek this union shall be presented before the Inner Sanctum of Senators in due ritual, and the blessing of the God Poseidon shall be brought down upon them."

News of the pending union sped through the Assembly – the first union since the Assembly had left the waters of Atlantis.

At the dawn of the fourth day, as decreed, Commander Zen and Scout Commander Lute waited to be ushered into the innermost sanctum of King Epiphanes and the eight of his Senators.

"Guard Commander Mio! Can you vouch that all those here assembled are of no less than of the fourth decree?"

"As so inquired, My King, as to that I cannot vouch," replied the Guard Commander.

"Have you sounded the alarm, Guard Commander?"

"No, my King. I have not, for that transgressor is none other than Scout Commander Lute whom you have this day summoned to present herself before you."

"Most Learned One, has this young Lute not reached the fourth?"

"My King, the young Lute, as you call her, reached the fourth some number of days past."

"Well, Most Learned One, let's bring her before me, and let us bestow the honour of the fourth on her as our gift on this day of her great union. Commander Zen, son of Senator Ira, Grandson of Zoa, present yourself before me, your King."

"As so ordered, as so I obey." The somewhat timid reply from Commander Zen was barely audible as he moved forward.

"Scout Commander Lute, daughter of Senator Irk, present yourself before me also." The call from The King had taken on a laboured tone.

"As so ordered, as so I obey," the ritual continued with Lute's reply.

"Most Learned One, present yourself before me," The King again ordered.

"As so ordered, as so I obey."

"Most Learned One, from that immense reservoir of all things past, entrusted unto those of the higher learning for safe keeping, can any justification be discovered as to why this union about to take place should not progress?"

"As so ordered, as so I have searched, and it is, I report, that this union has no weakness."

"On this day of unification we must observe that it was our God, Poseidon, who laid down the founding principles of the Creed that have endured with us from the beginning of our time." The words of King Epiphanes were indeed laboured.

"Senator Ku, father of Scout Commander Lute, I ask that you reveal the meanings of the fifth principal of this Creed."

"As so ordered, My King, as so of these secrets I will now tell. The fifth principle of our founding creed is to observe a due medium between avarice and profusion, to hold the balance of truth and sincerity with balanced equality, to moderate emotion and intolerance, and in all pursuits to always have eternity in view." Having delivered the fifth principle, the Senator retired.

"Senator Ira, father of Commander Zen, as I asked that Senator Ku reveal the secrets of the fifth principle of this Creed, it is of you I ask to speak of the sixth principle of our Creed."

"As so ordered, My King, as so I will tell. The sixth and final principle of our founding Creed is to agree to hold in reverence the original rulers and Gods of this universe and this our Assembly, and all further successors supreme and subordinate according to their rank, and to yield to the accords and proclamations as decreed by the Gods or their Supreme Council."

"Thank you, Senator Ira."

The Senator like Senator Ku before him then took his leave.

"Commander Zen and Scout Leader Lute, the fifth and sixth principles of our founding Creed this day have been read to you. I urge that you, having heard of these teachings, take heed; for as those who inhabited the Island of Atlantis failed to follow closely these teachings, they then did come to the attention of the God, Poseidon. And it was this God of the Sea that brought about the destruction of that land and all those who dwelt therein."

The King let the sombreness of his words settle over the two to be united. Turning to the Most Learned One, he gave further instruction.

"Most Learned One, I call upon you to bring down the blessing of our God, the Great God Poseidon, on these two before me."

"As so ordered, as so I must obey. Oh, Great God, Poseidon, God of the Sea and all that dwell here-in, I, your most loyal and obedient servant, ask that you in all your generosity grant to these here just joined, your gifts of procreation. Bring and grant to them in the wisdom of their youth, the gifts of an ever-lasting union, that they may be free of torment and hidden dangers. Grant to them your never-ending love, that they may go from this place of unification wiser and stronger in the knowledge that it is you who watches over them. Grant to these, your two Regents of the Deep, these things that I ask in reverence."

With the final blessings of the God Poseidon concluded, King Epiphanes recited the age-old completion of the ritual of unification.

"So let it come to pass," which was then repeated by the Senators.

"So let it come to pass."

"Commander Zen, Scout Leader Lute, as so you did request, as so it has now been recited and recorded by The Learned Ones of our Great Assembly, as so it is now complete. Go forth, united, and from this time to ten days hence you are both free from all your duties."

The newly joined couple, in a concluding tribute to their King and what had taken place before the gathered assembly members, then circled those of the inner sanctum three times. On each circuit, as written, they came to a halt in front of The King – their heads bowed in respect to this wise old man of the seas who had ruled over them both for the time that had spanned all their lives.

They too did recite the ode, "So let it come to pass," and then they did retreat to a place of solitude that would last for the following ten days.

Following the unification ceremony of Zen and Lute, King Epiphanes moved next to The Learned One.

"Most Learned One, call the Senate back to order, and I want them brought to order in the first decree." The King's mood had gone from the uplifting atmosphere of the unification ritual to one that could only be described as harsh and without formality.

"As so ordered, as so I will do."

"Without the formality is what I ordered; and without formality is what I demand it to be."

The Learned One was completely taken aback by the bluntness of the King's call.

"Senators, draw together as our King wishes."

"Senators! Thank you for your attendance."

The cutting short of The Learned One's call was unheard of by the gathered Senators. The Learned One, nursing his wounded pride, withdrew to the rear of the advancing King.

"I have decided the time has come that all Senators here gathered discuss the continuing problems caused by the widowed Dy." The King looked out at his Senators, sensing that they were far from happy to discuss this subject.

"Come, come! It is a matter that now has to be discussed, and a conclusion reached."

The King waited for some sort of reaction to his statement, and as there was none, he continued. "The widow Dy is again bringing disharmony to certain sections of the Assembly with her on-going complaining. Now, this matter must be clarified to the satisfaction of all concerned.

"What is she complaining about now? It cannot be the provisioning, as the food scouts are doing extremely well in that department."

Senator Viarka volunteered to speak. The King nodded his approval to the Senator.

"It is not the victuals; it is her son, Hur. Again, she claims that there is discrimination against him."

"By what means can the widow Dy substantiate these grave accusations? You seem to be the only one with a point of discussion, Senator Viarka." The King moved through the Senators, all of whom offered up nothing.

"Well! Do none of you have anything constructive to contribute? It seems to me that at this time not one of you wishes to add anything on the matter of the widow Dy or her son Hur." Hesitating for a moment, hoping there would be some sort of Senate interjection, but with none forthcoming, the King continued.

"I have, this day, decided that Hur will be promoted to Scout Leader, and accordingly, this is promotion is being bestowed upon him as I speak to you of these things." The King's delivery took the Senators by complete surprise.

"Furthermore," The King continued, "I have further ordered that he be given all of those commands and privileges that others of his rank are given and so enjoy."

The King could feel the disbelief and dismay rising in some of the Senators. Ignoring their requests to address him now, he continued on. "Furthermore, a patrol under Scout leader Hur is at this time undergoing final briefing prior to departing."

The King turned away from the Senators to address a Senate Runner who had scanned in for his attention.

"Thank you, Senate Runner".

"Now this will set off the volcanos within the ranks of my Senators," The King thought as he turned back to address the Senators.

"Scout Leader Hur has departed with his patrol, and so I dismiss you all."

The Senators responded as The King departed, "So, let it come to pass.

—— Ψ ——

With the ten days of their solitude now at an end, the newly united Commander Zen and Scout Commander Lute returned to the Great Assembly. First to welcome them back was Teacher Tia who had been taking time out from his daily tasks to swim alone, enjoying his own solitude.

"Greetings, my friends. It's great to see you both again." The affectionate words from their life-long friend was a very warming welcome back into the fold; however, the three friends' reunion was broken by the incoming scans of a Senate Runner.

"Commander Zen, welcome back; and my welcome back also extends to you, Scout Commander Lute."

"Senate Runner, Lute and I both thank you for your welcome. Now, what Senate member sends you out this far from their fold?"

Lute could not place the Senate Runner, but then again she thought, things are changing very fast.

"Senator Ova and Senator Opek have ordered your immediate attendance."

"Thank you. Inform the Senators I will present myself to them with all due haste."

Lute again tried to place the Senate Runner, thinking the youth seemed just that, a youth, as the Senate Runner left the three old friends and headed back in the direction of the Senate.

"Well, Lute, as so ordered, I will leave you two to continue catching up, while I go join the Senators. First day back, so had better start it in the best possible manner."

"Approach, Commander Zen. Firstly, let us welcome you home." The warmth of the greeting washed over Zen, and it felt good to be back in the fold

"Thank you Senator Ova." Zen noted the look of concern on the Senator's face.

"May I also extend my warmest greeting and welcome back to you my friend Commander?" offered Senator Opek.

"Thank you also, Senator Opek. Both yours and Senator Ova's greeting are warm and most welcome." However, the feeling of unease still radiated from Senator Ova; although now reduced in its intensity, it was still there. "Now, your good wishes and greetings are most welcomed, but I am sure this was not the only reason for you to call me this day before you."

"Well, to be perfectly honest, where it is always a pleasure to see you, there are matters that do need your attention with some degree of closer scrutiny."

Zen joined the two abreast in silence and waited for Senator Ova to continue.

"A number of days ago, Scout Leader Hur...."

"Scout Leader Hur!" Zen found himself interrupting the Senator, then apologised profusely for his breach of protocol. Zen struggled to keep his thoughts in check, knowing full well that any unwitting intensification in his opinion would open his own thoughts on Hur to appraisal by the Senators.

"Your apology is accepted, Commander. Your concerns about Hur's promotion we have just noted; and yes, we of the Senate were somewhat surprised at Hur's promotion. But the King overruled those Senators concerned by this promotion."

Zen felt slightly embarrassed that the Senator had read his thought pattern so quickly.

"Even an approach by both Senator Inca and myself, with the backing of Senator Opek here, fell on deaf ears. The King has decided that, by taking this course of action in promoting Hur, he would go some way to silencing his widowed mother's repeated outbursts. One thing we can all be thankful for is that it is the very bottom rung of promotion."

Zen nodded in agreement with the Senator's comments.

"Let us put this digression regarding Hur's promotion to one side, but not leave the subject of Hur entirely as Scout Leader Hur has, in the four days just past, returned from a long forward reconnaissance patrol. I think I will let Senator Opek speak of Hur's report, as it was directly to him that Scout Leader Hur reported on his return."

"Scout Leader Hur," the Senator began, "reports of landfall some sixteen days from where the Assembly is currently positioned. He further reports of a large mixing of fresh water." The Senator fell silent, as if letting Zen digest the first part of Hur's report.

"Was that all Hur reported?" Zen inquired of the Senator.

"Let me continue. Hur also reported a large bay, not too dissimilar to The Shallows that he believed is abundant in shoals of fish, and with this abundance he has recommended that the Assembly take up short-term residency there."

The Senator scanned for Zen's comments.

"On the face of it, Senators, the report does seem to have some credibility attached to it. Under the training regime of scouts at the basic level entry, they are taught to be careful. All scouts undergo training in using their scanners to check for all living things, both in the water and on the land. Now, please tell, what did Hur's report say of these things?" Zen watched and waited for either Senator to reply.

Senator Opek conferred with his fellow Senator, and then turned back to Hur.

"The Hur report said he had done these things, and found that other than the many shoals of fish that frequented the bay and the area immediately outside the bay, no scans confirmed any other form of life."

The two Senators waited for Commander Zen to comment.

"Well, as I can see, Scout Leader Hur carried out all tasks as laid down in that part of his training, but if you two Senators are not happy with his report, I will interview Scout Leader Hur and revisit his report."

Again, after conferring, Senator Opek turned back to address

Zen. "Yes! We do think that will be necessary, perhaps to calm our concerns, as it may well be we are just a bit too cautious. Maybe Hur has turned the corner, and we are pre-judging him just a little. Come, Commander. Come now and join the rest of the Senators. I am sure they will all be pleased to see you on your return." With that, Senator Opek turned and led the trio in the direction of the Senate.

The New Bay

6

In a special single moment in time, the little boy's laughter danced across the still waters of the bay like the dancing notes of the flutes that filled the night air with harmony. Again and again, the stick in the small boy's hand stirred up the water, and time and time again his laughter danced and floated its way over the bay. What captured his young imagination was the way his face was distorted by the disturbed water's reflection as he broke the surface with his stick. His eyes seemed to take on a world of their own. The black pupils shone like the black ebony that decorated his home and his round, plump, yellow-skinned face took on a fierce Warlord warrior look – and then as quickly as it had appeared on the water's surface, it disappeared.

The smell of cherry blossoms seemed to mix with the wisps of light fog to cast a magical spell in the early morning. For that moment in time, the little warrior of six summers stood proud overlooking all in his domain. The reflective. yellow-gold water of the bay with its floating cherry blossom flowers lay silent as if awaiting this little man's godly command.

"Ying Ying!"

"Oh why! Why can't they leave me alone? I am a mighty warrior with battles to fight, and demons to slay – demons like those I have seen far out in the bay." But the magic and tranquillity of the morning had been broken.

"Ying Ying! Where are you? Oh, there you are, Master Ying Ying. Your father commands your presence at the breakfast table. Come along, come now. I have much to do."

Grabbing the young man by the hand with a tug, they headed up the hill to the dwelling of the fearsome Warlord. The concubine's harsh tug brutally banished the last remnants of the little warrior's dreams of his pursuit of demons and dragons

—— Ψ ——

"Ying Ying, son of mine. Come, come! Sit down." Patting the chair next to him, the Jomonese Master Warlord beckoned his youngest son to sit.

"Concubines, concubines! Serve the food," the Master Warlord called, as he clapped his hands.

Ying Ying looked up in adoration at his father the Master Warlord who was the undisputed ruler of the small village that overlooked the isolated and tranquil bay.

"What has my Ying Ying been doing out so early in the morning?" The Warlord reached out and ruffled the hair of his young offspring.

"Father, I went down to the bay at first light." His little eyes took on a shine of excitement as he told of the monsters that lurked in the bay.

"You went where?" The Warlord's voice now rose as he realized where his young charge had been.

In the face of his father's anger, the brave little warrior was reduced to tears, for the little man had seen the anger explode before. On many occasions in the past, Ying Ying had seen a violent father melded into a frame of mind filled to over-flowing with fury.

"Where were your keepers when you went down to the bay?" the now inflamed Warlord demanded of his son. "Stop your crying, you little piece of dog vomit."

The Warlord reached across and grabbed his son by the hair and dragged him across the table, sending plates and goblets crashing to the floor in a shower of utensils and breaking glass. The large doors at the end of the dining hall swung open, momentarily interrupting the chastising of Ying Ying. The Warlord's face, now disfigured with rage, watched as three concubines shuffled in, each carrying steaming dishes of fish soup, rice, and rice flour bread.

"Which one of you allowed my son to go down to the bay by himself this morning?"

The concubines stopped in unison, all knowing full well the sound of developing fury in their Master's voice – a fury which had now imprinted itself across his face.

"No one took your son to the bay, Master. Your son climbed out of his window at first light." Yakari bowed as she spoke, praying to her god, begging him save her from her Master's rising anger.

"Is this true, Son? Did you disobey me again?" The tide of red again crept up the neck of the Warlord.

"No, Father, no! It was Minya who allowed me to go." The once brave warrior was now just a cowering little boy, terrified of the rising fury that manifested on his father's face. He silently begged to his god, – please make my father believe me.

"Minya! Did you allow my son to go to the bay alone this morning?"

"No Master, no Master," the now fearful Minya's meek voice uttered as she shuffled forward.

"Serve the food – I will think on this matter while I eat." The three women with their fear ever so slightly defused moved forward to serve as they were ordered.

In silence, Viarka placed her tray of rice bread before the Warlord and took her station behind her Master. Minya stood in silence, fearfully waiting to be called forward to serve her dish.

"Serve me the fish now!"

The Master's tone renewed the crushing fear in Minya as she gingerly stepped forward, and in her trembling hands, the serving ladle converted to a rattle against the side of the stone caldron. Silence stalked the dining hall as Minya served her dish, first to the Master, and then reaching across the table, she filled the plate of the snivelling Ying Ying.

"Leave the trays here and be gone. Get out of my sight!"

The Warlord seemed to have calmed down a little, and the red swelling of his neck had dissipated as the morning food service slowly returned to some form of near normality. Minya moved forward and placed the caldron of steaming rice to the right side of the Master, feeling somewhat relieved that the Master appeared calmer. Turning, she bowed to her Master, and then without warning, he grabbed her by the hair and unleashed his inner-dog of fury on her frailty. He swung his huge fist with a brutal force and smashed it into her face, splintering her fragile cheek bone, splitting open her flawless alabaster skin with ease, and sending a cascade of blood streaming down her face and neck.

Minya screamed and collapsed; she was only stopped short of hitting her head on the stone floor by the Master Warlord, who held steadfastly onto a handful of her long, obsidian black hair.

Again, the Warlord Master struck, and this time his clenched leather-bound fist found the mouth of Minya, shredding her lips as they were brutally forced back over breaking teeth. Again, and again the fury-fuelled Warlord swung his fist, and each and every blow sent another torrent of blood spurting from her once beautiful face, cascading down and saturating her once white kimono in a sea of red.

In a final indignity to the now semi-conscious Minya, the Warlord lifted her off her feet by her hair that he still held firmly grasped in his clenched fist as he stared at the bloodied woman as if thinking how he could inflict more suffering. His rage not yet abated; the fury-driven Master grabbed her blood-soaked kimono and ripped it from her body, exposing her nakedness to his son and servants. Dragging her closer so that her face was next to his, he spat a mouthful of half-eaten food that, when mixed with Minya's congealing blood, gave the concubine a grotesque look.

Through clinched teeth, in a tone that sent cold shivers through those present, he growled, "Don't you ever call my son a liar. Do you hear me? You, with the looks of an ugly pig's arse! You, daughter of the bitch dogs that scavenge on our pits of garbage!"

Then, with a flick of his arm, he sent the battered and bleeding Minya staggering backwards, and she fell to the cold unyielding stone floor in a blood-soaked heap.

"Crawl, you dog bitch! Crawl out of my sight."

In a final act of brutality, the Warlord swung his heavy leather booted foot, and the sickening sound of cracking bones gave a warning of how far the Master would go to instil his position of unquestionable dominance over all those in his domain.

"Get her out my sight, you women bred out of the arse of a pig. Get her out of here!" The Warlord's eyes bulged as if they were ready to leap out of their very sockets and attack the concubines themselves. Then, as if nothing at all had happened, the Master turned and resumed his place at the table.

"Eat, Ying Ying, my son. Eat! You do want to grow into a fine, brave, Master Warlord like your father don't you?" As quickly as the beast master of fury had risen in the Warlord, it had just as quickly been sedated and locked back in its cage of hate. Knowing his place, the boy just nodded and started on the soup. Other than the clatter of spoon on plate, the shuffling of shoes on the stone floor, and the occasional slurp, the meal was consumed in silence.

The Promotion

7

The storm gods had been slowly building up their forces, summoning in the wild clouds from their ice-capped mountain homes, putting on notice all heavenly things. It was as if all time stood still; the four winds halted in anticipation and filled the air with an eerie peace. Then, as the daylight dimmed, the storm gods sent forth their Trojans of war, free to attack with the greatest ferocity they could wield. Thus, the brewing storm broke, rearing up from a great depth. The sea-dwelling demons tore great pieces from the heart of the ocean and hurled these, as if in defiance, to the greatest God of all Gods himself. They drenched the heavens – throwing great walls of water again and again with ever-intensifying ferocity, as if teasing those heavenly bodies, only to drag soaring walls of water back to crush them again and again into a sea traumatised by the vengeance of the infuriated demons – seas that screamed as if pleading for mercy. A sound that only seas can make when those great bodies of water are ripped asunder, as they rise up in the air to be further attacked by the God winds that prowl the heavens, as if taking exception and revenge upon those that trespass into their realm.

"Commander Zen!"

The call to Zen was somewhat distorted during this time as the God storms vented their anger. Scans could be warped by the unseen fire that surged through the air prior to Thor voicing his anger.

"Senate Runner, I am here." As he watched the runner close in on him and Lute, Zen wondered what Senator in their right mind would be sending a runner out in this storm.

Lute looked across at the love of her life and said, "I have no doubt your presence is required by someone in the Senate – probably some small thing they should be able to handle without always calling on you."

Zen felt a tinge of the disapproval that, of late, was building in Lute.

"It seems any free time we manage alone is always interrupted by someone from the Senate with a problem that, with a little common sense, could be rectified without always calling on you to appear."

"Lute, now relieved of all her duties, is being that little bit difficult again."

"No! I am not being difficult."

Zen, having let his guard down, had his thoughts read by the heavily pregnant Lute.

"Commander Zen!" the Senate Runner interrupted.

"I am sorry, Senate Runner. What message do you bring me?" Zen shifted this thought train to the incoming scans.

"The Senators request your attendance at a special calling together of the Senate." The Senate Runner, having delivered his message, awaited a return reply from Zen.

"Thank you, Runner. Pray, tell me, did the Senators give any indication as to the urgency of my attendance?"

"No, Commander, as best I can recall, the only thing of note is that some of the Senators seemed a little agitated."

"Thank you, Senate Runner. Please convey to the Senators that I will be in attendance as they have ordered."

"Lute, come with me. I will not leave you way out here by yourself so far from the Assembly. Not in this developing storm; it is far too dangerous."

The thoughtfulness of Zen seemed to calm the soon-to-be-mother.

—— Ψ ——

"Approach, Commander Zen." The incoming call saw Zen being brought straight into the centre circle of Senators without formality.

"Thank you for your prompt response to our call, Commander."

Zen knew a call from the Senators was an irrevocable demand for attendance, but it was still good to get a thank you from Senator Opek.

"How is your dear Lute? I think I can speak for the rest of the Senators gathered here and say we do miss seeing her around."

Before Zen could answer the gift of praise, the Senator when on.

"Tell me, Legion Commander, how far are we away from hearing the good news of her giving birth?"

"The nursing matrons tell us both that her time is very close, and any time now we are expecting an arrival."

"The excitement of this pending birth is reflected in your voice, Commander."

Zen scanned a thank you to the Senator.

"The storm that is now descending on us is expected to get a lot worse. Even the Learned One who advised us of this is concerned at the storms projected magnitude." Senator Opek's words drew all in attendance back to the reason of their call together.

Zen knew that some of those of the Learned Ones had the ability to read the pressures that accompanied the strange noises the God Thor made.

"These findings, we all believe, are of grave concern to the wellbeing of the Assembly and, therefore, we must immediately put in place a plan to protect all." Senator Opek again waited for some response from the Commander. With none forthcoming, he went on.

"Before you say we have weathered bad storms in the past without succumbing to implementing any form of plan, let me make this very clear. The Learned Ones say we can expect this approaching storm to reach an intensity equal to the might of the storm our God Poseidon used to destroy Atlantis." The Senator let the full impact of his words sink in to the now fully attentive Commander Zen.

"Senator, what sort of time frame do we have before we can expect the worst of the storm to bear down on us?"

"Commander Zen, there is no time frame. Do you not feel the strength of the winds, for they increase in velocity as we speak? That alone is an indication of a time frame. To be blunt, Commander, we have no so-called time frame."

"Senator Opek, I must interrupt." Senator Inca, who had been silent until now, moved between the Commander and Senator Opek.

"Please do Senator. The more we all contribute, the quicker a decision on what needs doing can be made, and action taken."

"Ahh! Senator Opek, it is on a slightly happier and in a more joyous note that I interrupt you."

While the two Senators conferred, Zen became aware of how the winds now were ripping at the oceans. He thought to himself that if the storm were to grow as great as the Learned Ones predicted, then the Assembly might well be in for a time racked with danger.

"Commander Zen!" The command from Senator Opek called Zen's

wandering attention to heel.

"Yes, Senator Opek."

"Senator Inca has bought to this arena a call of glad tidings. It seems congratulations are very much the order of this day for you."

"For me, Senator? Why would I be in line for congratulations?" Zen scanned through his thought banks, looking for a reason why he would be in line for any good wishes.

"Come on, Zen! Stop looking! Senator Inca has this moment been informed by a runner from the nursing pod that your lovely Lute has just a short time past given birth to a happy and healthy girl. Here, I must add, mother and daughter are doing well." Senator Opek moved in close to the Commander and with a smile firmly playing across his eyes ordered: "You are dismissed, Zen. Go! Be with your Lute, but I want you to be back here at first light of the new day."

The warmth Zen felt from Senator Opek radiated out over all the others there gathered.

"Thank you, Senator. Your well wishes and congratulations are heartily received."

The warmth between the two Regents of the Deep was openly obvious to all.

"Thank you, Senator. I will convey to Lute your most warm well-wishes." Zen, with due ritual, turned to take his leave.

"Before you leave, Commander Zen, there is another task that has fallen on me to complete."

The call back of the Senator took Zen a little bit by surprise, but before he was given the opportunity to respond to the call back, the Senator continued. "The King has asked..." The Senator hesitated momentarily, and then proceeded. "The King, on the recommendation and endorsement of all the Senators, has decreed that the long disused rank of Legion Commander be reinstated."

Zen rode the ocean surges in silence. His mind vaguely recalled the rank of which the Senator spoke, but a rank that had long ago been dispelled.

"The King has also decreed that the rank not only be fully restored, but all the privileges that went with this prestigious rank are to be fully restored as well." Senator Opek watched for any reaction from the Commander, and again as none were forthcoming, he continued. "You have no comment on this matter, Commander?"

Zen turned to the Senator trying to read his thoughts which, as always, proved to be a fruitless effort.

"Senator Opek, as that is a matter for the inner circle and the King to decide, and as the Creed dictates, I will fully respect any and all decisions they arrive at."

The Senator allowed a faint smile to trickle across his thought patterns, thinking that the King was indeed correct with his decree – a very wise choice.

"Commander Zen, do you understand the privileges and status that go with this very rank?"

"Yes, Senator Opek. I am fully aware of those things or privileges as you call them."

"Commander Zen, is that a little impatience that I detect coming to the fore?"

"I am sorry, Senator Opek. I apologise for my loss of concentration." Zen again acknowledged the Senator.

"I am also sorry, Commander Zen, for it is not my, or indeed the rest of the gathered Senators' intention to further delay your reunion with Lute and your new-born child, but please present yourself before me."

"As ordered, as so I comply."

The tone in the Senator's scan, along with the instilled teachings of the creed, automatically drew both Senator Opek and Commander Zen into ritual.

"Commander Zen, on the instructions of the King and his Senators, I, Senator Opek, put the following question to you."

The sudden change from friendly bantering to the full format of ritual took Commander Zen by complete surprise.

"Commander Zen, do you accept the rank and privileges of Legion Commander?"

"Senator Opek, I, Commander Zen, accept and take up the mantle of the prestigious rank of Legion Commander."

"Legion Commander, is that a little hesitancy I feel in your reply?"

Zen felt the shroud of formality momentarily drift away from the Senator.

"No, my Senator Opek, not hesitancy. Far from it – surprise... total surprise that this honourable rank not only has been restored, but that the King has seen me as a fitting recipient of it."

Senator Opek looked across at he who was becoming The Great Assembly's favourite son, and nodded in approval.

"Go now, Legion Commander Zen. Go to Lute."

With those last words, the somewhat bewildered new Legion Commander took his leave from the Senators.

The Storm

8

The new day broke with the God winds in full attack. Anything that stood in their way was assaulted with unbending ferocity. The waters of the oceans screamed in torment as they bore the brunt of the wind God's anger.

Zen and Lute, with the newly named Cyan, were surrounded by the matrons who fussed as they did over all new arrivals. Cyan, already an able swimmer, had her mother on the run as the youngster quickly learned her mother was at her beck and call.

Zen scanned to Lute as the proud new mother once more swam after her offspring. "The Senate has instructed I present myself there this day."

With the tumult of the storm-causing chaos, Lute and Cyan were immediately lost in mountainous oceans and Zen was uncertain whether Lute had picked up his signal.

"Don't worry, Zen. They will be safe. You go to your appointment." The words of a passing nursing matron helped to somewhat reassure Zen.

— Ψ —

"Any hope of a time frame has gone. The storm is now upon us, Legion Commander." Senator Opek's words had a chill about them – a chill that cut to the very heart of Zen.

"I spoke with the Learned Ones a short time ago, and they told me that what we are experiencing at this time is just a small prelude of what we can expect over the coming days." The Senator allowed time for his words to sink in, and then continued.

"Legion Commander, what thought, if any, have you given to the imminent danger these Gods of the winds seem to want to inflict on us all?"

"Senator!" Zen had to increase his scan output for the Senator to receive and comprehend. "Senator! Can you understand me?"

The Senator nodded.

"I think we are at a loss as to a plan of action that will give the Assembly complete safety."

The Senator scanned Zen, requesting him to transmit with more intensity.

"Senator, can you understand me now?"

Again, the Senator nodded, but this time it had a lot more authority to it.

"I will repeat myself. Did you get that?"

Again the Senator nodded, but with conviction this time.

"Senator, I have taken the liberty to recall all the Scout Commanders, and have asked them to report here as soon as they can."

The Senator nodded his agreement. Zen knew full well that the Senator was at a complete loss; and, if he was being honest with himself, he had no idea whatsoever how they were going to handle this ever-increasing storm and the dangers that flowed from it.

"Senator, I have also told the Scout Commanders that during this crisis we will be dropping the formalities of ceremony. Do you agree Senator? Senator, do you agree?"

"I agree, Legion Commander."

"Thank you, Senator Opek."

Again, the Senator just nodded.

The winds intensified, then intensified again, then again; and the oceans reached for the heavens in anguish, as if petitioning the Wind Gods to be set free from the wind's torments. In response, daylight was struck from the heavens, and darkness rode the waves of doom.

"Legion Commander Zen!" The incoming scan of the first of the Scout Commanders beamed in.

"Thanks for your prompt attendance, Zarlie. Do you know how far away the others are?" Zen scanned back.

Scout Commander Zarlie broached next to Zen. Turning to acknowledge Senator Opek, Zarlie was unceremoniously picked up by a rogue wave and dumped ignominiously on top of the Legion Commander. Having temporarily lost some of her dignity, Zarlie surfaced next to the Senator.

"Sorry, Legion Commander, my mistake."

"Yes, it was your mistake," Zen reprimanded the newly promoted Zarlie.

"I was told in the earlier briefing that the water is now far too violent to stand on formality."

The chuckles of the other Scout Commanders who had joined the group unannounced brought Zen's brief reprimand of Zarlie to an end.

"Scout Commander, I, along with Senator Opek, have called you all here this morning to…."

"Excuse me, Legion Commander, but I am afraid I cannot read your scans," the late arriving Scout Commander Idyll signalled.

85

"Idyll by name, and idle by nature. I hope not, Scout Commander Idyll."

For some unknown reason, Zen felt a common bond with another of the newly promoted Scout Commanders. Scout Commander Idyll was one of the smallest in the Assembly, but he compensated for his lack of size with a raw strength that far outmatched any other member of the greater Assembly. So taken with this Scout Leader was Zen that he went to the Senator of Scouts and Guards with a recommendation that they take a chance and immediately promote the eager youngster to Scout Commander. To date, the call on which Zen staked his reputation had proved to be the right one.

"I am most remorseful, Legion Commander in my lateness, but it was my visit to the nursery that held me up. In fact, I would have been on time but for a cute little girl who caught my eye."

"Scout Commander Idyll, I am very disappointed in you. In these troubling times, you are thinking about your love life?"

"But, Legion Commander…"

The interruption came as a total surprise to Zen.

"This female that caught my eye is not five days old, and I have it on the very best of authority that she goes by the name of Cyan."

As a ripple of mirth encompassed the group of assorted commanders, Zen looked briefly at each and every Scout Commander in the troop, mentally thanking the Senate for their very wise selection of such a fine, able-bodied group.

As he attempted to continue, Zen had trouble getting the gathered group to understand him; the static that pervaded the air caused havoc with their communication scans. The towering seas were not only creating problems with their communication systems, but caused all to struggle with the elements. Ripping currents beneath the waves added to their uncertainty, for not only was the position of the other commanders unable to be plotted, but surfacing at speed, which was a necessity under the conditions, created its own life-threatening hazards.

"I can recall nothing in my past training that can give me any sort of guidance as to what to do under these conditions." The urgency of Zen's maximum scan reached all the commanders who could only respond with silence.

"Furthermore – and not wanting to add problem on problem – but after discussions with the Learned Ones who have consulted with those who have gone before us, it seems they also have nothing to offer by way of guidance."

For a fleeting moment, thoughts of a happy time now long past, along with the safety of The Shallow's protection, filled Zen's mind.

"If there is nothing of the past we can call on at this time, then what are your recommendations, Legion Commander?"

Idyll's scan quickly brought Zen back to the harsh reality of the responsibilities that came with the rank of Legion Commander. This, the highest non-Senate rank in the Assembly, was only bestowed upon the very few who were tested and proven in all levels of training. However, the fact that one had to achieve perfection in all these steps on the ladder of ascension to the rank did not automatically grant the wearer of the mantle absolute knowledge and wisdom.

The ever-increasing fury of the storm was now making communication very difficult, and Zen scanned all Scout Commanders to come in as close as safety allowed.

Increasing the intensity of his mental scans as best he could, Zen continued. "I have no miracle answers that will guarantee the safety of any of you; nor do I have answers to all those questions you are scanning in. All I can do is give you suggestions as to what action, or perhaps a better word is advice, may help you get through these troubled times."

"You had better make it quick, Legion Commander. We are all now struggling." The intermittent scan of Zarlie called in from a fading position, now some way to the rear of the gathered pack of Scout Commanders.

"Face into the storm! Face into the storm! Have you received that, Zarlie?" But all that replied to the Legion Commander was the roar of the terrified oceans; and Zarlie was gone.

"Go now, the rest of you. Go now, while you still can, and may our great God Poseidon reach down and cocoon you with his safety. So let it come to pass."

Again, only the wind replied to the Legion Commander, and it only answered with what seemed its never-ending roar.

—— Ψ ——

Ying Ying stood transfixed at the window, mesmerised by the torrential rains: fist-like raindrops that smashed and pounded the ramshackle village below – fist-like raindrops that demanded immediate entry. Those buildings that refused the rain entry were warned, and then warned again, by the unrelenting pounding. Then, one by one, those buildings that resisted the rain's demands had their flimsy thatched roofs ripped asunder. The swirling winds dragged down from the heavens the clouds that fuelled the fear-inducing rain, forcing the day to grow dim with darkening skies.

Ying Ying watched the fierce winds gulp down the airborne pieces of debris just as he had seen the wild dogs that roamed the surrounding wooded hills devour their prey. Then, as if on command of an unknown God, the swirling winds and rains disgorged the roof remnants spreading them far and wide across the countryside. Thankful that his father was a fearless Master Warlord warrior, and as such had the privileges and trappings that went with his hard-earned position, he felt safe in their big stone house high on the hill overlooking the village. They had many servants who attended to their every want and need, and there were also the many concubines his father kept in another part of the house – that part of the house he was forbidden to enter.

Ying Ying flinched in fright as a piece of the flying thatch slammed into the window as if, in some way, it was begging the little Warlord to grant it entry and shelter from the winds. With walls as thick as the young master's arms were long, Ying Ying knew he was safe in a house that could endure all the might the storm could muster. Of this he was sure. This instilled pride of position elevated Ying Ying above all those other children he had often watched through this very same window as they played on the cobbled paths that crisscrossed the village. The cherry blossom tree that stood as a sentinel outside his window bent and swayed, fighting not to submit to the unforgiving forces, its branches refusing to comply with the order of the wind. Then, as if offering up a compromise, it did give in and yield to those fierce winds one of its branches that now, stripped bare of its leaves and pink blossom petals, was sent spiralling down the hillside.

Then, in one gust that jolted even the stone house, the wind finally had its way with the cherry tree, ripping it from the earth and then spinning it over and over until it was flung without mercy against the high walls that surrounded the courtyard.

The little Warlord closed his eyes tightly as he tried to expel the memory flashes of times he'd seen his father unleash his wrath on the members of the staff – and their screams and pleas for mercy as he thrashed them until they could take no more and lost consciousness. At the height of his rages, the Master Warlord was known to continue to inflict his anger on his defenceless victims long after they had fallen unconscious. Ying Ying knew better than to ask his father why he was forced to watch as this brutal regime was imposed on all those around him. Ying Ying was called from his thoughts by the opening of the great door.

"Come, my young man, it is time for bed."

The harsh voice of the new maid who had replaced Minya was unlike that of the gentle young woman who, Ying Ying now realised, had not been seen since the morning of her beating.

He always received a silent response when he asked after the missing maid. Nobody seemed to know, or wanted to know, about the missing Minya.

The new maid, whom Ying Ying had secretly named the ugly dragon, grabbed him by the arm. Her vise-like grip caused the little man to cry out in pain.

"I said it was bed time, so come along. Bed time it is."

"You are not my keeper. Minya is my keeper."

The sudden outburst caused the ugly dragon to release her charge. Then she grabbed him again, this time by his clothing, and as if she was carrying a bag of rice, dragged him down the hallway towards his bedroom.

"Minya has gone! Minya is not coming back! The sooner you get to understand that, the sooner you and I will get along." The stinging words the ugly dragon threw at him brought a rush of tears to his eyes.

"Minya has not gone away. Minya is still here. I know she is still here." The little warrior's tears and sobs were now uncontrollable. "She is still here," His words were barely audible above the sobs. Ying Ying knew Minya was still here. The mound of newly turned earth in a corner of the compound told him so.

Maybe tomorrow, if the skies were clear and the storm had passed, he would again arise at first breaking light and steal out, down to the Bay. Once again to become that fierce Warlord Warrior fighting the unseen foes that lurked under every rock and behind every tree. But this time he would take another path, a path that would take the little man on a new journey. A new adventure, a little further around the Bay where he was sure there were even bigger monsters to find and put to the sword. And, if nothing else, a place the ever-vigilant concubines would not find him as easily as they had in the past.

"Scout Commander Diva, what are your instructions?" one of the scout leaders called, as they closed in on Diva.

"The only advice I can offer is what the Legion Commander passed on."

The raging seas were now rendering close formation impossible.

"We must keep facing the wind."

"Say again, Commander!"

This time Diva pulsed at maximum, repeating her instructions and adding, "Protect the young – at all cost, protect the young!"

There was no way Diva could know that the next few days would forever change the Assembly.

"Commander, may I have your attention for just a moment?" Hur rose close to Diva as the surging waves threw them together with a force that knocked Diva sideways.

"Back off, Hur! Back off! What are you trying to do – kill me?"

The brutal reply sent Hur scurrying out to a safer distance. Before Hur had a chance to say his piece, Scout Commander again spoke to him sternly.

"Where is The Most Learned One? Tell me you have not left him alone, Scout Leader."

"No, Commander, I have left him with four Scouts."

"How many Scouts have you left with the nursing mothers?" Diva's sharp interruption had taken on a softer tone as she asked, "What is it you have to report, Hur?"

Hur struggled to keep in contact with his Scout Commander. "On my last long range patrol, we found a bay…"

Contact was momentarily lost as the two regents were swept down into a mountainous hollow in the oceans with such a great speed that both required their full attention just to survive.

"Continue, Hur. What about this bay?" Diva waited for a response. "Hur, where are you? Can you hear me? Hur! *Always a problem*," she thought out loud.

"Here I am, Commander, and I take a little exception to your comments."

Diva castigated herself for letting her thoughts scan out.

"What is it you want to say about this so-called bay?" Diva let Hur's last remarks pass over her.

"Commander Diva, it is not a so-called bay. It is a real bay, and the finding of it was fully reported to the Senate on my return and …"

"I don't think this is the time, or in fact the place, to discuss a report that I was not privileged to hear," Diva interrupted the scout leader.

"Commander, all I am trying to tell you is what I believe regarding the bay of which I spoke. I think it is not too far from here, and I think I can find it." Hur fell silent waiting to see what sort of response he would get.

"Unless this so-called bay is directly in front of us, we will not be changing course; and furthermore, I cannot change direction to a bay I know nothing about." Diva let her harsh words sink in before continuing. "I am not interested in a bay you think is nearby, and then only think you can find. Now, Scout Leader Hur, go back to your position."

The finality of Diva's tone ended any further discussions on the matter of the bay. The last thing Scout Commander Diva needed now was some unsupported idea from a known-to-be unreliable scout leader.

Having to guide Scout Leader Hur in each of his tasks, and never knowing whether or not he would complete them, added to carrying the unexpected burden of the safe-keeping of The Most Learned One's understudy. Having Hur thrust on her – he who was being trained to assume the highest mantle, if and when the Most Learned One was called to account, just added to her increasingly precarious predicament.

"Legion Commander Zen, we are in trouble, are we not?"

"Yes, Senator Opek, we are in great distress."

The two were finding great difficulty in keeping abreast.

"I have lost contact with all the other groups. I cannot afford to send out scouts to try and locate them. Then again, I don't want to send them out for no other reason than my fear for their very safety." Zen could feel the mounting fear in the vibrations from the Senator.

"The last contact I had was from Scout Commander Diva, and she reported at that time she had lost four of the oldest members in her group."

"Lost, Legion Commander? Lost as in what? Lost as in lost, or lost as in death?"

"Senator Opek, the report was as lost in death by drowning."

The cold reality of what was going on around them hit the Senator hard. Zen felt the great sorrow build up in the Senator as he grew silent – as he struggled with the grave turn of events – as they all struggled.

"These are grave times, Legion Commander. Grave times indeed, and it troubles me deeply."

"The storm will pass, Senator Opek, of that I can assure you, and from this great storm we will emerge stronger."

"True as that may be, Legion Commander, what is of concern to me at this moment is far greater than any storm."

"Far greater, Senator? What could be far greater than the perils this storm is throwing at us? Pray tell me that, Senator."

The Senator looked across at Zen as they both broached the water in unison atop a powerful upsurge.

"You have come up through the trials and promotions very quickly, Zen, but you are still very young in other ways."

There was something in the tone that the Senator took on. It was something not unlike a hypnotic trance – an inner peace that all Senators seemed to have the ability to enter into at will. Zen waited for the Senator to continue.

"It was not a fear of the storm that radiated from me, Legion Commander, but my feelings for those who have died in the rage of this storm."

It was only then that Zen fully comprehended... and so did understand that as once they were all lost souls that had been rescued, now it was that some members of the Assembly had passed on – without guidance or direction – to the next stepping stones of life. The spirits of those members were now trapped, doomed to wallow in that place that was not here and was not there.

"I see you do now understand, Legion Commander. Just perhaps I was a bit premature in calling you a little young."

With that, Senator Opek was dragged away by the raging storm, and Zen's inner thoughts and great concern turned to his beloved Lute and daughter Cyan as he prayed to Poseidon to watch over them. Zen moved as best he could among the group, lifting their spirits as he gave each one a scan of encouragement.

Three days of an unrelenting wind and rain resulted in oceans being ripped apart into towering waves that crashed in huge avalanches of water.

"Senator Inca, can I have your attention?" The incoming call was from Scout Leader, Hur.

"Yes, Hur. What brings you to me?"

The Senator surfed down the large swell. Even in this dangerous storm, it still was a thrill to slide down the waves at high speed.

"What brings you to me?" Again, the Senator called to Hur.

Hur braced himself for the response that what he was about to say would bring.

"What response will that be Hur?"

Again, Hur had forgotten that Senators had the ability to read one's loose thoughts.

"Senator Inca, on my last long-range patrol, my troop found an uninhabited bay. This report was filed in full with both Senators Ova and Opek." Hur waited for the Senator to comment.

"Scout Leader Hur, why is it that you bring this up with me, and why now?"

"Senator Inca, I know that the bay of which I speak is not too distant from here." Again Hur waited for the Senator to comment, being careful to keep his thoughts in check.

"Again, Hur, why do you bring these matters up with me? Why do you not..."

Hur took a chance, and interrupted the Senator.

"Senator, I tried to bring it to the attention of Scout Commander Diva, and she dismissed what I had to say."

"Hur!" Now it was the turn of the Senator to interrupt.

"Firstly, don't ever interrupt a Senator when he is speaking, and secondly, if you brought this matter to the attention of the Scout Commander, then it is back to her you have to go."

The two Regents of the Deep rode the on-coming waves of the storm in silence.

"Have you anything else you want to bring up, Hur? If not, then I suggest you return to your duties."

Hur looked across at the Senator. "As a matter of fact, I have."

The audacity of Hur annoyed the Senator.

"Well, in this instance I will let you speak, but be warned that your demeanour this day will have consequences once some form of normality returns to the Assembly."

"I am prepared to face the consequences if you are prepared to face yours, Senator."

"Go ahead, Hur, please tell me what consequences I should be afraid of facing.

"As of now, we have lost all contact with the other groups, and we have also lost contact with half of this group. On top of this, all my remaining scouts are finding it nearly impossible to continue with the never-ending care of the young and aged. They are exhausted, Senator."

Hur waited for a response, and with none coming, he continued. "Senator, I am sure that given the chance, I can find that bay again."

So it was that at this time of apocalyptic, forbidding peril that Hur led the group to seek the protection that the bay of golden-yellow water offered.

The sanctuary of the golden bay was a welcome relief from the storm-torn seas that all had endured over the past six days. The waters, while not as clear as the open oceans, offered up strange new smells to the group. A smell of sweetness seemed to fill the air when the light winds flowed down from the distant shore. The smells of burning incense at day's end mixed with an array of unknown aromas.

All these signs gave an indication that, just maybe, God-like creatures, not dissimilar to those that once walked the Island of Atlantis, dwelt nearby.

As sure as light follows the darkness, so it was that calm followed the storm, bringing with it a peace and tranquillity for all and sundry that inhabited the land and the water.

$$—\Psi—$$

A great pall of anguish cast its cloak over the Assembly as they milled about waiting to be called together in a congregation of sorrow. Legion Commander Zen called the Assembly to gather together in open court. The Most Learned One called, and the murmur of the Assembly faded to silence as they waited for the next call of Legion Commander Zen. With no call forthcoming from the Legion Commander, the call went out again, and for the second time, the call went unanswered.

The Learned One turned to Senator Inca. "Why has the Legion Commander not answered the call, Senator?"

Senator Inca was at a loss as to where the Legion Commander was.

"I have no knowledge as to his whereabouts, Most Learned One."

"Most Learned One!" The interrupting call from Senator Ova released the penetrating stare of The Most Learned One from Senator Inca.

"Approach, Senator. Now, what can you tell me of this breach of protocol by the Legion Commander?"

"At this time, Most Learned One, the Legion Commander is out with a search group."

"Thank you, Senator. I understand and forgive his absence. I feel for the Legion Commander. He has not been the same since the storm, but then who could blame him, with Lute and Cyan still out there somewhere, maybe lost for all time, or at the worst, dead."

"Most Learned One!"

The call from Senator Ova broke into his thoughts.

"I am sorry, Senator. I let my inner thoughts radiate. In the absence of the Legion Commander, I instruct you, Senator Inca, to call the Assembly to order."

With his call made, the Most Learned One took up his position.

"Senators, members of the great Assembly, I call you all to order in the name of King Epiphanes. I call you all to order in the name of our God Poseidon, and in due respect to our God Poseidon, I now bring down upon all of you here gathered, his blessing. Then, with the blessing completed, the Senator bowed to The Most Learned One, and retired to join the grouping of the other six Senators.

"Senators and Assembly members! It is with great sadness that your Most Learned One has this day the unenviable of task of conveying extremely grave tidings to one and all."

His scans swept across the now flat, calm oceans that sparkled in a tranquillised serenity, freed from the tortuous winds that had at last released their grip of supremacy and allowed the Regents of the Deep to move about with their customary freedom.

The Learned One continued. "From the very bowels of the Gods of Darkness we have been granted a reprieve – a reprieve we know not when will end. Over the last days, the Storm God has gathered up a large number of our members to his realm. Even at this time, our King is suffering from the torments of these last days."

"Senator, Senator!" The cry, shrill and fear-laden, interrupted the address of The Most Learned One.

"I feel the death of The King is near." The call of Guard Commander Mio brought Senator Zoa into the presence of the Most Learned One, and directed her message to him, "Senator Zoa, your attendance must be with the King, your father. He is calling for you."

Guard Commander Mio turned to the Learned One. "My extreme apologies for the disruption, but I believe the King's time is near."

The Learned One nodded to acknowledge the interruption was acceptable, as he moved to the side of the Senator.

"Come, my friend Zoa, let us go to our King."

The Death

9

Staring with tear-filled eyes, Senator Zoa felt numb horror at the sight of his beloved father, King Epiphanes, as he slowly breached the surface then drifted down beneath the waves. The white of his underbody had changed to a subtle shade of blue; this colour change onset was an early sign of the rigor mortis which was beginning to steal into the patriarchal body, even while yet he lived.

"Guard Commander Mio, you must go and bring forth all those of the Senate, for the Most Learned One has foretold that Our King will soon depart his much-loved Mother Earth. Before the passing of the coming day, the King, I believe, will have left on his final journey. I feel his departure is very near, and we have little time to prepare to guide him to that next place of final resting. We must prepare him, so go now, quickly."

Golden shafts of light speared through the oceans as the sun blessed the new day. Frozen moisture in the cold air reflected in a multitude of colours from the prisms formed in the great blocks of ice that floated on the surface. The members of the Senate raced through the chilled waters in answer to the call of the Most Learned One.

The rasping, croaking sounds of The King, struggling to get his breath, filled the still air and greeted them on their arrival. As they surrounded their beloved leader, they could only watch as the Most Learned One moved in close to scan the bodily functions of The King who was now in a state of semi-consciousness, but supported by those attending in a state of semi-sensibility.

Floating on the surface of the ocean, his tired old body, now took on the appearance of one that had suffered the hardships of life, and his great age now revealed itself in him. It was with no fear that The King accepted what fate was shortly to bestow on him. He had lived his life in accordance with the beliefs and teachings of a creed, and according to those beliefs, his future was assured. The King laboured with his breath, and in his conviction that he was shortly to embark on his final journey, to take his place – along with those who had gone before him – at the side of their God, the great Poseidon, he sought the guidance of The Most Learned One.

King Epiphanes looked across at those gathering and some semblance, some fleeting look of happiness flittered across his face, as he saw circled around him the Senators. It was he who had given the final word on their promotion to their office.

The Most Learned One moved still closer in to his King, uttering soothing sounds that allayed any fears. According to the pre-ordained ritual, the Most Learned One went about his sombre duties. Senator Ira called the remaining Council Elders to close attendance. He then ordered the returned Legion Commander Zen and Guard Commander Mio to call forth the highest ranking scouts, and then to take those scouts and form them into a protective barrier around this arena of the dying. Then, it was that the sad, sombre ritual of death began its mournful dirge.

"Oh, great God of Death and Dying, we call upon you to show mercy in guiding this, the very humble spirit of our King. Guide him in reverence to that place that has been set aside by our Great God of the Oceans, and assure his place therein. Lead him to that place of rest."

As the chanting droned on, a strange peace began to descend upon the body of The King. His breathing became less laboured, and those who read the scans he sent out felt the surge of tranquillity that was now evident in the body of their beloved leader.

"Oh, Great God of Death, the spirit here about to depart this body, we entrust into your care, to be prepared for the final place of resting."

The Most Learned One's chanting continued. "Oh, spirit of King Epiphanes, King of all Dolphins, we call you to leave this place of dwelling here on the good Earth, and rise to those heavenly bodies. Take your place at the side of our Great God, Poseidon. Your time to release yourself from the labours of this place and take up your due abode in the refectory of the universe has come."

The breathing of the King grew very shallow and faint. The Most Learned One had now moved in to help to support the body of this old man of the sea as it rose back to the surface. With each shallow breath, the tide of life slowly ebbed from King Epiphanes. His chest's heaving became less and less prominent. Then, as the Most Learned One continued with his chants, The King gave one final short gasp; his body stiffened and then sagged, as the last of the life-giving air wheezed its escape from the now still body, and the silence of his death ruled the oceans.

And so it was, that in the one hundred and seventieth day in the twenty-first pass in the time of the King Epiphanes, King of all Dolphins, his spirit departed from its temple of life to begin the final journey to the heavenly bodies.

The word of the death of this beloved Regent of the Deep swept through the Great Assembly as the four strong God Winds, Boreas, Zephyrus, Notus, and Eurus that swept the seas, and carried with them waves of their sadness and despair. As this great sorrow overcame those in the Assembly, they were moved to tears. The Learned Ones, helped by the Senators, slowly lowered the body of the departed King toward the ocean's floor where, with great care, they lay him down amongst the coral. The Most Learned One placed a stone under the jaw to hold the mouth shut, and draped a branch of coloured kelp over the open but unseeing eyes of the dead body. The Most Learned One circled overhead, looking down at his departed friend of many passes. Being, as he was, of the highest possible training, he watched the aura – that strange glow that surrounds all living things in a cloud, a swirling mass, a multitude of colours that fluctuate and shift with the changing moods and wellbeing of its host. The once-vibrant colours now took on a dull grey appearance as it faded from around the body. The swirling mass slowly rose and collected as a spiritual entity some five lukmar above the now empty temple of the dead, although it was still tied to the lifeless body by a strand of silver-coloured silk.

The Most Learned One watched this spirit entity, now in the form of a much younger Dolphin King, lift to the end of the silvery cord, then settle back down, only to raise itself again to the end of its tether. Then finally, after many attempts, it broke free to make that final transition from a being in an earthly body to one of the spiritual kind, and to begin the great journey to its rightful place in the heavens.

The Most Learned One, on seeing the King finally free himself of his earthly form, droned out the farewell ode.

"Oh, now free spirit,
liberated from the bonds of Earth,
freed from the shackles of life
and floating free before me this day,
go forth in peace,
taking not your troubles nor pains of this place.
Be not afraid of what you see along this path
which you now must follow,
as so you have been instructed, as so you must depart."

The hovering entity moved slightly towards the Most Learned One in a gesture of acknowledgment and recognition of his lifelong friend, then slowly and gently rose to the surface of the water, and was no more. The Most Learned One followed the ascending spirit, and as it hesitated just above the surface of the ocean, he uttered the final chant.

"Oh spirit, that from this place of your former dwelling
and from which you have just departed,
whose wisdom and deeds we have cemented
into the deepest emporium of our memories,
lodged that they may be retrieved
when it is your guidance we seek.
Oh spirit, this day departing, we bid you farewell.
So let it come to pass."

And so ended the time of King Epiphanes, King of all dolphins in this place of all earthly dwellings.

The time-honoured edict, as was written into the laws of their creed, took immediate effect with The Most Learned One assuming the mantle of leadership over all those of the Great Assembly. A mantle he would hold until times of calm, that invariably follow the trauma of death, returned to the Assembly. So it was that the Most Learned One, as his first instruction, decreed that the next two days be held in mourning for the departed King.

Over the next two days, each and every member of the Great Assembly passed over the resting-place of their beloved leader, the departed Dolphin King; and in tribute, each placed a small piece of coloured coral on his body. So it was that at the end of the two days of mourning, the body of their so-loved, departed King was completely covered and garnished in coloured coral.

It was the time-honoured rituals of mourning that filled the hearts of the Assembly with great sorrow as one last time they were called together for the final prayers of farewell, to be led by The Most Learned One. The mournful prayer call that expounded the teachings of the creed reverberated out over the arena of death. Then it came to pass, the final farewells to the now departed Sovereign Regent of the deep drew to a close, and the mortal remains of the departed King Epiphanes, King of all Dolphins, were left for the crawling and burrowing creatures of the seas to feast upon.

In the fullness of time, the cycle of life had travelled its full circle; for as it was written in their doctrine, those of the flesh would, in due course, be called to return to that place from whence they first came.

The Sanctuary

10

It had been sixteen days since the group arrived in the bay of yellow-gold waters, and all were now well rested and in good spirits having survived a storm greater than any could remember. This bay of golden water was abundant with fish that swam in from the oceans in great swarms, feeding on the weed that flourished on the seabed.

Senator Nara called on Hur, "I feel it is time we made preparations to move on."

The Senator felt reluctance radiate from the self-promoting Hur.

"Let us remain a little longer – the waters are warm; the group is happy." Hur broke the surface again, sliding up next to the Senator. "Come on Senator, relax. When have you seen such a hospitable place? Why, we don't even have to send out the food scouts to find our food anymore."

Something deep inside the Senator's storehouse of knowledge set off a cautionary alert, something faint that he could not readily recall or react to.

"The other Senators will be most concerned that we have lost contact with them."

Again, Hur was reluctant to take the words of the aged Senator as anything more than ramblings.

"You worry too much. The remainder of the Assembly will have, I am sure, sheltered somewhere from the storm. They will send out Scouts if there is any thought of us being in peril," Hur said as he pushed the very boundaries of his importance with the Senator.

"You are just a silly old Senator who I was lumbered with looking after. You would not be here – or you might even be dead – if it had not been for me," Hur thought to himself as the Senator dismissed him by turning and moving away.

Lute leapt high out of the water, calling to Cyan to watch. The sun reflected off her streamlined body as she somersaulted mid-air. "Come on! Show me how high you can jump."

The unresponsive youngster ignored her mother's calling. "You promised me that we could explore the bay. I don't want to play." Cyan swam away knowing full well her mother would soon catch up.

"Oh, all right!" Knowing how stubborn the youngster could be, Lute thought a break away from the rest might be just the tonic Cyan needed.

"Let's go over to where the fresh water stream falls down over the rocks," the young one called, as she sped off across the bay.

With mother in hot pursuit, leaping and dancing across the yellow-gold waters, the two Regents of the Deep sped across the bay. Reaching the far side, mother and child were invigorated as the cascading waters fell onto them. With great affection, Lute looked at her daughter and marvelled at the fast growing body gleaming in youth's vigour. Her father would be so proud.

"Let's return now. We have been away long enough," Lute called to her youngster.

"Two more! Just two more sweeps, please?"

"All right, just two more, and then we must go. The last thing we want is for the Senator to send a scout to look for us," said Lute, shifting the onus.

The slapping of Cyan's body hitting the water drowned out the muffled splashes and squeals of delight that fluttered across the surface of the yellow-gold bay from somewhere on the shoreline, not too distant.

Aspiring Warlord Ying Ying stood on the prow of his giant ship, watching for the great sea monsters that slunk and hid under the rolling oceans, awaiting their chance to attack him and his warriors. He was prepared – the stick he held in his hand transformed into a magical sword that could slay all things. Then he spied it. The huge green head, breathing fire, as it reared up out of the water.

"Row, row!" the Young Warlord screamed at his slaves. "It's getting away!"

Just then, the monster turned. Diving deep, it disappeared, only to resurface at the side of the boat. Then, reaching in it struck at the rowers, taking three of them in its huge mouth and dragging them screaming from their seats, to disappear beneath the waters forever.

The little Warlord was not afraid, as this was a fight to the death. Just like his father and those before him, he would protect his men, one and all. Just when he thought the great beast had escaped, back it came – this time twice as big, twice as strong. Again the heavy burden of protector fell upon the shoulders of one so young. Charging at the boat with eyes glazed in anger, great streams of fire bellowing from its nostrils, the monster now knew it had met its match.

Ying Ying waited, waited, waited. The beast drew closer and closer, larger and larger. The young man could now feel the searing heat from the streams of flames on his little face. The vile smell from the beast's body filled the air. Ying Ying stood his ground, unflinching, waiting for the right moment to launch his attack, knowing full well that if he miscalculated, the great monster would win, and all would be lost. With a blood-curdling roar, this great beast reared up to strike the brave warrior – to smite him down.

The little Warlord, having watched his father training, struck – slashing out and across, slicing open a gaping wound on the neck of the monster, sending blood spurting into the air. Then, as the monster fell back onto the water, the little warrior lunged forward to plunge his magical sword into the heart of the fallen monster. With full and lasting victory a mere stroke of the sword away, a surge of pride filled the small body.

"Victory is mine!" he called to the skies, sending an acknowledgment to his God. He then swept his sword down with such great force that the weight he exerted snapped the branch he was standing on. As fate had dictated, the greatest and bravest Warlord warrior that had ever lived, plunged headfirst into the cold deep waters, reduced in that moment to the small, helpless, little boy he was – a boy of only six summers, whose life now ebbed away.

Lute's sensors tuned into the thrashing vibrations resounding from some six sigmar away. In a flash, her brain took in the impulses, deciphered them, set out a course of action, and executed the plan.

"Cyan, go to deep water and wait."

Cyan felt the snapped changes in her mother that signalled the games were over; then, without question, she moved as fast as her little body could, and dived deep to safety. Lute raced through the murky waters toward the source of the distress signals. Five sigmar out, the signals had lost some of their intensity – the thrashing weakened. At four sigmar, Lute's sensors had already confirmed the target was a young boy drowning in twenty lukmar of water, one dikmar from water's edge. At three sigmar – source four lukmar under the water.

At two sigmar – nine lukmar under water, stomach partly filled with water. At one sigmar – fourteen lukmar under water, stomach full of water, left lung filling with water, brain signals weakening.

At twenty dikmar – on sea floor, body convulsing, stomach contents ejecting, left lung full of water, right lung filling, brain signals down. All movements then stopped.

Ming Lee, concubine mother of Ying Ying, had been up since dawn, having the night before endured the assaulting anger of the Master Warlord. Ming Lee dragged herself up from her sleeping platform to perform her daily ritual of creeping from her room long before daybreak to check on the nocturnal wanderings of her son, Ying Ying.

To her fearful consternation, the boy had gone. The vision of Minya lying on the stone floor with an ever increasing halo of blood radiating out from her head brought urgency to the finding and return of the favourite son. Already, the kitchen was a hive of activity as the servants prepared the morning meals for the Warlord Master and his many guests who had been arriving from the hinterlands over the past few days. Ming Lee called to three of her most trusted friends.

"Come quickly, please! You must help me. Ying Ying has again gone. We must find him before the master arises."

"Ying Ying!" The frantic callings of the concubines and servants echoed out over the still waters of the bay, as the search widened.

"Please, Buddha, please help us find Ying Ying," Ming Lee pleaded. "Please help us find him before the master awakes."

— Ψ —

Lute dived down, grabbing the boy's baggy clothes. She lifted him up, and then with a great thrust, she heaved the limp body onto the edge of the beach. Scanning the lifeless body, Lute detected a weak heartbeat labouring under the pressure of water-filled lungs.

Having watched the drama unfold before them, the women of the Jomonese people raced to the aid of the fallen youngster. The wailing sounds momentarily distracted Lute in her efforts to bring life back into this small boy.

"Ying Ying!" Ming Lee wailed, as she watched the regent from the deep flip over her son and begin striking down with her head onto the back of this tiniest of warriors. With each thump, water flooded from the little body, and it was then that the young warrior's god, smiled. And so, the little Jomonese Warlord began his resurrection from the jaws of certain death, and so was returned to his people. Tears of immense joy tumbled down the face of Ming Lee as she fell upon her boy's saviour, the majestic lady from the deep. Lute and Ming Lee spoke in silence and each understood – as caring mothers united by a bond of love and understanding always do.

It was a very different matter with the Warlord and his warrior men for they had little sympathy with these Regents that had entered, uninvited, into their waters.

This race of Jomonese people had been created by their gods to replicate those that had walked the land of Caucus; but unlike those people, the yellow-skinned, slit-eyed race of this country the gods now called Jomon were cruel and unyielding. They now planned to bring about the destruction of those members of the Assembly who had ventured into their waters. These people sought to inflict barbarous cruelty to bring about the demise of the intruders, partly to try and appease their god, and also to rid their bay of these monarchs of the oceans who had taken up uninvited residence in their waters.

So, to catch them easily, they would take advantage of the very thing the Assembly was most honoured for – their maternal love.

To accomplish this foul deed, it was determined that first the Jomonese must gain the trust and acceptance of the Assembly. Those treacherous, slant-eyed butchers went out each day in their small craft, rowed effortlessly across the water, and cast fish caught in their nets to the Assembly. By this deception, the people quickly gained the right to move freely amongst the Assembly who had no thought of any danger that might be brought upon them at the hands of these men. They looked upon the yellow-skinned people as they had looked on their Gods: as compassionate colleagues who happily joined in celebrations. And so, with this naiveté, on the morning of the twentieth day since arriving in the golden bay, they sowed the seeds of their own destruction.

Without warning, a lone fisherman did strike swiftly with deadly aim. The hurled bronze harpoon, his most deadly weapon of the hunt, struck. The first to feel this onslaught was the youngest, Cyan, only daughter of Lute and Zen. With deadly precision, the harpoon did enter deep into her left eye, splitting it. Shuddering with great pain, and knowing not how or why it was received, the young Cyan reeled back, and diving deep in bitter torment, afflicted with tortuous and agonizing pain, begged in a dying lament, calling her mother to her side.

These pusillanimous warriors did not squander their own energy to restrain the convulsing Cyan, or attempt to pull her to the surface by force. They waited, and let the line attached to the harpoon run out until she tired; knowing the lack of air would force her to the surface. Cyan was exhausted by her struggles with the barbed harpoon. Her calls of pain brought many from the Assembly to her aid, as had been expected by the slit-eyed Jomonese. Through all this, the barbarous men watched Lute, as she tried in vain to assist her mortally wounded infant, and they smiled with the perfection of their deed. They listened to Lute's cries of anguish as she helped her dying daughter to the surface. Many of the Assembly followed, torn in distress as they circled about, crying aloud as if they were the ones suffering. Other young ones closed in to watch, and they were manoeuvred away by the elders, away from the unseen danger.

When at last Cyan reached the surface exhausted, she was slowly hauled by the lone butcher into the ring of the circling small craft. Her mournful cries filled the air, and those who had followed them in the crowded water fell victim to the hunters' trap.

Vicious, and with sinful treachery, the hunters, with neither pity nor sorrow, and in defiance of the distress about to be put upon the multitude who had answered the call of anguish, did not bend their hearts of iron. Instead, en masse, they rose up from their places of hiding in their boats, and their deed of destruction played out its final hand as they did strike with swiftness and brutality at all those who had gathered on the surface of the water.

Lute, trying to stay close to Cyan, was the next to feel the pain of the bronze harpoon deep in her side. Then it was the time for Teacher Tai to fall to these foul deeds, and the air was filled with the cries of terrible suffering as the harpoons struck with deadly efficiency. Cyan, with mother Lute, now both held fast by the bronzed harpoons, were dragged up and across the water. Lute, without thought of her own heinous suffering or peril, reached out to comfort her dying daughter. As the bastardly butchers pulled them up from the water, they touched, invoking a rush of unspoken understanding and love that surged between them. This brought to them both an inner reconciliation and a sudden tranquillity in the face of their impending death. As this serenity settled over them, the hunters plunged their blades deeply and slayed the child and mother together. Their flowing blood turned all the waters red as it merged with the floating flowers. The cries of all the dying sang a mournful serenade to the empty heavens.

From that day forth, those of the yellow skin who prayed to a lump of stone they had made in their own image and named "God" could no longer stand next to the Gods as a welcome sacrificer, nor could they touch their altars with clean hands. For they had polluted all those who shared the same roof with them, as equal to human slaughter, the Gods of the Heavens abhorred the deadly destruction of the Regents of the Deep who had long been held by these Gods as symbols of swiftness, diligence, and love; and great anger was felt as they were cast aside. When the God Poseidon did hear of this deed, it was in great sadness that he wept, and his tears fell from the heavens in great torrents.

His fellow Gods, broken with grief, did then gather up these rains of sorrow, as they fell from the skies, and with great hostility they hurled them at the Jomonese people with the slit-eyes.

And so it was that this storm of tears brought immense devastation and havoc to these inhabitants. Then the great God, Poseidon, did so decree that throughout all eternity, these storms of destruction would return again and again, to thrash those of the slit-eyes and yellow skin as a reminder of these past grave deeds inflicted on those the Gods so loved. Then it was that Zeus, the King of all Gods, in a final act of revulsion sent forth amid this typhoon of tears, a multitude of forked lightning bolts, and these lightning bolts did destroy even the houses of stone and all those who dwelt therein.

He did then send down great lightning bolts of flame, and this new onslaught did sweep through and ignite the ramshackle buildings that housed these barbarous people, incinerating all in its fiery blast.

For as it had been written in the thirteen houses of the zodiac of the heavens, the yellow-gold waters of satisfaction turned red in hostility and brought the great tears of rain that turned into fires of remorse.

And so it was that the first of the great God Poseidon's heavenly writings had come to pass.

The Found

11

The six young scouts had been gone three days; their search patterns ever increasing as they crisscrossed the ocean floor. Scout Leader Sola, a young and robust sibling of Zen in his first command, set a new course. He scanned out the new locks, and then dropped back into trail, hoping to grab a little rest. Twenty-four days had passed since the fierce storm had spread the four groups far and wide. Three of the groups had reformed, but the fourth seemed to have vanished from the face of Mother Earth. Twenty-six times since last contact with Senator Nara had been made, the sun God had blessed the assembly with its warmth

"Where were they? Storm direction – ocean drift?" Mindlessly speculating as he did, Sola pondered the whereabouts of the lost; but the answer evaded the young scout. The calculated judgments as to where to look next and thoughts of the impossible kept racing through his mind.

Night slowly began its task of stealing the light from the skies, and then one by one, the Gods lit their candles to cast a twinkling sway across the darkening heavens, and dragged the scout leader into slumber.

Scout Leader Sola, Scout Leader Sola!" The call from his second-in-command nudged him out of his controlled slumber.

"Yes, Mina?"

"Your turn to move up. There is nothing to report – no signs of transgression – friendly, or unfriendly."

Sola detected tiredness creeping into Mina. He scanned to her, "Rest now."

Moving up through the Scouts, Sola scanned for all to close in. "We are now in our fourth day of searching, with still no given sign." Sola felt at a loss. All his training told him that hope of finding the lost group was fading fast. "We know there is land; the long-range scouts reported that to the Senate before the great storm."

The scouts waited for the leader to continue.

It was Scout Aplo who spoke next. "It may be that they sought refuge there. If you seek our view, I for one, think that while we are this far out, and because this place just may turn out to be of some significance, and it is within our range limits and our briefing, then we should explore all possibilities... and this is a possibility."

Sola looked across at the Scout Aplo, who was not known for having much to say at the best of times; however, this time he had given them all food for thought. Breaking the water in unison, a reflective silence settled over the group.

"This unknown land, and its reported bay, seem altogether too far off course from the path the lost group were ordered to follow," Scout Leader Sola countered. *"No, it's not possible! It would have added a number of days to their trip – that is provided they could find the land at all,"* Sola thought out loud in open scan.

"If the scouts were disorientated by the storm, they just may have headed in the wrong direction, and, if nothing else, what have we got to lose other than time?"

Aplo did make sense in some ways, but the unknown lands were still a reasonable distance away.

His fellow scouts again took in Sola's thoughts as they kept in their tight closed formation, waiting for the scout leader to decide on the next segment of the search.

"I do not think it should be overlooked that we think the impossible just may have come to pass – maybe we consider what Aplo is thinking. I, for one, am prepared to set course in that direction, if only to satisfy myself that we have ruled out the possibility that what Aplo is surmising has happened." Mira's comments added fuel to the discussions.

"The rest of you! What contributions, if any, would you like to make? Jove, Sui, Zeta! Are any of you prepared to go to this unknown place, adding many more days to the patrol, on the off-chance that Aplo might be right?"

The young scout leader was finding his first command more difficult than he had first thought it would be, and Aplo was somewhat taken aback at being propelled into the centre of ongoing discussions.

"Zeta! What are your views?" Sola turned to the only female in the patrol.

"We have searched in every conceivable place, not alone, but with many other scout groups over many days, and so far, what has any group found? Nothing! Not a sign! Nothing! So what have we got to lose? Again, nothing – nothing but our time and our efforts." Zeta looked across to Jove and Sui, more than happy to see both of them nodding in agreement.

Sola felt somewhat relieved that the decision to go beyond their brief had been taken from him, even if only by consensus. However, he knew that in theory, as in practice, if anything should go amiss while out of their dictated area of search, he would be called to account for his action.

Regardless of what others of the scout group may have contributed to the decision to go to the unknown islands, the decision had to be his and his alone.

—— Ψ ——

As darkness, again in its time-honoured ritual, began returning the stolen light back to the day and lighting the new day sky, a new course was locked in. So, it was in earnest that the search-and-find scouts set out.

Four days into the journey, Sola, while on forward lead, detected a small group of reefs ahead. He immediately relayed his scans to the rest of the scout group, and then called them to close formation.

"I think the reefs ahead may offer us a temporary lay-up, and a place to rest out of the swells and drifts. If the Gods are smiling upon us, somewhere among all that coloured coral, we will find food."

The returning sonar signals confirmed a consensus.

"Aplo and Zeta – to food detail. Sui and Jove – scout the reefs." Sola sent off the scouts, still not comfortable with being so far off the pre-determined course.

"Just hope it will be worth the effort," he thought..

"Sola! Sola!"

The sudden scans broke into the second thoughts Sola was having about his decision to head this far afield of the search plan.

"Sola, Sola!" Mira's excited scans, now hitting him at maximum impulse, thundered across his brain.

"Sola, Sola!" Mira, scanning the signal of in-heading fish, snapped Sola into life. All second thoughts vanished, and instinct took control, sending Sola racing in to help herd the mullet school into catching circles. The thrashing fish drove him and his fellow scouts into a feeding frenzy.

The swaying, coloured plants that clung to the reefs offered a much-needed tranquil place of rest so Sola planned to spend at least one day here before the final drive closer in to the lands.

First light heralded a grey heaven, the oceans taking on an air of serenity, darkened by the skies. The group, now refreshed, milled around waiting for the scanning instructions from the scout leader. The first warning that a transgressor had moved into the patrolled area was in-scanned by Jove, who had spent the darkness as sentinel, stationed at six sigmar. Sola read the alert.

"All scouts – into close formation!" Sola found his training automatically taking control.

"Jove, stay where you are and track the unknown. Mina, you follow me. Aplo, take your place at watch, and take Zeta with you."

Sola sent two of the best scouts out to stand off two sigmar each side of Jove.

"Sui, you stay tail."

With his scouts drafted to the caution positions, Sola and Mina moved out to link up with Jove, whose unrelenting scans were tracking the transgressors' approach. Jove's scans were trans-scanned to all the scouts as they closed in towards her position. At four sigmar, the shadowy figure was an unrecognisable blur to Sola.

"Aplo, Zeta, move up! See if you can get a little closer, but be careful," Sola signalled to the two.

The remaining troops broke the surface in unison.

"What do you think it is?" Sui inquired, as he drew up alongside

Sola.

"You were ordered to stay astern. Now fall back and monitor the rear. Now!"

The sharp rebuff sent the youngest scout in the troop scurrying in haste rearward.

Sola winced. Just maybe he was a little sharp with the youngster.

Zeta was the first to recognise the figure slowly moving towards them. "It's one from the lost group – we have found them." The excited scan messages filled the water.

Zeta and Alpo increased closing speed. At two sigmar, Zeta scanned, and confirmed the recognition status of the lost member, then relayed the same back to scout leader, Sola. At one sigmar, the excitement from the two closing scouts was subdued, as the incoming body scans begin to tell their own story.

The Grieving

12

The Most Learned One called the Assembly together; as he made his report of the great tragedy to them, all were stunned to silence and disbelief. As day left the heavens and darkness strode the skies, the oceans grew still as they mourned for the lost Regents they had taken on their last fateful journey.

Not one member of the Assembly was unaffected by what had taken place. Then it was that the Most Learned One called Legion Commander Zen to take seven of the Assembly's most experienced scouts, and at the night's darkest, go into the yellow waters of the Bay of Death – to see what there was to see, and report what there was to report.

"Legion Commander Zen, before the Sun God, Hyperion, rises from his sleep and lights the day ten days hence, you will confirm these sightings and reports. The grave voice of The Most Learned One permeated the Great Assembly.

"As so ordered, as so I will comply," responded Legion Commander Zen.

Then, taking seven of the finest scouts, and with Lido as Scout Leader, Zen left the Assembly and started the long, anguished journey to the Bay of Death. As the darkened depths of the sea flowed under them, not one word passed between the scouts, as each was engrossed in their own sullen fears of what lay ahead. Little did they realise that before this patrol would end, their endurance and understanding of the creed would be put to the great examination of life.

The scouts raced on, skimming over the waters, oblivious to the surrounding schools of fish. Schools of fish that, in the past, would have darted from sight to seek refuge in the many cracks and crevices that offered a sanctuary in the twisting and turning coral, watched undisturbed. The scouts passed them by. It was as if on this day the fish had been pre-warned they were free from peril, that the quickly passing scouts were on some mission far more important, and so they went about their daily existence, untroubled by the events taking place around them.

Five asmar into the journey, Zen scanned a three lock course change to his troop – a course change that would take the group to the reefs that lay four sigmar to the west of the entrance to the Bay of Death. Once inside the calm waters that separated the reefs from the land, Zen planned a short rest to brief his six accomplices on a plan of search that was now formulating in his mind. The seven made good time, and it was in the sheltered waters that Zen broke the silence of the trip and ordered his companions into a tight formation. Once all were in tight, he explained in very great detail the references he wanted undertaken in a grid search. Under the command of Scout leader Lido, four members would follow the land's edge towards the east for twelve asmar, then move three asmar from land's edge, and then return to the entrance to the bay. They were then to continue on this course for another twelve asmar west of the entrance, and at that point, again turn and move in closer to land's edge, and then follow this course back to the bay entrance.

The entrance to the Bay of Death was just two asmar wide, and one dikmar deep. Its floor was constantly swept clean by the tides that flowed in and then turned and rushed out in a torrent of water that scoured the ground; thus making it inhospitable to any life form that attempted to establish itself.

Zen spoke to his scouts, giving them warnings on what was expected of them in this, the most trying of times. Then, he reminded them of the words and teachings of the creed.

Finally, Zen offered each and every one the opportunity to stay in the protected waters and wait at the reefs until all returned after completing the grim task ahead. Zen awaited each scout's response; then, as he had expected, led the first group out from the calm protected waters into the channel, moving with the tide towards the unknown.

Scout Leader Lido watched as the Legion Commander and his scouts disappeared from sight, and then ordered his three scouts to follow him. He led the way across the bay channel toward the start of their search area. Once clear of the entrance, Lido ordered the three to form a line abreast, taking the most dangerous berth nearest land's edge himself, and struggling through the breaking seas that pounded the land's edge with a relentless fury, throwing, as it did so, sheets of fine spray into the air.

And so, the search for the lost souls began.

As Legion Commander Zen's group approached the channel end, a distinct feeling of foreboding filled the water with the lingering chill of death. This uneasy feeling, in turn, was now invading their senses. An eerie silence engulfed the scouts as they moved quietly through the waters of death, still darkened by the night.

Twelve asmar up the land's edge from the entrance to the Bay of

Death, Scout Leader Lido ordered a ten lock course change that led the scouts out from land's edge for three sigmar. Then, at this three sigmar point, another ten lock change and the scouts headed back along the land's edge.

Once through the narrow channel that gave the bay access to the open oceans, Legion Commander Zen ordered his scouts to span out into their pre-planned positions and to move forward in scanning arcs of twenty locks. Their first priority was to seek out any who might have escaped the heathen slaughter. Using their sensors, each scout moved forward, unsure as to what to expect. And as they scanned, a sight of terrible carnage began to unfold before them. With each sweep, the scouts registered the many dead who rolled backward and forward on the ocean floor, caught in the surging tide, their white under-bellies reflecting the faint light of dawn that had now penetrated the shallow waters.

Zen slowly moved over the many dead, mentally blocking out the grief tearing at his heart. With each of his scans, the tally of the dead increased. With no mechanism of selection, the barbarous Jomonese people had inflicted their cruelty on the entire Assembly – males, females, young, and old. All had fallen victim. Zen turned and retreated back toward the entrance to the bay. His task now complete, he did not want to linger for any longer than was necessary in this place of death. It was in the very last lock of his final scan that one more body registered – a body out some two dikmar from the rest, caught up, and partially hidden, in the kelp. Zen moved in closer to make formal and positive identification.

Scout Leader Lido's patrol moved across the entrance to the bay, as they continued their search for any members of the Assembly who might have escaped the vicious ambush of the Jomonese butchers. Any who might have sought refuge among the rocks or in the many small inlets scattered along the land's edge that offered sanctuary. One asmar on the westward tack, Scout Nimo's excited signal called alarm to Lido.

"I imaged a fleeting response from the group of rocks six dikmar in lock three of my scan," he reported to the Scout Leader as he broke the surface next to him.

Lido intensified his scan, bouncing his ultrasonic waves off the myriad of rocks ahead that were being doused by the pounding seas. Lido called to the other two scouts to take up positions to the rear of the circle of the rocks; then again, Lido scanned the rocks with his sensors – again without a response.

As Legion Commander Zen approached the partly obscured body, a feeling of numbness and shock sickened him. Again, and again he scanned the lifeless form, refusing to register and confirm the silent shape of a lifeless Lute lying in front of him. Zen cried aloud in anguish as he settled next to his beloved Lute. He saw the terrible wounds where the harpoons of death had been hacked from her body in a great hurry, to again wreak further destruction on another of the defenceless monarchs of the deep. The gaping wounds were now the asylum of the flesh-eating and crawling insects of the deep. Zen observed the numerous incisions where the swords of doom had been plunged, again and again, as they emptied Lute's reservoir of life into the oceans – slits that were now great indents in her once streamlined body.

Zen repeatedly cried aloud in anguish. His wails quickly brought the other two scouts to his side. The two scouts moved in close to console their comrade and commander in this his time of grief. Lifting Zen to the surface, the two escorted him away from the body of Lute and toward the channel and out of the bay.

Scout Leader Lido moved to the extreme edge of danger offered up by the jagged rocks and pounding seas, and then audibly vibrated a call to the rocky outcrop. Without a moment's hesitation, a positive recall was received. And so it came to pass that Hur, the lone survivor from the Bay of Butchers, was found and delivered from the malicious seas.

Legion Commander Zen, with the two scouts linked tightly together, reached the open sea, then turned and headed once again to the protected waters of the reef. Zen, having now regained some composure, called on the other scouts to report their findings. Lido responded first to report the finding of one hundred and three dead. Those of the Assembly known best to all included Teacher Tia, and Scout Diva. No trace was found of the little Cyan, and the heavy toll of personal loss added to the burden crushing down on Zen.

Ruz then reported his findings: ninety-six dead including Senator Inca, and Senator Ku, father of Commander Mio. There was no sign of any survivors, and he too reported no trace of Zen's daughter, Cyan, or the Most Learned One's two most highly trained subordinates.

The new day was heralded by the dawn of a painted red heaven.

The seven scouts moved out from the protected waters of the reefs and made their way back into the channel – and into the Bay of Death once more.

Zen moved ahead of the group, leading the way over the rocks that marked the path to where Lute lay intertwined in the kelp. The ghostly figures of the dead cast unseeing eyes at the seven as they slowly passed overhead, left, as their souls were, to pursue their own direction to the God Tellus who received all the dead before they departed on the great voyage to that place of final resting. Spirits who, without the guidance of the Most Learned One to calm and set them on their plotted course, swirled around as entities lost again in the corridors of time.

Lute's body loomed in the darkened water, her whiteness acting as a homing beacon to Zen. With compassion and tenderness, Zen and Ruz dived down, and with one on each side, lifted Lute to the surface. Then together, they carried her out of the Bay of Death, through the narrow channel, and across to the calm waters of the reef. Here, the two laid Lute on the white sands that surrounded the base of the reef. Then, on Zen's instructions, the other scouts circled overhead. In total silence, Zen moved about collecting small rocks and pebbles, and with each of these he carefully adorned the body of his beloved Lute until she was completely covered. With his labour of love completed, Zen, in a ritual he had observed on numerous occasions, attempted to assist her spirit to navigate its way out into the independence of the oceans and on its course to the beyond.

As the third day since finding the dead drew to a close and the day slipped from the skies, for one last time Zen visited the resting-place of Lute. Here, his tears mixed with the salt water as he spoke to her of his love and sadness – and of the good times gone by.

He spoke of Cyan, their only born, and he thanked Lute for this precious gift of life, and the short time they'd had together. Once again, his tears mixed with the cold waters of the oceans. Then, in response to a call from Lido and Ruz, his very finest scouts, he bade one final goodbye to his Lute, and joined his patrol on the new course that would lead them back to the Assembly.

As the scouts passed the entrance to the Bay of Death, Zen called them to a halt. Then, in a final lingering farewell to those who had perished, Zen scanned a blessing he had carried from his training way back in the fourth decree and to which for his lost daughter, Cyan, he now added words from his heart.

"Goodbye, my little girl; for now I weep that you have gone. You have cemented your place in my heart as you swim through the treasured memories of my mind. Two passes ago, on your birth, I laid my dreams before your so diminutive self, and being the perfect little lady you always were, you swam carefully, for you knew you swam among my dreams. For I, who am now left alone, will still dream the dream – for to dream the dream is to live the dream in my mind."

As the sea was washed with the tears from the Regents of the Deep, Legion Commander Zen of the Sixth Order of a creed that spanned all time, ordered all to leave this Bay of Death for the last time. All were draped in cloaks of unyielding sorrow that seemed to be crushingly unbearable.

The Lost Souls

13

From the beginning of time, the Great Assembly had demonstrated the fortitude to continue when it seemed the great adversities of life called into question its very existence. Now, such times of uncertainty and leaderlessness were harshly thrust upon them. The fleeting calls of Lute haunted Zen for many days. Her cries to him in the dead of night while he rode the swells in sleep brought with them black clouds of grief that spread their wings and enveloped him. Zen was engulfed in a pall of self-pity and heartbreak that seemed to have no end in sight. As each day began, and then ended, those of the Great Assembly milled about in groups as if time had reduced them to what they had once been: lost souls that aimlessly wandered the oceans.

Without the guidance of their beloved King, the members of the Assembly were left to wallow in their gloom. Senator Opek watched with growing concern the effect the turmoil of the past events was taking on the Most Learned One. His mantle of leadership had triggered in him changes for the worse.

"Guard Commander Syle, can you vouch that all gathered here are trained in the degree of Senators?" The Most Learned One called.

"As so you have sought of me, as so I can vouch," the somewhat nervous new Guard Commander replied.

"Guard Commander Syle, take up your position."

"Legion Commander Zen, open this gathering of Senators, and

deliver the prayer."

The change in due rituals was one of the many changes instigated by the Most Learned One, and Zen responded automatically: "Senators, I call together this meeting in the name of our Great God, Poseidon. Let us take this moment to pray for guidance. Oh, Great God, Poseidon, I, your most humble of servants, beg you in all your wisdom to bestow your blessing on these Senators here gathered."

A sharp challenge of Guard Commander Syle to the approaching three assistants of the Most Learned One interrupted the proceedings.

The Senators awaited the Legion Commander's continuance of the prayer, and an uneasy silence spread across the Assembly. Against all protocol, the three uninvited intruders took up a position behind the Most Learned One, as if sentinels. The silence was broken when the Legion Commander continued with the opening sacraments.

"Oh, Great God Poseidon, we, the gathered …"

"There shall be no further prayers this day, Legion Commander."

Senator Opek called out, "The creed dictates that prayers to our God must be recited. It is a matter…"

The Most Learned One quickly silenced the interruption from Senator Opek. "It is now two passes since the death of our King." The Most Learned One circled the Senators as he scanned. "I have studied the Heavens and read the circle of stars, and then in total solitude, I have visited that emporium of Past Wise Ones and have determined the selection of a new King must be delayed." The Most Learned One let his words settle over the gathering.

Senator Ira broke the surface.

"With all due respect, Most Learned One! As you say, it is some two passes since that time of great sorrow, when we farewelled our most beloved King as he passed to the Heavens. It is also now one pass since we were last called together to discuss the appointment of a new King."

Hesitating for a moment before proceeding, Senator Ira felt the quiver of retort, albeit very small, but nevertheless a quiver of retort from The Most Learned One.

"What is the point you are trying to make, Senator Ira?" The interjection by The Most Learned One brought with it a sharpness that sounded a warning to Senator Ira.

"With all due respect, Most Learned One, it is my thought that full consideration must be given to this appointment. No more, no less!"

"Let me remind you, Senator Ira, no call to seek a new King will be made until such time as the heaven's readings confirm that time. And, let me add, until that time is here, there shall be no more talk on this subject."

Senator Opek broke the surface next to The Most Learned One.

"With due respect, Most Learned One."

"Proceed, Senator."

"I, Senator Opek, along with a number of my fellow Senators, have a growing concern at some of the decisions that have been taken without any recourse to us, or to the Great Council of Elders."

"Let me remind you also, the governing of this, the Great Assembly's mantle, has fallen on me – for that is what is written in our foundation creed." The Most Learned One's sharpness had now taken on a dictatorial, chilling arrogance.

"Senator Opek, pray tell me! What decision have I made that has affected The Great Assembly, has somehow failed to appease you?"

Only the swishing of the sleek bodies breaking through the surface interrupted the silence. "Well, Senator Opek! I am waiting for these startling revelations you have seen fit to bring to this forum."

"With all due respect, Most Learned One, it is not so much a decision that you have cast into law, but your courses of action that we have not had time to study – or make recommendations on – before you cast them into law."

"With due respect, Most Learned One!" Senator Ira breached the ocean's surface next to Senator Opek and the Most Learned One.

"You may speak, Senator Ira."

"With due respect, Most Learned One, I concur with Senator Opek. There are a number of issues that we, as Senators, feel required our input."

"Senator Opek! Senator Ira! I ask you for the last time, what decisions have I taken that you feel aggrieved by?"

"With due respect, Most Learned One." Senator Ira was the first to speak. "There are two decisions that bother Senator Opek and myself – and I must add, a number of other Senators as well. Senator Ira felt the support of Senator Opek, which gave him encouragement to speak his mind.

"The first of these decisions, which bothers us the most, is the promise that Hur, son of widowed mother Dy, may be promoted to Guard Commander. Here, I must add, to be totally honest, the rumour is that Hur will be promoted. What say you to this, Most Learned One?"

Senator Ira was somewhat taken aback by his own forthrightness towards the Most Learned One. Then, riding on his newly found candour, he continued, not giving the Most Learned One any opportunity to interject.

"While I am on the subject of Hur, no formal enquiry has been held into the happenings at the Bay of Death. In my mind, there are far too many unanswered questions."

Not wanting the outspoken Senator to gain the upper hand in their verbal exchange, the Most Learned One took on an arrogant posture.

"Rumour! You dare come before me with nothing more than rumour, Senator Ira?" The cutting edge of the Most Learned One's voice grew cold and contemptuous, in a manner that fell far outside all that was written and taught in any level in their creed.

"From where does this rumour emanate, Senator?"

"From none other than the widowed mother Dy, who has made no secret of these promises to her son: promises, she claims, made to her by you, with all due respect, Most Learned One."

"What of the second decision, Senator Ira? What of the second decision that seems to bother you? Maybe we should hear from Senator Opek, for I have felt his support of you. Senator Ira, let him now speak." With this, the Most Learned One dismissed the rumour of Hur's promotion with a tone of distaste for the Senator that was felt by all within the Great Council of Elders who, unnoticed, had now joined the rest of the Senators.

"Senator Opek," the Most Learned One scanned to the Senator. "Senator Opek, come to the front, and present your views so that we all may see you are not a puppet to any other Senator."

"I will do as you ask, Most Learned One, not for the reason you give, but to protest at the tone and insinuations you have made in an attempt to cast aspersions on both my character and that of Senator Ira. With all due respect, Most Learned One."

Senator Opek moved to the fore of those assembled as he continued: "The number of those whom you have chosen to begin the training as

Learned Ones has tripled since the death of our King."

"Is that a problem for you, Senator?" The Most Learned One's interjection was barbed and brutal.

"With all due respect, Most Learned One, it is not I, or better still, we, who have a problem with this influx of those choosing to take up this calling. But we all do foresee a problem with those joining for they are from that pool who are struggling with their lessons."

The Most Learned One took his time in replying. "Senator Opek, it may well be that by joining in the group of Learned Ones, their talents may be better utilized." The Most Learned One seemed to have softened in his manner towards the Senators.

"With due respect, Most Learned One, where it is not our privilege to question the wisdom of your very self, we raise these matters only out of concern."

Senator Opek again felt the repressed wrath of The Most Learned One as he spoke. "Senators, we have heard from both Senators Ira and Opek. Do any of you assembled here have other matters you feel need to be brought to this forum?"

"With due respect, Most Learned One..."

"Approach, Senator Ark!"

The Senator, known as the quiet one among the other Senators, broke the surface next to The Most Learned One.

"With due respect, Most Learned One, these matters raised by my two fellow Senators still lie unanswered, and no clarification has been made on those subjects so raised."

"Senator Ark, you seem to have aligned yourself with Senators Ira and Opek in questioning my judgement."

"With due respect, Most Learned One, on these matters, which I view with some gravity, I certainly have."

"Let there be no more talk on these perceived rumours," The Most Learned One decreed; and so ended that discussion before the Senators.

"There is a subject of much more importance I wish to broach at this time." Again, the tone of The Most Learned One cut to the heart of the Senators.

"We have decided that it is time to make a change to our being …"

"With due respect – we? Who are we?" The interjection from Senator Ira caught The Most Learned One completely by surprise.

"The Learned Ones! The Learned Ones! That's who we are. Are you satisfied now, Senator Ira?"

Senator Ira withdrew. "With all due respect, Most Learned One."

The Most Learned One then continued: "After due deliberation and readings of the heavens, I have been sent a clear message, and that message I am going to follow.

Firstly, I am going to reorganise the Learned Ones. This is to be undertaken forthwith. As we are now growing in numbers, any reorganisation will be a better reflection on us, and indeed the Assembly in its total."

With all due respect, again, Most Learned One." Senator Oly spoke for the first time. "We, as the Great Council of Elders, and in this body I include all the Senators, will need time to reflect on this proposal of yours. In fact, Most Learned One, there are many things we must now consider and discuss amongst ourselves before we can approve or disapprove of any such changes."

"To approve or disapprove, you want time to think? If you will approve or disapprove of what I have already decided, you overstep your authority in questioning my decisions!" The stinging rebuke of The Most Learned One stunned the Elders and Senators to disbelief.

"I, The Most Learned One, this day, have declared that from this time forth, all Learned Ones shall revert to the name that Poseidon removed all that time ago."

"I protest!"

"Protest all you want, Senator Opek, for as I have instructed, so it shall be. From this time on all Learned Ones, shall be known as Priests, and the title I bestow upon myself with or without your blessing…" The Most Learned One hesitated, as if he was having second thoughts on continuing his enforcement of change, but then he spoke. "I, the Most Learned One, from this point onwards shall be known as High Byzefu."

The Senators of the Great Assembly were shocked to silence.

"In the name of the great God Poseidon, I call this meeting to end."

"Most Learned One we want …"

"Byzefu! Byzefu! I will be known as Byzefu! You will never again call me Most Learned One. Do you understand? As so I have decreed, so I will enforce." The full strength scan of The High Byzefu sent a sharp shock wave through the water and knocked Senator Opek sideways.

So it came to pass that The High Byzefu did, that day, chisel in stone his destiny.

Senator Ira, and Senator Opek, decided to meet with Senators Oly and Ark in the solitude of the shallow mountains some one day's travel from where the Assembly had made their home for the last two passes.

"Senators, I give you thanks for your attendance." Senator Ira was the first to break the silence. "I have taken the liberty of inviting Legion Commander Zen to join us." The other Senators nodded their agreement with Ira's decision, and acknowledged the Legion Commander's presence.

"It gravely concerns me, my friends of old..." Ira let the opening words give an indication of the tone he sought to bring to this covert meeting. "It gravely concerns me that the Assembly is becoming very unsettled: rife with rumours and the onset of ill feelings that are beginning to fester in some of the younger ones, all of which is bringing disharmony to the rest of the Assembly. Even the food scouts have to be pressured to carry out their appointed task."

After a brief silence, the Senator continued. "The time has come. There must be a calling together of all Senators at a place of solitude, and we must elect a new King."

A quizzical expression crept across the face of Senator Opek. "Tell me, is this wise, Ira? After all, Byzefu has decreed that at this time, his reading of the heavens tells him the time is not yet right to take this step."

"Senator Opek, we all have been informed of the thinking of Byzefu; and I, for one, say the time is now. I cannot believe for one moment that our God would want us to continue on, leaderless."

Senator Oly scanned to speak. "I agree! Byzefu has delayed the appointment of a new King to suit his own agenda. Furthermore, by changing his name, and introducing teachings outside the creed, I now firmly believe he has abdicated his responsibilities, and he no longer has my respect as The Most Learned One, leader of the spiritual teachings of this our creed."

The brave, sombre words of the soft-spoken Senator struck a chord, albeit a silent one, in all those in attendance.

"The Senator makes a very good point. The feelings of despair that are invading our people are of major concern to me as well." Senator Ark's statement confirmed the creeping veil of mistrust in The Byzefu.

In unison, the group surfed the long rolling swells as Ira continued.

Ira scanned to speak: "Widow Dy, mother of Hur, last day did approach me. She has requested that I seek all Senators' approval to allow Hur to renounce his Scout Leadership rank to join the group of Priests."

"Hur join the priests? Why, Ira, do you bring mirth to this discussion?"

"My friend, Ark, it is not in mirth that I raise the matter."

"I think it may be a wise move if Hur is allowed to join them," Ark added.

This was an answer not expected by Ira.

Then Ark continued: "He has always been a wayward one. I did not agree with him being promoted to his current rank, and I feel we were somewhat manipulated by Byzefu. But nevertheless, Hur did survive the brutal slaughter in the Bay of Death. So yes, if this is his calling, who are we to prevent it?"

Ira nodded in agreement.

"I am to meet with Byzefu at day's end, and at this time I will raise this matter," concluded Ark.

Ira again nodded in agreement.

A lone seabird circled over the Regents of the Deep, its grey and white body silhouetted against the crystal blue heavens, its cries giving a somewhat strange solace to them all.

140

"Now, Ira, let us get back to the main reason for this call together, and away from the subject of Hur. What must we do next to bring about a settlement of your troubled mind?" Opek waited for Ira to respond.

"There are many things that my troubled mind must come to terms with. The most important is the on-going delay in the beginning of the selection ritual to find a new King. The thought of having to consider the replacement of The Most Learned One adds to the weight."

"I agree with you, Ira, but we are somewhat at a loss. Byzefu, by our law, is the only one with the ability to read the cosmos and decipher the writing, and so we must await his pleasure. I have watched the rapid raise of one of your prodigies, Ira. Teacher Notris, I understand, is ready to take the next decree. Even in this time of great turmoil, he has progressed, and done so very rapidly."

"I agree with you, Opek. He is one of the brightest shining stars we have amongst us, and it may well be that he will be called on before his allotted time."

"Yes, I suppose you are right, Ira. I have no doubt that grave times are just ahead of us, and we must not rest at ease while we are without a King."

"Legion Commander Zen, I thank you for your attendance."

"Thank you, Senator Ira, but I am at a loss as to why you extended the invitation to me."

Senator Ira thought for a moment, not wanting to put the Legion Commander in any position that would put his standing and rank within the Assembly in jeopardy.

"As you have heard here today, there is a growing discontent within the Great Assembly, and we Senators seek to remedy it." Senator Ira looked over at his son, and then choosing his words carefully, he proceeded.

"You, as my son, may well be put in the position where you will have to decide into which group you will place your faith. The group you choose must be one chosen based on logic and the teachings of our creed."

The other Senators now fully understood the gravity of the path their most senior Senator was advocating in his subliminal way.

"I did, I must admit, have some inclination of what this call together was about, and by my very attendance I have given clear indication of where my loyalties lie, father of mine."

For twenty-one days, those newly recruited to the priest training were deprived of all nourishment and sleep – twenty-one days of endless bombardment by learning scans. Lessons of the mystic were scanned in over and over again – wave after wave of scans that knew not an end. The lack of food and sleep took an ever-increasing toll on the young minds, and in this way, the doctrine of the Byzefu pushed aside the teachings of the creed and supplanted them with a new teaching.

The young protégé, Teacher Notris, already trained to the sixth degree, felt the change creeping into his fellow teachers. He was somewhat glad that Byzefu had separated him, and those of the higher teaching skills, leaving them to continue their daily rituals as before.

The remaining group, championed by Byzefu as the future spiritual guides of the Assembly, sent a quivering chill down his flanks whenever they passed by. But who was he to think further on these matters, as he had no doubt the Senators had given this new direction their blessing.

Priest Rabiz watched the four new apprentices being prepared for the first of their lessons. These four would be added to his group once they reached the standards as laid down by Byzefu. A faint smile forced back his bottom lip.

"Priest Rabiz!" The call from Byzefu broke into his train of thought.

"As summoned, Byzefu."

"How fare these new inductees?"

"As those before them passed, I am left with little doubt that they will do as well."

"I have decided that there shall be no further additions to the group."

"May I enquire as to why you have reduced the projected numbers, Byzefu?'

"The Great Council of Elders is becoming concerned at the numbers that are opting out of their training to join us."

Priest Rabiz knew when not to speak.

Byzefu continued. "I have set a number of no more than four new priests for every house of the heavenly Zodiac."

Both priests broke the surface in unison. "Then the number shall be set at fifty-two, Byzefu?"

"No! No! The number is set at forty-eight for the twelve houses of the Zodiac in the Heavens."

"But Byzefu, our God Poseidon spoke of thirteen houses in the Zodiac."

"I have read the heavens, and nowhere is there any sign of a thirteenth house."

"Our God Posi...."

"You question me?" Byzefu cut the priest off in mid-word. "Back to your task, Priest!"

As Priest Rabiz turned to leave, Byzefu called to him, "Ensure all the training goes well, for I will search the Heavens for new names to be bestowed on these, the last, at their induction."

With that, Byzefu turned away.

"So mote it be, Byzefu."

$$——\ \Psi\ ——$$

"So Hur seeks an audience with me? Maybe I could use him. Yes, I will see the wayward one, and let's see for what purpose he has sought me out."

As wished by Hur, so it did come to pass that Byzefu did set to meet with the wayward Hur in solitude.

Byzefu's growing position and hulking demeanour caused a ripple of fear to pass through Hur, making him wonder whatever possessed him to seek this audience.

The approaching Priests called to Hur, "You are Hur?"

Hur could only nod.

"I am Huela, Priest Huela. As you have sought a meeting with High Priest Byzefu, it is my given task to brief you on the protocols that are expected of you before and during this meeting."

Again Hur could only nod.

"We will take you to the outer sanctum of Byzefu." The priest hesitated, and then continued, "When his pleasure is known, an attending Priest shall scan for you to approach."

The nervous fear that had gripped Hur was now starting to subside.

The priest continued, "You will approach Byzefu from directly in front. You will only speak when spoken to. Keep your answers brief and to the point. Do you understand?"

Again, Hur could only acknowledge his agreement with a nod.

"Then follow me." With that command, the three headed to the outer perimeter of the Assembly.

"Come abreast!"

Priest Huela's call to Hur banished all thoughts of escape, replacing them with a cold fear of the unknown. Priest Huela broke the water next to Hur.

"I hope for your sake that this audience you seek with Byzefu is important." A sharper harshness had crept into the priest's tone. "Byzefu is extremely busy. There are many things he must attend to, and a meeting that has no important substance will bring down his wrath."

Hur was now having second thoughts as to why he had decided to join the mystic priests. These second thoughts were now reinforced with a fear brought on by the tone adopted by the Priest, Huela.

"Wait here!" Huela ordered. "Wait here, while I announce your arrival to the Byzefu. Do you understand me, Hur?"

Hur looked across at the Priest without answering.

"Do you understand, Hur, or would you have me tell Byzefu that you have grown weak and taken fright at the thought of meeting him? Well, Hur!"

The sneering attitude of the Priest Huela fortified Hur's resolve to meet with Byzefu. "No, Priest, I am not afraid to meet with Byzefu. I,

Hur, am not afraid of any such meeting."

"Then wait here as I have instructed you." The sneer now had with it a sense of ridicule that put a little boldness in Hur's demeanour. "Your attempt at bravado does not impress at all. We will see just how brave you are when you are face-to-face with Byzefu."

Hur felt the attitude of the Priest contemptible at the very least, as he awaited, with the second silent Priest, the pleasure of Byzefu.

"The Byzefu will see you now." The quick return of Priest Huela took Hur somewhat aback.

"Follow me!"

At four sigmar from the place of meeting, two further Priests joined the entourage. Then, at two sigmar from the place of meeting, a further four Priests flanked the group. At one sigmar, the Priest Huela scanned a slowdown – and stop. Turning to Hur, Huela again informed him: "Wait with these Priests until you receive my scan to approach."

Hur again found a mental block prevented him from replying, so he nodded his understanding. The water seemed to chill with presence of the Priests and Byzefu nearby.

"Hur, only son of widowed mother, Dy, you are now summoned as per your own request, to approach and appear before The Byzefu in due ritual."

From whom or where the scan had come, Hur knew not.

The calling words, as if by some magical power, put Hur into a state of automation, whether by his own mind playing games with him, or by his own self-induced fear. Hur was thus drawn into the presence of the Assembly's most feared, Byzefu.

"Byzefu, I, Priest Huela, present to you, Hur, only son of widowed mother Dy, who has humbly requested to meet with you."

Then, with head bowed in ritual, Huela retreated from the presence of the two.

"Hur, only son of widowed mother Dy, I have granted you audience with me. This audience is now upon us." The voice of Byzefu matched the cold staring eyes he cast on Hur.

Hur, now engulfed by the aura of cold fear emitted by Byzefu, found no words forthcoming.

"Come, Hur, speak of these things that bother you. Fear not me, feel fear only of any untruth you may speak."

Hur felt a softening in Byzefu's demeanour that in some small way began to lift the invisible veil that somehow had choked and paralysed his voice and thoughts.

"I, Hur, only son of widowed mother Dy, give thanks to you for allowing me into your revered presence." Hur racked his brain, wishing now to have taken more notice of the tuition in ritual training in the first decree.

"High Priest of the Universe, I, Hur of the third decree, only son of widow…"

"Stop! Stop! Hur, your knowledge of ritual is somewhat poor. Your address is in the wrong context and terms. Stop now!"

Hur felt a shaming disgrace, and went silent.

Byzefu looked at Hur, his mind ranging over ways for how best to use him. Hmmm! He would be just the sort of individual who could be used in his plan – as one who was dispensable.

"Your training in the first degree is somewhat lacking. It is an insult to my position and to all those past who have held this position that you let this training fall on unhearing ears. But I can forgive you."

Byzefu let a little feeling creep back into his voice.

"Hur, it is told that you wish to give up all rank, and then to undergo training as a Priest – how say you to this?" Byzefu and Hur broke the sea surface as one.

"Yes, Byzefu, it is my wish to join your noble Legion of Priests." Then, not knowing what to say or do next, Hur rode the long swells in silence with the dark and foreboding Byzefu.

"I have scanned the very inner sanctums of your mind, and I see there are things that bother you. Hur, I want you to now speak of these things. It may be best if you tell of these things freely, and without prejudice."

Fear grabbed Hur in its fist-like grip. What does Byzefu know of those things hidden deep?

Byzefu felt the sense of fear building up in Hur; a creeping sense of trepidation emitted by Hur revealed that, perhaps, Hur had a number of secrets hidden in his auditorium of memories.

The silence deafened Hur, now caught up in a vortex of swirling emotions that were being driven by the cold stare of Byzefu – a hypnotic stare that ripped aside the mental barriers as it entered the reservoir of memories.

"Tell me, Hur. Tell me of these things you hide," Byzefu's voice droned. "Tell me, Hur. Tell of these shameful deeds which you try to hide. Tell the omniscient one. It is best that these tellings come freely from you."

So, it came to pass, like the streams that cascaded, bubbling and talking, as they flowed over the rocks in a bygone Atlantis. So it was that Hur, only son of widowed Dy, did tell of his misdeeds which led to the happenings at the Bay of Death. And in this telling of all these things that for so long he had hidden, Hur, only son of the widowed Dy, did seal his fate.

—— Ψ ——

"Legion Commander Zen." The incoming call from a Senate Runner brought Zen out of his morning slumber. Of late, it seemed the ongoing tension between The Byzefu and the Senate was the only reason he was repeatedly called to the Senate.

"Sorry, Senate Runner, I was somewhat distracted by my own thoughts. Now, what brings you out this far?"

The young scout moved in closer. "Senator Ira has requested your attendance at a Senate meeting he has called to take place when the sun is at its zenith."

"Thank you, Runner. Please inform the Senator I will be in attendance."

With a nod, the Senate Runner retired.

"Teacher Notris!" The incoming scan drew the teacher away from his young students. "Yes, Senate Runner, to what do I owe this unexpected scan. The young teacher's mind starting to race a little, as it was only the third time he had been called to face the Senate. The Senate Runner moved in close to the teacher.

"Senator Ira has requested you to present yourself to a meeting he is calling today when the sun is at its zenith."

"Thank you, Runner. Please inform the Senator I will be honoured to attend his meeting, as so instructed."

With that, the Senate Runner departed, leaving a somewhat bewildered teacher at a loss to understand why the Senator wanted to see him.

"I suppose all will come to the fore in time," he thought to himself as he turned back to the tasks at hand.

"Guard Commander Mio!" The Senate Runner scanned a call to Mio, who was with a group of her female friends engaged in their customary pastime of chattering, whilst they enjoyed the warmth of the new day.

"Come in closer," Mio scanned to the waiting Senate Runner. "I don't bite, and I will go as far as saying my friends don't bite either."

Again, the Senate Runner felt he was the subject of the group's chattering mirth.

"Guard Commander Mio, Senator Ira has requested that you attend a Senate meeting he is calling today, when the sun is at its zenith."

"Thank you, Scout. Please convey to the Senator, as ordered, as so I will obey."

With a nod for a response, the Senate Runner moved away as quickly as he could, thinking, *"Females! Who needs them?"*

The thought was read by the chattering females, inducing a response of more chattering mirth.

"Hello, Senate Runner." The incoming scan of Guard Commander Zarlie startled the Senate Runner.

"What brings you so far from the Senate?"

"You do, Guard Commander, you do. I bring a message from Senator Ira. He has requested your attendance at a meeting he is calling this day."

"And when is this meeting to be held?" the young Guard

Commander interrupted.

"When the sun is at its zenith, Guard Commander."

"Thank you. Tell the Senator, as instructed, as so I will obey."

With a nod of acknowledgement to the Guard Commander, the Senate Runner retired.

"Legion Commander Zen, bring the meeting to order in open harmony." The solemnity of Senator Ira's voice gave an indication of the gravity that he was to bring to this calling together.

"Our Great God, Poseidon, please bring down your blessing upon those of your humble servants of the deep here gathered."

With the shortened prayer appropriately recited, Zen took up a position to the left of Senator Ira who looked out over those of his most faithful friends of old, his most trusted Commanders.

"Guard Commanders Zarlie and Mio, gather together quickly those Guard Commanders and Scouts you most trust. Then take them, and set in place a protection barrier that gives those here assembled greatest protection from all intruders. Furthermore, under no circumstances is this call together to be interrupted for any reason. Do I make myself clear to you both?"

"As so instructed, as so we will comply."

The unison scans got the nod of approval from the Senator.

"Gathered Senators, Legion Commander Zen, Teacher Notris, I give you thanks for your attendance, and I will immediately give you the reason for this meeting I have called..." The ominous shriek of a lone sea bird as it passed overhead interrupted the Senator in mid-sentence

"Since the passing of our King, the Great Assembly has suffered great hardship. Not only have we lost our King, but we have lost many of our Assembly."

The words of the Senator triggered Zen's memories, and again he felt the pain of finding his Lute. Blinking back his tears, the comforting scans from his father brought only small comfort.

"The time has come that we, the Senators, take back the position of guardians of our Assembly, and insure that we move on from these recent times of sorrow." Senator Ira waited for his scans to be read, and then continued.

"The Learned One, who now insists on being called The High Byzefu, is leading us away from our creed, and more importantly, by stealth, we are being denied our given rights to worship our God Poseidon."

"With the very greatest respect, Ira!" The Senator of Scouts, and Guards, Senator Ova, breached the surface next to Ira. "The Byzefu has grown all-powerful. I will even go so far as to say that The High Byzefu, as he now wishes to be called, has grown more powerful than our past King ever was. With this power he has, I believe, grown mendacious." The Senator's words had a sobering effect on the gathering.

"Senator Ova, the matters you have raised, if proven true, I tend to agree with; however, raising them and proving them are two very different things"

Senator Opek let his scans sink in, and then continued: "I think we have not been as forceful as The Byzefu has, and in so being, The Byzefu has managed to override us. Maybe we should try a little harder, and exert our authority. The Senate must first ratify all decisions before they come to pass, and then it is the Senators who instruct the Teachers in the changes that the Senate approves of, and sends out. Is that not true?"

"What is your point, Opek?"

"My point is, Ira, I see no reason that anything The Byzefu has said, or done cannot be redressed, and redressed quickly. Rectification of these perceived wrongs is easily rectified – easily rectified."

"Easily rectified? That is a lot easier said than done." The harsh interruption by the normally mild Senator Ira took all by surprise. "Pray, tell me how? I can assure you I will follow any of your recommendations that will expedite this developing standoff. The Byzefu has informed us all that his reading of the heavens prevents all call togethers of the Senate; so with call togethers out of the question, this lull has strengthened his hand, and by that very act, has weakened ours. What say you to that, Senator Opek?"

"Before the Senator speaks, may I speak?" Legion Commander Zen, breaking all protocol, scanned his request to Senator Ira.

"Granted, Legion Commander! Speak your mind. We are in open call together."

A somewhat nervous Zen broached next to Ira. "I have listened to you all speak on the matter of The Byzefu. It is on this matter that I wish to speak." Taking a moment to collect his thoughts, Zen looked at those who now had him in their focus.

"Continue on, Legion Commander." The sudden input from Senator Ark's scan had certain urgency in it.

"There are a number of trends that are developing within the priest followers of The Byzefu. The first of these is the growth in their numbers – at this time, they outnumber all scouts and guards combined."

"That is news to me, Legion Commander, and of major concern. Why is it that The Byzefu wants so many priests?"

"It is not just the numbers that The Byzefu is surrounding himself with, Senator Ova, but the character of those who have joined his group. These new members, along with the main group of former Learned Ones, now number some one hundred trainees. These trainees have been gathered from those of the Assembly who have either failed at the first decree, or have been bought to the notice of the Senator of Discipline and Goodwill."

The Legion Commander now had the full attention of the call together and continued.

"Not only has this number grown, but they are now showing absolute contempt towards the Teachers and Senate Runners."

"How are they showing this contempt to these ones, Legion Commander?" The scan of Senator Opek indicated a loss of some of his attitude of appeasement towards The Byzefu.

"The Byzefu is now insisting that all messaging, be it from the Senate or the Teachers, must, in the first instance, be directed to one of his appointees. Then, to add insult to the conveyers, the appointee is making them wait, sometimes for a full day, before taking in the scans."

"Legion Commander Zen, are you saying what I think you are saying?"

"Yes, Senator Ova. The Byzefu is controlling the flow of information from the Senate to his trainees."

"Who is the appointee?" Again, Senator Ova interrupted.

Zen waited for full effect, then answered, "None other than Hur, only son of widowed Dy!"

"Senator Ira, Senator Ira," the incoming scan stirred Ira from his sleep. "Senator Ira it is I, Hur, only son of widow Dy."

"Yes. I know who you are," the now fully alert Ira invited Hur to come in closer.

"What is it you seek of me, Hur?"

"I bring a message from The High Byzefu."

"And why cannot the Most Learned One bring the message himself rather than send one of his pawns?"

The stinging tone of the Senator's scan passed right over Hur. After all, he was now someone of stature within the growing band of those whose allegiance had been sworn to the High Byzefu.

"Well, answer me, Hur. Why does your so-called leader Byzefu not show me the respect I have earned as Senior Senator, and deliver his message in person?"

The thwarted Hur could do nothing but listen to the irate Ira.

"Now, you go and tell The Byzefu, and yes, from now on I will call him The Byzefu as well, for no other reason than he is no longer fit or able to hold the standing of The Most Learned One. Now go, get out of my sight!"

Hur, with his facade of bravado ripped away by the stinging words of the Senator, slunk away.

With all hope of returning to his slumber, Ira returned to the Senate.

"Senate Runner."

"Yes Senator Ira."

"I want a message to go to Senator Ova and Legion Commander Zen. Tell them I want a call together with no others but them, and I want this call together to be before this day's end."

"As ordered, as so I obey," responded the Senate Runner as he sped away to carry out his instructions.

Zen closed in on his father, scanning in a greeting as he did so.

"Welcome my son. Thanks for your prompt attention to my call together."

"Senator Ira." The incoming call of Senator Ova interrupted the chatter of the father and son.

"Greetings, Ova."

"And I reciprocate those greetings to you, Ira, and my greetings to you, Legion Commander."

"Thank you Senator Ova." Zen nodded to the incoming Senator as she broached next to the two of them.

"Now, you old fossil of the ocean, what great importance so dominates your mind that you saw fit to drag me away from my Senate duties?"

Zen felt the quiver of warmth that always surrounded his favourite Senator who, all through his youth in The Shallows, took the place of the mother he never had.

"It is good to see you have lost none of your sense of humour, Ova. And me an old fossil? You are not that many passes younger than me."

Zen watched the two verbally jostle in the calm waters, listened to their friendly banter, and wondered why these who were such close friends had not taken their friendship to the next level.

"Zen, you keep those thoughts to yourself."

One of Zen's faults was that his mirth was always so transparent, and radiated out for all to read.

"Sorry, Senator Ova, but when you and my father are together away from the pressures of Senate life, you both radiate a contagious happiness."

"Thank you, Zen. I do enjoy the company of your father, but I am sure that this idle banter is not the reason we have been called here. So, out with it, Ira. Why have you called us together?"

"You are right. There are matters I want to discuss with you, or more to the point, I have some news I want you two to be the first to hear. That's not to say your company is not always a highlight, Ova."

A more solemn tone had crept into Senator Ira's voice. He waited, thinking carefully about the words he would choose.

"I have decided that in the overall interest of the Great Assembly, the time has come to choose a new King, and to fill the vacancies of the two murdered Senators along with those Senators lost in the great storm."

As the three rode the oceans in silence, it was Ova who spoke first.

"Have you thought it through, Ira? After all, The Byzefu has read the heavens, and he claims the heavenly bodies are not in an alignment that would permit a new King's appointment."

"Your words, Ova, I always take with the highest respect, but in this instance, I ask you, in whose interest is it to delay the appointment of a new King? I do believe, if you answer this question in the faith of our creed, you will have to agree it is none other than the so-called High Byzefu."

Ira's words completely removed any remaining hint of mirth that had lingered around the three.

"I agree with all you have said, but the question is what can be done now? Can a call together be held without the blessing of the Most Learned One, and can the raising of any new King be completed without the final raising of obligation and installation secrets only known by the Learned One?"

"I have given these concerns you have raised my utmost attention, and it will not be easy; but I am of the mind that it can be done."

Senator Ova watched as Ira took in her comments, and then continued.

"Pray tell me Ira, knowing you as I do, I'm sure you will have formulated a plan. I think it is time we three know just what this course is that you want to chart to bring about any elevation of a new King."

Zen watched and waited for his father to reply.

"As the most senior Senator, the training I have undertaken over many passes – unbeknownst to all but the past King – allows me to take control should the unthinkable happen to the current King.

This news came as a complete shock to Senator Ova.

"Are you saying you are trained to the level of a King?"

"No, Ova, I did not say that. What I am saying is that I was trained to elevate any approved candidate to the level of King."

Ova watched Ira, seeing the inner turmoil her friend of so long now faced with the path he had chosen.

"Thank you for your thoughts, Ova. And yes, there are worrying times ahead. Not only for me, but for all of us."

Zen again felt the warm vibrations these two held for each other seep back into the call together.

"Legion Commander Zen."

The full formality of Senator Ira's scan stole the joviality from the two Senators, and started a chain of events that would change the course of the Great Assembly forever.

The New King

14

"Teacher Notris, call this Council of Elders together in the fifth order of our decree," Senator Ira called.

The somewhat nervous Notris, called to account, kept saying to himself, "Don't be nervous. This unexpected call to serve the Council of Elders is a proud moment."

"As so ordered, as so I obey."

A nod and a quiet reassuring scan from Senator Ira removed the last lingering shreds of self-doubt.

"Guard Commander Zarlie, take up your position."

"As you have ordered, as so I will comply, Senator Ira."

Zarlie scanned to Teacher Notris as she positioned herself to the right of the teacher, "Scout Commander Zarlie, can you confirm that all here present are of the fifth decree of our creed or higher?"

"Teacher Nortris, as so asked as so I can confirm that all present here are as you ask."

Guard Commander Zarlie then took her leave to join her trusted scouts, to keep all but those of the fifth decree out of the call together area.

"Senator Ira, as you have instructed, as so I have opened this call together of the Council of Elders in the fifth decree."

With a nod of approval from Senator Ira, the teacher retired to take up his position to the right of Senator Ira.

"Senator Ova, present yourself before me and bring down the blessing of our Great God Poseidon upon the Council of Elders gathered here."

"As so ordered, Senator Ira, as so I will comply."

Zen was always amazed that Ova and his father were able to keep their feelings at bay during these times of due ceremony, and he held them both in the highest esteem. Having opened the call together with her blessing, Senator Ova nodded to the Senior Senator and retired to join the other Senators. Ira waited as Ova returned to the fold, and then turned to those gathered, knowing the words he was about to speak had to be chosen very carefully so as not to cast aspersions on any member.

"Senators, Council of Elders," again, Senator Ira was hesitant in choosing his words. "As the most senior Senator of this Great Assembly, I have ordered this call together as the first step in the process to determine a new King."

The underlying murmur that was always present, even in the most solemn of meetings, was suddenly sucked from the call together auditorium.

Senator Opek was the first to break the silence. "Senator Ira, why is it that the Most Learned One, or The Byzefu as he insists on now being called, why is it that he is not present at this time?"

Again, Senator Ira thought very carefully in choosing his words. "The Most Learned One has decided that the heavenly readings were not conducive to any call together."

"Then why do you proceed and go against his readings, Senator Ira? Why?" The words of Opek had taken on a stinging rebuke.

"Senator Opek, I, along with Senators Ova and Ark, have made repeated requests to the Most Learned One, or The High Byzefu as you call him, to start the process of King determination, and each time

160

we make this call, his answer is always the same. Here and now I will not bore you with his repeated replies; you know them as well as I do – as well as we all do." Ira stared across at Opek and felt his growing resentment, the reason for which he could not fathom.

"Well, maybe he is right. Just maybe he, in this instance, is right. What say you to that Senator?" Again the strength in Senator Opek's rebuking tone cut to the heart of the mild Senator Ira.

"In all my time as…"

"Before you continue, Senator Ira," Zen interrupted, broaching between the two. "Senator Opek, as Legion Commander, one of the many tasks the Senate has bestowed on me is to ensure that all formalities of any call together are strictly adhered to."

Senator Opek knew what was coming next.

"Senator Opek, your demeanour and tone is totally unacceptable to this gathering, and to all that is taught in the creed." Zen watched as his words had their desired effect.

"Senator Opek, you will apologise to the Senior Senator, and then you will withdraw from this call together."

All eyes now fell on the disgraced Senator as he rose up to remedy his folly.

"Senator Ira, Legion Commander Zen, esteemed members of the Council of Elders, I apologise to you all, and as instructed by Legion Commander Zen, I will remove myself from this call together." With his apology tendered, the Senator nodded and turned away to withdraw.

"Senator Opek, your apology is accepted, and I would ask the Legion Commander to revoke his order for you to withdraw. Your contribution to this call together would be greatly appreciated." The

Senator turned to the Legion Commander, awaiting his decision on the withdraw order.

"As it is your request, Senator Ira, then I, on reflection, rescind my withdraw order."

Ira nodded this thanks to the Legion Commander. The last thing on his mind was to alienate any Senator at this time.

"Now where was I? Oh yes! In all my time as a Senator, and that time is now of some many passes, we have never had to wait this long to have the heavenly readings in our favour."

Ira saw Senator Opek rise up as if to speak, and then drop down as if he thought better of it, not wanting to test the patience of any member of the call together.

"As to those of you who are at a loss as to why the Most Learned One is not here, I have no idea why he is absent; he was invited to attend, but as only a silent observer. As I had expected, he is not here, and I don't really care."

For all those gathered, it was the first time any of them had heard Senator Ira speak of anyone in this tone.

"I have called you all here this day so that we can put into motion the instruments of elevation that will see a new King ascend to the throne of Epiphanes."

An exciting chatter swept through the call together in anticipation that, at last, some sort of order would return to the Great Assembly. Legion Commander Zen scanned for silence; and order – other than that low hum of chatter – returned.

"The first order of business…" The Senator waited till the chatter had subsided further and he had the full attention of all. "The first order of business is to elevate from the Great Assembly eight members to fill the ranks of the Council of Elders."

Sadness suddenly swept over the call together, as they remembered those who had fallen to the storm and in the Bay of Death.

Reading the feelings of these regents, Ira responded: "Once we have elected a new King, his first duty will be to pay tribute to honour those departed ones."

All nodded in agreement at the words of Senator Ira who then continued: "I charge each and every member of the Council of Elders to seek out, and then present to the Senate for consideration, those candidates who have met all as is laid down in our creed. Remember that the responsibilities of the Council of Elders are enormous, and must be continued in the same vein as in the past. All must be blessed with dignity and great nobility."

Elder Ramcy scanned for permission to speak to Senator Ira.

"Your contribution is always welcomed and respected, Elder Ramcy."

Ramcy circled in close and broached next to the Senator. "With all due respect, Senator Ira, as it is written in our creed, we have three days in which to make these far- reaching decisions. I feel that this may not be long enough, taking into consideration what has befallen us of late."

"I have given this matter great thought, Elder Ramcy, and I am glad you have raised it. I am of the opinion that at a time like this, we will gain great strength in knowing we have followed the writings of the creed, even in these times of great anxiety."

"I take your point, Senator Ira, and I for one will do all in my power to meet the deadline of three days."

Senator Ira watched as Elder Ramcy returned to his former

position, thinking that one of the vacancies in the Senate could be best filled by this elder.

"Elders!" Senator Ira's scan again drew the attention of the call together. "Before I dismiss you all with the charge to bring before the Senate those candidates who seek higher office, I…"

"Challenge, challenge!" The distant scan of Guard Commander Zarlie cut in and silenced Senator Ira in mid-sentence.

"Challenge! Challenge!" Again the scan of Guard Commander Zarlie raked across the call together.

"Scout Commander Idyll, report, report!" The intensified scans of a call to protect from Guard Commander Zarlie sent a wave of uneasy anticipation sweeping over those gathered.

"Legion Commander Zen, report!" The call from Senator Ira brought Zen to account.

"Legion Commander Zen, find the reasons for these challenges."

The uneasiness of the call together was heightened by Scout Commander Iydll and six of his scouts racing through the Elders' call together, on track to the source of the challenges.

"How dare you call me to challenge. How dare you! Don't you know who I am, Guard Commander Zarlie?" The High Byzefu's intense scan and threatening stance failed to intimidate the young Guard Commander.

"Yes, with all due respect Most Learned One, I know exactly who you are. You are the Most Learned One."

"Byzefu! Byzefu! I am The High Byzefu, and your refusing to acknowledge this is an insult on my position and to me. You will call me by my now given name, The High Byzefu. What don't you understand, Guard Commander Zarlie, about that the very simplest of instructions?"

The violent, verbal outburst from The Byzefu did not faze the young Commander from her duty.

"Yes, I know who you are, and in saying that, you know who I am, and the tasks that Senior Senator Ira has entrusted me with."

"Get out of my way." The Byzefu went to brush past the Guard Commander.

"Challenge! Challenge!"

The Byzefu again was stopped by the strength of the young Guard Commander's scan.

"Move aside, Guard Commander. Get out of my way. I am The High Byzefu, and have the given right to proceed unhindered."

"Scout Commander Idyll, on guard." The order of the young unflinching Guard Commander to the fast approaching Scout Commander Idyll and his troop of scouts raised the tension between herself and The High Byzefu.

"Scout Commander Idyll, escort The Byzefu away from this place of call together."

"You cannot do this to me. I am The High Byzefu. I cannot, and will not be denied my right of passage."

"You will go on your way now, Most Learned One, or I will order that you be forcibly removed from this place of call together." In that brief moment of time, the Guard Commander knew she had the full measure of The High Byzefu.

"Guard Commander Zarlie, report." The incoming scan of the Legion Commander was a welcome relief.

Zen surfaced next to the Guard Commander, and then as protocol dictated, he first scanned a greeting to the Most Learned One.

"Proceed with your report, Guard Commander Zarlie."

Zen sensed the relief in the demeanour of the young Commander.

"As directed by Senator Ira, a protective barrier was placed around the area of call together, with instruction that it was not to be breached under any circumstances." Zarlie hesitated, not wanting to over-dramatize the events that led her to challenge the Most Learned One.

"Continue, Guard Commander."

Zarlie felt the encouraging scans of the Legion Commander.

"The Most Learned One, along with two of his priests, approached the protection area with scant regard to the scouts and guards who were on patrol."

Zen looked across at the Most Learned One who had now moved away in open defiance to the authority of the Legion Commander.

"The two challenges from the scouts went unanswered, as were the challenges issued directly by myself to the Most Learned One. With the attitude shown by the Most Learned One towards both the scouts and myself, I called in reinforcements, and issued an on guard directive to Scout Commander Idyll."

"Thank you, Scout Commander Zarlie. Your task, as difficult as it was, has been carried out with the highest level of professionalism and diligence. I will take up what seems a blatant breach of etiquette with the Most Learned One myself. I ask that you now resume your patrol duties."

"Thank you, Legion Commander Zen."

Zarlie moved away, somewhat relieved at the timely appearance of the Legion Commander; at the same time, she signalled for Scout

Commander Idyll along with his troop of scouts to stand down. Zen watched as they moved off, somewhat relieved that the Senate had taken up his recommendation and promoted her to Guard Commander.

The thought of the so-called High Byzefu being challenged by any other may have had very different consequences. Now, the unenviable task of dealing with the apparent blatant breach of protocol by the Most Learned One filled the mind of Zen as he set off in the direction taken by the disappearing Most Learned One.

"Legion Commander Zen!" The incoming scan of a Senate Runner called Zen to a halt.

"Yes Senate Runner."

"Legion Commander Zen, Senator Ira calls you to report on the call to guard."

"Thank you, Senate Runner. Report to Senator Ira that I have attended to the call to guard, and will fully brief the Senator as soon as his call together ends."

Zen watched as the Senate Runner disappeared, and then set out again in search of the now vanished Most Learned One, a little reluctant to try too hard to locate the elusive Byzefu, as he was of little doubt that a confrontation would ensue.

—— Ψ ——

"Teacher Notris, present yourself before me." The first call of Senator Ira silenced the gathering together of the Senators.

"Teacher Notris, can you vouch that all present here are trained to the seventh degree?"

Again, the time-honoured rituals in calling together the Senators of the Great Assembly began.

"As so asked, as so I can confirm, Senator Ira."

"Teacher Notris, how can you vouch that all Senators here gathered are protected?"

"As so inquired, as so I will tell. This Senate is protected by two of our finest Guards and Scout Commanders, namely Guard Commander Zarlie and Scout Commander Idyll, along with fifty of their hand-picked guards and scouts that have set up a protective band that surrounds this gathering as I speak."

"Thank you, Teacher Notris. I now ask that you take your leave from this place and await further instructions."

"As so ordered, as so I obey, Senator Ira"

"Senator Ramcy!" The call from Senator Ira took the newly promoted Senator by complete surprise.

"Senator Ramcy, I charge you with reciting the sixth principal of our creed."

A somewhat nervous Ramcy broached next to Senator Ira. "As so instructed, as so I will comply, Senator Ira."

Senator Ira sensing the nervousness in the new Senator scanned him encouragement.

"The sixth and final principal of our creed is to agree to hold in reverence the original Rulers and Gods of this Universe and this our Assembly, and all further successors supreme and subordinate according to their rank, and to yield to the accords and proclamations as decreed by the Gods or their Supreme Council."

"Thank you, Senator Ramcy. Please take your position with the other Senators."

"Senator Nova, I charge you with bringing down the blessing of our great God, Poseidon, on these gathered Senators."

"As so instructed, as so I will comply." Senator Nova's quick response and move to the front was somewhat surprising to Ira.

"Oh! Great God Poseidon, ruler of the oceans, we beseech you, we your most loyal and humble servants, to give us the fortitude and strength to help us through these troubled times. We, your most beloved Regents of the Deep, ask that you bring down upon us your blessing, and grant us your wisdom that we may make the decisions that will best enhance our beliefs and creed." After a brief pause, the Senator completed the prayer with "So mote it be."

In unison, the Senators replied. "So mote it be."

"Thank you, Senator Nova. Please resume your position in the Senate." Senator Ira nodded his thanks to the departing Senator, waiting until the new Senator had accepted the congratulations on his maiden address to the Senate, and taken up his place next to his mentoring Senator.

"Senators, I have called you together this day to begin a Senate session that will require us to make decisions that will have far reaching ramifications – ramifications that will change the course of history for all time to come."

Hail the New King

15

The Great Assembly was a hive of activity, for this was the first time that all but the very old would have witnessed the raising of a new King. Senator Ira had left a message with a Senate Runner for the Legion Commander to meet him out beyond the outer security ring of the assembly when the sun was at its zenith. Whilst he waited, the Senator found himself taking the time to enjoy the solitude of the open waters as he rode the long swells. With each slide down the water embankments, his thoughts were taken back to an earlier time. A time that now seemed so distant – that now seemed only a figment of his imagination: that beloved place, The Shallows.

"Senator Ira."

The incoming call from the Legion Commander snapped the Senator back to reality.

"Legion Commander, firstly let me apologize for interrupting your busy schedule."

The Senator waited until the Legion Commander drew up alongside him before continuing.

"Sorry Senator, but I did not comprehend your last scan."

"I said I was sorry for having interrupted your busy schedule, but there are a number of pressing issues that are bothering me, and their importance is far greater than your allotted tasks." The Senator looked across at his son, knowing full well Zen's disappointment in not been raised to the Senate still hung like a pall of gloom over him.

Zen remained silent, waiting for his father to continue.

"Firstly, I want to explain why I vetoed your promotion to the Senate."

A scan of absolute disbelief radiated out from the Legion Commander.

"Yes Zen, it was I, your father, who cast the sole negative vote."

Again, the Senator felt the wave of Zen's disappointment.

"Senator Ira! Father, why? Why did you do this? You, of all the Senators whom I thought I could trust for their vote!"

"Zen, I know the disappointment you feel at this time weighs heavily on you, as it does on me." The Senator hesitated a moment; he wanted to choose his words carefully as he looked at his son and felt his disappointment.

"The tasks facing any new King are far greater than you anticipate. Firstly, the Most Learned One, or Byzefu as he insists now on been called, has made it very clear that he will refuse to take part in any ceremony, and he has promised to disrupt the proceedings. Then, on top of this, there has been a whisper... now, before you say anything, I know that it is only a whisper, but whisper or not, the talk is that he is preparing to break away from the Great Assembly if this raising of a new King goes ahead."

"Father, I know all this, but I don't see how these so-called rumours, or whisperings as you prefer to call them, of the Most Learned One leaving would have caused you to cast a negative vote. Explain that to me."

The Senator was somewhat taken aback by his son's tone.

"Zen, I want you to listen to me, and listen carefully."

Zen looked at his father, a little angry with himself for allowing his failure to be raised to the Senate to create ill feeling towards him.

"Your apology is accepted."

"You know, Father, I keep forgetting that even my innermost thoughts cannot be hidden from you."

"Legion Commander," the formality in the Senator's tone drew the meeting of the two back into ritual. "During our time at the Shallows, whilst you were still very young, the last Legion Commander who went by the name of Legion Commander Roe passed on. At that time, the Senators decided that the need to fill his position was uncalled for." After a brief hesitation, the Senator continued: "But we live in a very different time now; there are new trials and tribulations to contend with. Not only is there unrest in the Assembly, but many are still grieving for all those lost in the Bay of Death. I must add, we still have not resolved whether anyone contributed to this loss."

The Senator looked across at his son, feeling again his sorrow at the loss of his family, and then continued, "At this time, it is most imperative for the good of all that we have a strong Legion Commander in place, and that is the one and only reason I cast my vote as I did. I want you to remember that your time will come."

Senator Ira watched as his words had their desired effect on Zen.

"Father, yes I am coming to terms with what you are saying, but I still fail to comprehend why you vetoed my raising."

"Zen, let me explain further. Firstly, you are now trained to the seventh decree, so it is that you enjoy all the benefits of a Senator; yet by your very rank, you enjoy all the benefits of an Elder. What I am saying is that you are the only one to have the freedom of taking part in any call together, be it of the Senate or the Council of Elders."

At last, the Senator could see the dawning of understanding in Zen.

"Further to these two privileges, you are held in the very highest respect by every member of the Assembly, from the very young to the very oldest – all of whom you have been endeared to in some shape or form."

"Senator Ira, Senator Ira!" The incoming call from a Senate Runner interrupted Ira.

"Excuse me, Legion Commander, while I attend to the runner."

After a brief discussion with the runner, the Senator returned.

"Nothing important, I hope, Father."

"No, my son, nothing that cannot be taken care of later. Now where was I?" The Senator moved into unison with the Legion Commander. "Hmm yes! With your rank and standing, I thought it... no, I will rephrase that; it will be in the best interest of us all for you to remain as Legion Commander."

The words of the Senator now started to make sense to Zen.

"So, as you can see, if the rumours of the Most Learned One come to fruition, and he is successful in his endeavours, then it is at this time any new King will need a loyal and trusted servant, and this burden can fall upon no better servant than you."

The full impact of why his father had cast his negative vote in the way he did was now fully understood by Zen.

The Assembly was a sea of excitement, with flashing bodies that darted here and there, all the time chattering with a racket that at times reached a crescendo that in all circumstances would have been heard by all the Gods in their heavenly realm. This day, from the very moment darkness was swept from the skies, the Senators had been put into quarantine. They were guarded by the Assembly's finest Scouts and Guards who had their numbers increased to two hundred and fifty under the joint leadership of Scout Commander Idyll and Guard Commander Zarlie. The day passed its zenith, and still the chatter showed no sign of abating; in fact, if anything, it had increased as time went on. All awaited with eager anticipation the naming of the new King.

The excitement of the day was not lost on those Scout and Guard Commanders who had not been drafted into duties.

"Mio, news has it you and the Legion Commander are spending more and more time together, and alone as well." The cheeky scan from Zeta bought a chattering giggle from the rest of the group.

"More time on things, other than official business," Alex chipped in, as one would expect from the newly appointed Guard Commander whose reputation as a jester was already well known throughout the Assembly.

"Come on Mio, tell us – after all, we are friends."

Mio looked across at her friend, Zeta.

"Yes, and as I hear it, alone." Again, the little insert from Alex.

"Well, not that it is anyone's business but mine, I will tell you something that will enlighten you all on the matter."

The rest of the group crowded in close to Mio. After all any bit of gossip is always good gossip when the water is calm, and all chatterers are at peace with each other, and besides all this, it was a waiting game.

"Now, come on, Mio! Don't you dare leave any morsel out. We all want it in full, don't we?" Zeta, now taking on the role of spokesman for the chattering entourage, pushed her way to the front and closest to Mio.

"Now, I can only tell you if I have your absolute promise that not one word of what I am about to tell you will be spoken to any other, apart from those of us here." Mio's scan was now only just above an audible level.

"Yes, yes, we promise. We promise, don't we?" Zeta frantically scanned to all those gathered, who now pushed in as close as they could, not wanting to miss the smallest morsel of the pending revelations.

After all, it was about the Legion Commander who, if the truth be known, not one of the available females in the Assembly, at one time or another, had not secretly lusted after.

Again Mio lowered her audible signal. "Just last night I…"

"We cannot hear you. Louder please, Mio." The somewhat desperate scan of Sola interrupted Mio.

"Just last night I met with Zen. Can you understand me now, Sola?"

"No, no we cannot! Louder please, Mio." A quiet desperation was creeping into the group – after all, this was gossip straight from the source, and it did concern the Legion Commander.

"Just last night I met with Zen, and he told me to tell you…"

"Mio, please! If you are going to tell us, at least tell us all and not just those in close." The call from Alex brought a chorus of similar calls from the others.

"What did Zen tell you to tell us Mio? Come on, don't keep us in suspense." This time it was Jove getting in on the act.

Then, as loud as her sensors would allow, Mio replied, "To mind your own business."

Then with a chatter of mirth, Mio dived deep and raced away with all in full pursuit.

"Guard Commanders, Scout Commanders, report." The incoming scans of Legion Commander Zen bought the frolicking gossipers back to alert.

"Guard Commanders Mio and Alex, report."

Zen was quick to notice a certain amount of mirth being exchanged between the two Guard Commanders as they approached.

"As ordered, as so we comply, Legion Commander."

"Thank you, Guard Commander Mio. Before you ask, I cannot speak of what stage the raising of a new King is." Zen watched as the mirth subsided between the two of his favourites before continuing: "Guard Commanders, it is very important that you find Teacher Notris and escort him to the Senior Senate Runner."

The two Guard Commanders nodded their understanding before turning away to begin their search for the teacher.

"Back here, you two!" The sharp call back from the Legion Commander dismissed the last remnants of mirth from the two chatterers.

"Let us not forget the very formalities that our creed was founded upon."

The two Guard Commanders looked at each other, at a loss as to what the Legion Commander referred to.

"I am sorry, Legion Commander, but I am not sure, or should I say we are not sure what we are remiss about?" The scan from Alex was full of apologetic retort.

Zen looked at the two Guard Commanders. Alex now showed a little nervousness that was starting to manifest in his posture. Switching his gaze back to Mio, Zen let a little warmth creep in and radiate over the two.

"When I was trained, I was always told to wait until I was dismissed when before those of a higher decree."

Mio was first to respond to the Legion Commander. "Legion Commander, your recollection and recall of the creed training differs somewhat to mine. It may well be that I will need some sort of refresher course, preferably private."

This whole conversation was totally lost on the new boy, Alex. Zen looked at Mio, and her black beautiful eyes stared straight back at him.

"Maybe, just maybe I will have to arrange a lesson."

The feelings that flowed between the Legion Commander and Mio were obvious to all, but went right over Alex's head.

Once more, light was ripped from the skies and darkness stalked the heavens. Still, the Senate kept its secrets on the progress of raising the new King. The chattering that swept back and forth in anticipation of any announcement had somewhat diminished as many of the Assembly members settled in to rest for the night. Only the most ardent remained grouped on the protection ring awaiting the news.

"Challenge, Challenge!" The distant call alerted those of the Assembly closest to the ring of security.

Challenge, Challenge!" This time, the new call of challenge was delivered with a chilling intensity that allied with the growing tension to bring most of the Assembly from their slumber.

"Challenge, Challenge!" Again and again the challenges raked across the Assembly, and then to add to their apprehension, the call "On guard!" was heard and then repeated, echoing in from the different sectional Guard and Scout Commanders.

"Guard Commanders, Jove, Mio, Alex report! Report under

urgency." The exigency in the Senior Senate Runner's call was added to the anxiety and brought all Assembly members to full alert. Alex and Jove were first to report to the call, followed closely by Scout Commander Mio.

"Senior Senate Runner Zuke, as called, as so we report." Mio, being the most senior of all Scout Commanders, as expected, took upon herself the responsibility of speaking for the trio.

"At this time, the Most Learned One has..." The toll of age and the sprint from the Senate had taken its toll on the aged Senior Runner. The trio of Guard Commanders waited while the old gentleman of the sea regained his composure.

"The Byzefu has called together all his followers and deployed them to offensive positions on the outskirts of the security ring surrounding the Senate. He is threatening to disrupt the raising of a new King – by whatever means he has at his disposal."

Again, the trio waited for the Senior Senate Runner to catch his breath.

"You are all ordered to report under urgency in the eighth alert, to the Legion Commander, along with all available Commanders and their scouts and guards. Now!" Having finally got his message out, the old-timer at last had time to catch his breath – he was getting just a little too old for all this racing around.

"What urgency?" The intensity of the scan from Mio dispersed the thought train of the old runner, Zurk.

"The eighth, the eighth order," he responded.

"The eighth order! Are you sure, Senate Runner Zuke? Are you sure – are you very sure?"

The old runner looked at the stunned Mio.

"Yes Guard Commander Mio, you read me right. The alert is of the highest order of security – meaning it is none other than our newly raised leader whose life is under threat."

"The new King is raised? A new King is raised, you scan? When did this happen? Why was the rest of the Assembly not informed of this?" Mio bombarded old Zuke with her questions.

"Who am I to question the integrity of the Senate, when by their very orders all communicational scans were ordered latent? And who am I to query the very wisdom of the Legion Commander who recommended this silence of the Senate?"

Mio looked into the tired eyes of the Senior Senate Runner and her thoughts concurred; after all, who was she to question this old man who had the wisdom of the aged? She had to remind herself of the teaching of their creed, and show him the respect that went with his great age. Mio glanced over at the other two now somewhat tense Commanders, reading the multitude of thoughts filling their minds, and then back to Zuke. Her first undertaking would be to ensure this loyal servant of the Senate was kept out of harm's way.

"Senior Senate Runner Zuke, you will remain here. I order this for your very own safety, my old friend." Mio let a scan of warmth sweep momentarily over Zuke, before turning back to Alex and Jove.

"Guard Commanders, remember you are by your very training among the best of the Assembly's very best." Mio used her words to reinforce the status of the two Commanders before continuing. "Alex, I am assigning you and your Guards to Assembly protection. Guard Commander Jove, call together all Scout and Guard Commanders and all those under their command and then report back here. Go now!"

Both Commanders hesitated, as if this surreal moment in time had stunned them into inefficient drones.

"Let your training guide your actions, and may our great God Poseidon always be beside you. Now go!" Mio's scans snapped both back into the reality of these grave and dangerous times.

Mio turned back to the old Zuke. "There are troubled times ahead if this escalates, my old friend."

"Yes, Mio, that I do know. We are all in unchartered oceans and times. I secretly yearn for those days when we were all back in The Shallows – a time that will always have pride of place in my hall of memories."

"Before you go, Zuke, who was raised to King?"

A look of knowing darted quickly across the old timer's face. "Mio, my dear Mio, you know better than to ask me that, but what I will tell you..." Zuke, always the one to prolong the moment, hesitated mid-sentence for effect and then continued... "All I can tell you is that you will be surprised by the choice; of that I am sure."

"I thought knowing who we are to protect would be better than not knowing."

Seeing nothing was going to entice the old runner to depart from the strict Senate rules, Mio scanned, "Zuke, I want you to follow Guard Commander Alex into protection."

Not wanting to give old Zuke any chance of getting into a ramble of monologue about the good old days, for which he was well known, Mio again scanned her orders to Zuke. "Go now! Follow Guard Commander Alex into protection."

Old Zuke sensed the very urgency of Mio's scan; and so without further comment, set out after Alex muttering, "Nobody's got the time anymore; always in a hurry; give me the old days."

A smile briefly flitted across Mio's face as she watched the old timer slowly move away, and she mentally noted that when life returned to some form of normality, she would take some time and spend it with Zuke. After all, he did have a repertoire of wonderful stories; but this was just not the time.

"Guard Commander Mio."

Mio turned to address the incoming scan of Jove.

"Approach, Guard Commanders." Mio was pleased to feel the aura of urgency with which the accompanying Guard and Scout Commanders approached. The legions of Scouts and Guards turned the oceans white as they milled around behind their respective commanders and awaited further instructions.

"Commanders, I will keep this message brief. The newly raised King is under threat, and we are called to protect."

The sudden crescendo of chatter completely drowned out Guard Commander Mio, much to the disappointment of all the assembled Commanders.

"Silence!" The ferocity of Mio's scan slammed the chatter to silence.

"That's better. Just remember who you are." The strength and intensity of Mio's scans carried a cold, unyielding statement that reinforced the fact that this was indeed a dangerous time.

Mio hesitated, watching as the effect of her sternness started to sink in; and then she continued: "The message delivered under urgency from the Senate is that a new King has been raised, and at this time the Most Learned One, or High Byzefu as he now wants to be known, has threatened this new King's very survival."

Again, the sudden rising chatter had to quickly be put to silence.

This time it only took angry glares from their respective leaders.

Mio waited until the silence was complete before continuing. "Guard and Scout Commanders, you will take your respective troops of Guards and Scouts and report to Legion Commander Zen on the…"

"Attack!" The cold, distant, single command that emanated from Legion Commander Zen shocked Mio to silence. This solitary word of his command engulfed all, without exception, in a cloak of frightened anticipation.

The Farewell

16

The inevitable tranquillity of calm that follows a storm cast its shroud of despair across the oceans and those Regents of the Deep that dwelt therein.

"Report all Guard Commanders, report all Scout Commanders!"

The scan from Guard Commander Mio went out via the Senate runners. The pall of surreal disbelief of what had come to pass this day enveloped each commander as they reported to Guard Commander Mio.

"Guard Commander Alex, you will file your report first."

"As ordered, Guard Commander Mio." Alex broached next to Mio.

"The task of protecting the Great Assembly from any rear intruders was carried out without any incident worthy of reporting." Alex waited for any further call from Mio; with none forthcoming, he returned to the assembled fold of commanders.

"Thank you, Guard Commander Alex. Guard Commander Jove, report."

Mio waited for Jove to broach, and then scanned him to begin his report. The gathered commanders felt a great sadness emanating from Jove even before he began his report. It was obvious that he was troubled, and silence ruled as Jove sought to gather his thoughts and calm his emotions. Mio moved closer to the distressed Guard Commander; her very low scan sent out an assurance.

"Remember our creed. Remember the teachings of our Great God Poseidon."

Jove looked across at his friend of so long, tears filling his eyes.

"Come Jove, start your report." This time Mio's scan was shepherded by a warm embrace, and again the scan was at a plane that only Jove could monitor.

"As so ordered, Senior Guard Commander Mio, as so I Guard Commander, Jove report. On the sound of alarm, my troop was ordered to assist in the reinforcement of that area of the outer ring forward of the place of raising that was reportedly under attack." Jove's report trailed off to silence; the great burden of responsibility in these troubled times was taking its toll on the young Guard Commander.

"Come, come, Guard Commander Jove. You must continue. It is important that you continue." Mio's firm, yet assuring voice gave encouragement to the youngster.

Fortified by her soothing words, the youngest ever Guard Commander continued: "On arrival, a full skirmish was underway with a large number of those loyal to Byzefu aggressively attacking the Outer Ring Guards with a barrage of high speed rushes. Each one of these rushes was repelled with ease, using nothing more than a medium level self-protective scans." Guard Commander Jove slowly breached, and then as ordered, he continued his report. "It was during one of those frontal assaults that I received a call from Legion Commander Zen requesting urgent assistance for the new King's Guards."

The Guard Commander hesitated, as he sorted through his vocabulary looking for the right words.

Again, Mio sent in a soft scan of encouragement to the young Jove.

"On the Legion Commander's orders, I, along with the rest of my troop, was sent to assist. On arrival at the predetermined area, it quickly became obvious that the attack on the outer ring was nothing more than a subterfuge." Jove again breached before continuing.

"While this subterfuge was being enacted, The High Byzefu along with four of those closest allied to him had, undetected, managed to breach the outer protection barrier."

"It's Zen! It's Zen! They got him... he's dead... I think he's dead.

Again, the tragedy of what he had witnessed choked the scans of the young Guard Commander. Mio, realising that she had to give the somewhat traumatised youngster a little leeway to finish his report, remained silent.

"Guard Commander Jove, stand down." Mio, now concerned at the toll the trauma of the last day had taken on the young Guard Commander, called him to move aside with her to privately confer.

The remaining Regents of the Deep called together by Mio surfed the waves in silence, as they all waited for Guard Commander Jove and Senior Guard Commander Mio to return.

The Time Weaver

17

Zen felt as if his life had been torn from his body; the water that rushed past his sensors roared like wild winds as he struggled for breath; his torso was gripped in an ever-increasing tightening band. Racked with pain, down he spiralled – deeper, deeper into an all-encompassing black abyss.

"Poseidon, my great God, why have you abandoned me? Poseidon, I beg you." Zen's call to the great ruler who watched over all things that dwelt in the known universe went unanswered.

A black swirling mist that distorted time and direction was rapidly replacing the stability of consciousness, but Zen fought the engulfing blackness to no avail and his known world floated away. Then, bright distant lights rushed in and offered solace: brightness, clear bright light, swirling brightness, peaceful light that cast its mesmerising spell over Zen as it leisurely sucked him into a slowly rotating vortex of a dying brightness that was now quickly fading. He disappeared – drawn deeper and deeper into the black nothingness of death.

"Zen, Zen."

From a place far, far away, a strange voice wafted, filling all the surrounds – a voice floating, intermingling with sounds of a lone flute. So far, far away; calling, calling to him.

"Zen, Zen."

The beautiful soothing sounds of music calling, calling him back from the black abyss.

"Zen, Zen."

The floating sounds: music, sweet music – a sweet beauty wrapped in the arms of an alluring mystic charm. Zen drifted alone, floating cocooned in an inexplicable serenade of peace and tranquillity.

"Zen, Zen."

The sounds of the distant callings became sharper, louder. Zen fought to stay in Utopia – no more worries, no more pain, no more grieving. Just sleep, deep ever-lasting sleep.

"Zen." The voice, was now much sterner.

"Zen, Zen." Slowly, ever so slowly, the mist of sleep lifted its veils of secrecy.

"We are glad you have found your way here – pleased that Somnus, the God of Sleep, has graciously released you from his shackled charms, Zen. Come, come! Wake yourself up, Zen. We have no time to waste."

Zen shook off the last remnants of his enforced slumber.

"Where am I? Who are you?" Zen struggled to disguise the alarm that had welled up and put a quiver in his voice.

"Fear not, for you are in a place only a very privileged few have been given the opportunity to visit." The floating voice had a strangely calming quality. "Follow me." Again, the voice surrounded Zen, totally engulfing him. "This way."

"Which way?"

"This way. Follow me." Again, the voice filled all space, but where was it coming from?

Zen was lost, his mind now racing. *Where am I to go? Follow me! Who is me? Follow me - follow what, and to where?* As confusion was layered on top of bewilderment, doubt started to creep in and cast shadows of fear across Zen's troubled mind. Zen thought insanity had thrust itself unwittingly into the equation... somewhere between those fine lines of sanity and lunacy.

"Over here, this way." The voice now seemed to come from a direction that he could at last zero in on.

Slowly Zen turned, dreamlike, his eyes still not focusing as quickly as they should. He was fast becoming aware that no matter how hard he tried to do anything, everything just moved in very slow, hallucinatory motion. Lifting his eyes, Zen captured the first sight of the proprietor of the voice. Not six lukmar in front of him was a golden-haired young nymph dressed in a flimsy, whisper-thin toga that provided her no modesty whatsoever. Zen, still not fully aware of what was happening to him, focused in on what the nymph sat astride – the strangest looking creature he had ever seen.

"Follow me." The golden-haired nymph astride her steed of unknown origin stared at Zen, her dark eyes flashing. Again, the warm voice seemed to radiate from nowhere, but yet everywhere, filling the void of his troubled mind with her enchanting, melodious voice.

Slowly turning, the nymph rode her strange two-legged apparition across an abyss of the unknown. As if by silent command, her creature rolled aside a large boulder exposing a narrow, dimly lit tunnel, and Zen felt himself being irresistibly drawn towards the gloomy passageway. The nymph reined in her mount at the very rim of the mysterious entrance, and then slowly turning her head, she fixed her shining black eyes firmly on his, and Zen found himself involuntary following as if drawn by some sort of mysterious magnetism.

"Follow me, follow me."

The mesmerizing words that seemed to fill every available space drew Zen deeper and deeper into a trance as he followed the fleeing nymph astride that thing of unknown origin. Then, without warning, all three of them were sucked into a vortex that sent them cascading down, down deep into the unknown. Deeper than any living mortal had gone before; deeper, sucked along faster and faster, falling deeper, deeper. Falling. Lost. Captivated by the musically enriched voice that urged him on – faster, faster, faster – falling deeper into the great nothingness.

—— Ψ ——

The brightness of the large cave was in direct contrast to the dark tunnel. Zen's eyes ached from the sudden exposure to the glare.

"Who have we here?" a great booming voice echoed around the large cave.

"I found him asleep at the cave entrance." The nymph that Zen had followed suddenly reappeared.

"Found him sleeping you say? Found him sleeping?"

Zen's eyes, now accustomed to the bright light, could see clearly the source of the voice that had now taken on a more subdued tone. The darting nymph, now completely divested of her flimsy wrap, settled on a rocky ledge above the owner of the booming voice.

"Yes, Master, I found him sleeping and he followed me here. Can we keep him?"

The very thought of being kept, locked up in this unknown place far from the Assembly, increased the tension that was slowly building in Zen.

"Where am I? Why have I been brought to this place? Who are

you? Have I died? Where is my God?"

The old man lifted his head, his long, white hair and unkempt beard highlighted in the bright light.

"Who am I? Who am I you ask?" A puzzled look fell across the old wrinkled face. "Who am I?"

The nymph floated down from her perch, patting the old man's arm.

"There, there. We all know who you are, Master. Take no notice of the impertinence of this stranger. I still think we should keep him." Turning to Zen, the nymph now clothed in a gown of flowing gold glared, "How dare you ask?"

"Yes, how dare you ask?" The old man's sudden interruption surprised the nymph who, for a brief moment, looked lost for words.

"But who am I?" The old man ran his thin, aged fingers through his long, white hair, as if pondering that very question.

"Master, we all know who you are. You are the Time Weaver." The nymph, now only just protecting her modesty in a shimmering veil of swaying silver threads, seemed to reassure the old man with her reply.

"Yes, of course I know who I am. I am the Time Weaver, and a master Weaver of Time at that, I will have you know." The old man, having now regained some of his lost composure, took control, and dismissed the nymph with a flick of his head. "And no, we cannot keep him. Don't be absurd! Now, away, away with you, you gratuitous wench."

Turning back to Zen, the old man focused on his guest now suspended between life and death. For the first time since entering the tunnel, the realization occurred to Zen that he was suspended in a place between somewhere and nowhere. He could hear, far in the

190

remoteness of his mind, the voices of his beloved Scout Commanders calling him home. Just so far away – so far, far away. Zen fought to hang on to the last of his sanity as he desperately tried to respond to the call of his scouts... and then they were gone. He was lost; but lost to where?

With no surrounding water to support his body weight, Zen could only hazard a guess as to why he felt no pain or uneasiness. If anything, a small feeling of contentment was slowly sweeping over him.

"I can see what you are thinking – wondering how you got here." The voice that filled his mind came from everywhere, yet nowhere.

"My dear friend, Zen, welcome. It is good to see your mind is still very much alive. You are thinking how you can move by only thoughts, without the help of your body." Again, the soft floating voice of the white-haired one filled every part of Zen's mind and body.

"How it is I can speak directly into your mind? Are you dead or alive? So many questions! I ask that you just show a little patience; these questions will all be answered in time. In time, my friend, in time. For now, you must rest, my Legion Commander Zen; for rest you now must take."

So it was that living time ever so slowly stopped and faded away, leaving the hood of darkness to tighten its grip on its reluctant host. Unwillingly, Zen was dragged back into the blackness of nothing.

"What are we going to do with him, Master?" the nymph called to the old man, as he shuffled towards his chair.

"What are we going to do with who?"

"This one you have called Zen, Master. This one that now sleeps – sleeps at your command. Can I keep hi ...?"

"No! You cannot keep him. Now, away with you; and take that smelly Usala with you." The Master Time Weaver's interruption cut the nymph off in mid-sentence.

"Come on, my friend! We know when we are not wanted; and you are not smelly. Don't listen to that old man. You are not smelly, I promise. You are not smelly."

The old man watched as the nymph chased and finally caught the fleeing Usala, letting her mutterings go unanswered.

"Hmmm! What am I going to do with you, my friend? Just what am I going to do with you?" The Time Weaver again ran his bony hand through his long white hair, as he contemplated the future of this Regent of the Deep.

Light gently, like the dawning of a new day, filtered through Zen's awakening mind as slowly the curtain of his enforced slumber was lifted. Zen was gradually coming to the anxiety-laden realisation that wherever he was at this moment in time, he was trapped. But where was *here*? With no sign of the Dream Weaver or his Nymph, Zen let his eyes wander around this strange cave that was now his prison. Over to one side there was, partly hidden, what looked like a veil that swayed ever so slightly back and forth without a hint of a breeze to move it. Mesmerised somewhat by the hypnotic swaying effect of the veil, Zen felt the need to explore. Maybe it was the way back to the Great Assembly. No sooner had the thought entered his mind than he felt his body start to move towards the swaying veil.

In a moment of panic at his sudden move forward, Zen called "No!"

With the call, Zen's movement towards the veil stopped. Once the last remnants of panic had dissipated, Zen again nervously concentrated on the veil. The more he did this, the more he felt himself being drawn across the room towards it until he was close enough that, when the veil swung in, it touched him. Through the veil, Zen could see what looked like a darkened passage.

He was now sure this was the way back – back to those of his own kind. Zen closed his eyes and concentrated on the passageway, feeling the veil pass over him as he moved into its darkness. Slowly and cautiously, Zen moved further and further into the passage. Then, without warning, he found himself being dragged along against his will, faster and faster – until suddenly, his body was slammed, without forgiveness, into a clear wall.

Through the clear wall, Zen saw a great multitude of people – yellow people with slit-eyes, black people with curly closely-cropped hair, and those of fair colouring – all devastated by fear. Like great schools of fish that were herded together, they were joined by each and every ogre Zen had stored away in his halls of knowledge.

The great oceans before him were being torn asunder as those condemned were thrust up in their multitudes: land dwellers of every conceivable colour, shape, and size from the most hideous and darkened to those most striking; the brightly coloured and the strangely shaped; those that lived in the water; those that dwelt and crawled along the sea beds; not even the land dwellers' young children were spared, as each and every one was cast into a fiery Hell.

Zen watched, transfixed in stunned silence, as the living, in great numbers, were engulfed in fires that were breathed down from the heavens. As they died, their forsaken bodies twisted into grotesque, tortured silhouettes of their previous selves. The living begged; pleading with eyes that melted in the raging torrents of fire that raged with unrelenting ferocity. The silent screams of the dying filled Zen with revulsion.

The stench of burning flesh permeated the air as Death engulfed all those who stood before the flames. Zen struggled to shut out the cacophonous symphony of death that played out before him. He tried to turn away, to mentally block out the terrible scenes. As if frozen in time, unable to move, Zen's eyes were locked into an unblinking stare; he was trapped, unable to turn away – trapped as much as were those caught up in the incinerator of the doomed – trapped, forced to watch and hear death. Rivers of sweat streamed down Zen's face. The heat was now fast becoming unbearable. His eyes were racked with the pain inflicted by the searing heat those before him had to endure. The vice-like grip of an invisible hand tightened around Zen, holding him steadfast, mandating him to watch as the Director of Death took his toll. Zen's screams, mixed with those of the dying, surged to the heavens, seeking forgiveness from any quarter. But the unhearing Gods remained passive and muted as they watched from their heavenly domain, oblivious to the pleading cries of the dying.

Then, from the fiery depths of this God-made hell, a figure materialised, silhouetted by the billowing smoke and seemingly unaffected by the stench or the searing heat of this furnace of doom. With sword drawn, this nameless unidentified evil in white flowing robes strode among the dying, screaming profanities, slashing with his great sword at those who leapt into the air in attempts to escape his inferno. With each sword swipe, heads and limbs were severed and blood cascaded onto the white-hot embers to add to the steam and the stench. With each scream and slash of the sword, the robe-covered, malevolent spirit moved closer to Zen – and then, unexpectedly, it stopped as if it sensed his presence.

As if in slow motion, in a manner that sent cold shivers of absolute fear surging through Zen's overheated body, the personification of all things evil turned its attention toward the trapped Regent of the Deep. Zen saw nothing but malice and hate written in its eyes. From the evil one's black beard to the strange strip of cloth that was wrapped around and around its head as a covering that hid all signs of hair, evil oozed from its every pore. Death now courted Zen, dancing as an evil ballet across his trapped body. The noise of the dying beat a tempo into his head. Zen's body pounded with fear as he prepared to meet those who had gone before him, praying that the Gods would give him safe passage and guidance in the great journey upon which he was about to embark. The sword of death was raised above him, ready to swing down and impose its seal upon him – its next unwilling victim. Then, suddenly, the energy that had crushed Zen against the very face of death relinquished its grip, and now released, Zen fell – away from the scorching heat, away from death's grip.

Falling faster and faster, into the waiting cloak of solitude and darkness that was provided by Somnus, Zen felt wisps of a cool breeze caress him in a mantra of serenity that slowly spread its haze of awakening over his entire body, stirring him from his stupor.

"He is awake, Master! He is awake!" cried the nymph, now reunited with her strange beast that seemed to have but one task in mind – to dislodge its rider. Zen was not yet lucid, and his developing anxieties showed in his eyes. Looking around, he saw the Master sitting at the table. The nymph, having been dethroned from the beast, sat on the ground, a dejected expression plastered across her face.

Meanwhile, the beast, now happily riderless, sashayed out of sight, no doubt looking for somewhere out of reach of the nymph. Zen stared at the Master Time Weaver. Nothing made sense any more – this place, the nymph, the beast. The gap between realism and delusional visions slowly began to close.

"Please help me!" Zen's tears welled up, blurring his vision. "What is happening to me?"

The old man pushed back his chair and moved forward. Supporting himself with an old, gnarled walking stave, he reached out and placed his hand on the head of a bewildered Zen.

"Be at peace, my Zen of the sea, for you have travelled far, and seen much – maybe more than one would have wanted you to see."

The Time Weaver looked down at Zen, quelling the fear that had welled up in the now lucid Regent of the Deep.

"Sleep on, my friend, sleep on. Time is close, and time will return you once again to the living. Let that old companion of mine take you under his spell."

Zen felt his world spinning faster and faster then, and again, Somnus spread his cloak over the troubled one from the deep, and sleep, once again, took precedence.

The Time Weaver looked across to the nymph and said, "I think it is time we returned our friend to his life. Nymph, take him back to where you found him."

"But Master, it was I who found him, and as the finder, I think I should be able to keep him." The nymph, now again completely naked, let a little pique creep into her voice.

"Take him back, I tell you, and do it now."

The nymph was somewhat startled by the sharp tone of her Master.

"Do I have to?" Her question was in vain, and she dejectedly tried, without success, to catch her ever-evasive steed.

"Yes! You do, but as I weave his life, I promise this will not be the last time we have the pleasure of this one's company."

The nymph, now somewhat mollified by the words of the Time Weaver, gathered up Zen and moved away from the light.

"For as it had been written in the thirteen houses of the heavenly zodiac, the fires of torment did sear time; so the elevating of two to the mantle for one had surely begun."

And so it was that the second of the great God Poseidon's heavenly writings had come to pass.

Why? My God

18

The two Regents of the Deep surged through the slow, low-rolling swells – one in bottomless shock, the other in profound sympathy, searching for answers to comfort the other.

"Guard Commander Jove!"

Mio sent a soft scan to her young friend, then watched and waited for a response.

With a scan laced with hopelessness, and sorrow the only reply, Mio moved in closer, all but brushing up against the young Guard Commander.

"Jove, in our training, there was nothing that could have prepared any of us for what has come to pass since we left our bay of birth." Mio momentarily paused and watched for a reaction from Jove. With none coming, she continued. "I have struggled myself, as no doubt the majority of the Assembly has, to come to terms with the cruel fate that has, at times, spread its shroud of despair over us all." Mio sensed a response rising in the young Guard Commander.

"Mio, why Zen? Why Zen? Why has this happened to him?"

The sudden outpouring of grief from the young Guard Commander was not totally unexpected. Mio remained silent, leaving the way open for Jove to set free the great burden of grief that gripped him in a pall of anguish.

"If I had got there quicker, Mio. I tried, Mio. I did the best I could. Why Zen? Why Zen, Mio?"

Mio looked across at the distressed young Guard Commander as he swayed, torn between the emotions of grief, self-blame, and pity.

"Come, Guard Commander Jove! This is not the time to wallow in grief or self-pity. What is done is done." Mio thought the only way to get Jove back into the mode of highly trained member of the Assembly was to take a tougher line.

"But Mio!"

"But who, Guard Commander?" Mio's sharp interruption silenced Jove. The sudden switch, by Mio, to the severe regulatory conventions of the Assembly's creed of hierarchy and compliance to order of status, took Jove by surprise.

"Guard Commander Jove, present yourself before me," Mio scanned to a somewhat taken aback Jove.

"As so ordered, Senior Guard Commander Mio, so I must comply."

Once in ordained unison, Mio increased her speed, being extremely mindful that a very vulnerable and at risk Guard Commander was struggling to come to terms with the tragic circumstances of the last days.

"Guard Commander Jove, there is very little one can do to lessen your grief, other than to refer to the training that you, along with many others both here and long since passed have received." Mio's sternness, laced with a little compassion, started ever so slowly to have the desired effect on the young Guard Commander, and she let a long silence deliver the required impact before continuing.

"Now, I can spend a great deal of time reminding you of this training, and what is expected of each and every one of us. Guard Commander Jove, I know you were charged with a task to undertake, and I must add here, it was a very difficult undertaking at a very difficult time, but from all the reports filed, your tasks were executed with valour and extreme professionalism."

Mio again paused, noticing a calmness had now cocooned Jove.

"Senior Guard Commander Mio, I thank you for your patience with me at this time." The growing resurgence of self-assurance and confidence echoed in the scan from Jove.

The two Regents of the Deep, together in silence, rode the long white swells, as if lost in a peace reminiscent of a time and place long past. Mio was the first to draw back this tranquil cloak of security to bring both of them back into the realms of responsibility.

"Guard Commander Jove, now it is time for us to return to the call together, and then you will be expected to complete your report." Mio watched for any sign of an adverse reaction from Jove, and with none forthcoming, continued. "Jove, I want you to remember something that I was told a long time ago by our beloved, now past, King Epiphanes."

Jove moved in close to Mio.

"It was at a time when one of the Assembly members whom I had grown very close to disappeared – and most sadly, was never found again."

Silence momentarily ruled the oceans.

"I was alone, trying to come to terms with my grief that seemed to be everywhere within me. It was then that I unexpectedly crossed the path of The Most Wise One, as he was known then. As my memory recalls, he was also out there all alone, enjoying the beauty of solitude – as he, at the time put it to me. I actually saw the King long before he had seen me, so as protocol dictated, I started to discreetly withdraw and move out of the area he commanded. It was just as I was leaving that the King saw me, and scanned for me to approach."

"You mean you had an audience alone with the King?"

Mio let the interruption of Jove go unrebuked, and continued.

"The King helped me through my troubles at that time with words of comfort and wisdom: words that have held me steadfast and loyal from that time until now." Mio watched Jove with a growing feeling of confidence that his past stumble was nothing more than an aberration.

"Just before our King dismissed me, he asked me to remember one thing, and that was, dying is not a privilege of the aged alone."

Mio hesitated, letting her words have their desired effect on the Guard Commander before she continued. "These were wise words that his father, and his father before him, had passed down through the ages, and he passed them on to me."

Mio again studied the young Jove, convinced more than ever that the young Guard Commander would come through the trauma of the last days to resume his duties, a little older and a little wiser.

"Now, Guard Commander Jove, I order you to come abreast." Mio brought a formality to the action. "Now, let us return to the call together. Once there, I will expect you to complete your report in its totality without further hesitancy or interruptions."

"As so ordered, Senior Guard Commander Mio, as so I will comply."

The New Reign

19

"Zuke, is that you Zuke?" The incoming scan from Mio brought Zuke from his daydreaming past.

"It most certainly is, Senior Guard Commander Mio. It most certainly is."

"Where are the rest of the Commanders, Zuke?"

Before Zuke had a chance to continue, Mio cut him short. "Those missing Commanders were issued with specific instructions to remain in this vicinity either until we returned, or they were further advised."

Zuke felt a slight annoyance creeping into Mio's tone.

"Senior Guard Commander Mio, I am but a humble Senate Runner who has spent more time than I care to remember running messages for those who were gifted with a higher plane than myself."

Mio felt the vibration of Zuke's exasperations, realising that her frustration with the failure of the Commanders to heed her instructions was no reason to take umbrage with the old Senate Runner.

"Zuke, my old friend, let me apologise without reservation. My tone was totally uncalled for." Mio felt the tension slide in Zuke.

"Senior Guard Commander Mio, your apology is accepted, and yes, it is accepted without reservation as well."

"Thank you, Senate Runner Zuke. Now, pray tell me what brings you this far out from the Great Assembly?"

"Senior Guard Commander Mio, the new King as his first decree, has called together all members of the Great Assembly without exception, and like I said, without exception. So, those Commanders you ordered to remain here were thus recalled, and so it is that I have waited here to deliver to you two, the King's message."

The three Regents of the Deep cut through the long swells with ease, as Mio and Jove followed the mature Senate Runner toward the place of meeting.

Taking advantage of the silence, Mio unwittingly tested the integrity of old Zuke.

"Tell me, Senate Runner Zuke, who was raised up to bear the arduous mantle of King?"

Even before Mio completed her scan to the old runner, she knew that a knowing look would be the only response she could expect.

— Ψ —

The heaven-coloured waters of the oceans had erupted into life, fuelled by the surging flashing bodies of the Great Assembly as they gathered en masse on the direct decree of their new King.

"Senior Guard Commander Mio, Senior Guard Commander Mio!" The incoming scan from Alex brought the three Regents of the Deep to a halt.

"Senior Guard Commander Mio, am I pleased to finally see you!"

"Excuse me, Senior Guard Commander Mio." Zuke's scan interrupted the approaching Alex. "Senior Guard Commander Mio, please let me remind you that you are ordered to report immediately to Senator Ark." The old Senate Runner had not let his long passage of service to the Senate go by without learning a number of tricks to get his message across. Tricks like pausing in the middle of a message, to ensure the full attention of the receptor was held. With the attention of the three now fully focused, old Zuke continued.

"Also, let me further advise you that this Senator is now the new Senator responsible for all Guard and Scout Commanders, and all those ranked below that order. He is also the new Senator for Discipline and Wellbeing; so if I may be so bold, I recommend that it may not be the wisest thing to do to keep the new Senator waiting."

Then, to add to the growing drama of anticipation and excitement of those assembling and filling the auditorium, the old scoundrel of the oceans, not wanting to let the opportunity pass without adding his own touch of verbal theatrics, paused and then added: "Senior Guard Commander Mio, let me further remind you that the new Senator Ark is well known for his strict disciplinarian views."

Again, Zuke cemented the moment with a brief gap of silence before continuing. "This new Senator Ark is the very same Senator who is also well known for his pet phrase of, never forget and never forgive."

"Thank you, Senate Runner Zuke. I will advise the new Senator Ark of your prompt and expert delivery of his summons." Mio let a little mirth steal into her scan, thinking she would amuse herself at old Zuke's expense with a little of her own style of his mind games.

"But! But, Senior Guard Commander Mio, I meant no disrespect to the most honourable and new Senator Ark. In fact, Senior Guard Commander Mio, I hold the new Senator Ark in the very highest of esteem."

Mio was a little astounded at just how quickly old Zuke went into verbal retreat.

"Yes, Senate Runner Zuke, I think I just will sing your praises to the new Senator." With Zuke now in full recoil, Mio just had to add to the squirming runner's misery. "I do believe the new Senator Ark would also be most interested to hear how you pass on his pet phrase."

Mio watched as Zuke momentarily writhed, before putting him out of his self-induced misery. "Senate Runner Zuke, let me assure you that your secret is safe with me. Now, tell me where will we be able to find the new Senator Ark?"

"Thank you, Mio, thank you very much Mio. Please let me take you to the Senator now."

"You really don't have to, Zuke. We are quite able to seek him out. All you have to do is just point us in his general direction, if you would, please."

"No, no, Mio, I insist! I insist! You just follow me. This way, if you please." Old Zuke was somewhat relieved that Mio was jesting; or he hoped she was just jesting – yes she was jesting.

Mio let her mirth pass. After all, it was not every day that one got the better of old Zuke.

The remaining journey to execute the call of Senator Ark was left to silence.

Some two asmar out from the main assembly, Senate Runner Zuke brought the three to a halt.

"Please, remain here while I seek the pleasure of Senator Ark."

Senior Guard Commander Mio acknowledged the scan from the Senate Runner.

Jove waited until Zuke had disappeared and then breached next to Mio. "Mio, tell me what do you think has happened to Zen? It is as if no one knows the answer, or at the least, no one wants to talk about him."

Mio turned to Jove, again feeling the sorrow building in the youngster. "My friend, I know not the answer to your question. We are experiencing very sad times, and it may well be that you are the only one with the answer to your own question."

Jove rode the swell, drawing up alongside Mio.

"Mio, what I was to report has left me in no doubt that Zen was…."

"Senior Guard Commander Mio, Senator Ark has asked that the three of you report to him now."

The incoming scan of the old Senate Runner cut Jove short in mid scan.

"Thank you, Zuke, and believe me when I promised you your secret is totally safe with me, so it is." Mio saw the relief reflected in the bearing of the old ocean rogue, disguised as the oldest Senate Runner. As he left the trio, they were all subjected to his usual muttering of being hard done by, with utterings of being the hardest working Senate Runner, along with no one having the time anymore to stop and reminisce about the good old days.

"Greetings, Senator Ark, as you ordered, as so we present ourselves before you," Senior Guard Commander Mio scanned to the waiting Senator.

"Thank you, Guard Commander Mio, and those warm greetings I reciprocate to you and to your companions, Guard Commander Jove, and Guard Commander Alex."

Jove and Alex acknowledged the Senator in silence, with the approved appropriate nod.

Then, without any further formality, the Senator ordered his three visitors to draw in close as they headed away from the Assembly. Once all four were clear of the multitude of scans that permeated both the skies and water, Senator Ark ordered the three Commanders into close formation.

"Firstly, I must thank the three of you for your prompt response to my directive. Secondly, and this order only concerns you, Guard Commander Mio, and yes Mio, it is Guard Commander."

The Senator waited for a reaction from Mio, and with none forthcoming, continued... "During the crisis that befell the Assembly, during the ceremony of seeking out and installing a new King, a special rank of Senior Guard Commander was bestowed upon you, Mio. Now, it is with a mixture of regret and joy that I have to revoke the temporary order of Senior from your rank, regret that I must do so, and a joy that the crisis has passed and passed very quickly. So, it shall be. Do you understand the reasoning for this decision, Guard Commander Mio?"

"Yes, Senator Ark, I do understand, for at the time of my raising to the rank of Special, I understood that it was only to be a temporary measure."

"Thank you, Guard Commander Mio. Now, I want to move on to more pressing matters."

"Before we do, Senator Ark, and of course with all due respect, can I seek any information that you may be in possession of regarding the fate of Zen?"

The Senator toyed with letting the totally out-of-character interruption by Mio go unchallenged. Then, taking a softer approach, he replied, "I know how close you two are Mio."

"How close we were, Senator Ark, how close we were." Mio's second and sharp interruption not only took the Senator aback somewhat, but also presented an extremely poor example of discipline to the other two Commanders present.

Senator Ark again let the interruption of Mio go uncensored, knowing how close of late, she had grown to the Legion Commander.

"Guard Commander Mio, I ask that you take a moment and remember just who you are, who you are addressing, and most importantly, your training to the creed."

The gentle rebuke by Senator Ark quickly had its desired effect on the somewhat distraught Guard Commander Mio. The Senator allowed Mio a little time to regain her composure before he continued.

"It is the decision of the new King that there shall be no formal induction ceremony for his ascension to the throne. This decision, because the current circumstances we find ourselves in, has been fully agreed to, and thereby ratified, by all the Senators."

The Senator gave a little time for his scans to be fully understood.

"Furthermore, the new King has also decreed that Teacher Notris of the sixth, shall be elevated to the rank and standing of the former Most Learned One. This installation has already been completed, and according to our creed, all within the Assembly will embrace the new Most Learned One. This is to be without exception, as so directed by our new King."

"As so ordained, as so we shall comply." The response, in unison by the three Commanders, pleased the Senator.

Guard Commander Mio scanned for permission to address Senator Ark.

Senator Ark, not being one to agree to the interruptions of any subordinate, looked across at Mio. Then, after a moment's deliberation, acknowledged her right to address him.

"Senator Ark, with all due reverence, I respectfully admit that we three ordered here before you are completely mystified as to the happenings within the Assembly of late."

Guard Commanders, Alex and Jove nodded their agreement to Senator Ark.

After a brief pause, Mio continued. "I think I can speak on behalf of both my compatriots when I say I, or as would be a more fitting description, we, are at a complete loss as to our direction. We were directed into an area out from the Assembly during the selection process for a King."

Mio felt the scans of support from both Alex and Jove, as they moved in closer to reinforce their allegiance to her statements. Mio scanned her appreciation for their support – a scan that did not go unnoticed by the Senator.

"Senator Ark, the last thing we know with any certainty is that Guard Commander Jove here was called to assist the Legion Commander. When he arrived, it seems that he was too late to stop an attack on the Legion Commander – an attack that he believed saw the demise of Zen at the behest of Byzefu."

Mio felt the sorrow ever so slowly building up from deep inside her and, try as she might, her tears flowed, mixing with the ocean's salty waters.

Senator Ark moved in close to his faithful servant, soothing her with his scans.

"Mio, my very dear Mio, let not your sorrow blind you to your life. Let me assure you, what Guard Commander Jove saw was indeed true, and the Legion Commander was felled by a foul deed, and yes it is true that this foul deed was instigated by Byzefu."

The four Regents of the Deep breached the oceans together in united sorrow, and then just as quickly disappeared beneath the heaven-blue waves. The three Guard Commanders waited for Senator Ark to gather his thoughts and continue.

"The attack on the place of call together was believed, by the Senators, to be nothing more than posturing and bluff that got steeped in violence by either Byzefu or Hur. Whether or not it was deliberate, or an accidental act, the King, on the urging of all Senators, and here I must reiterate most vigorously, all Senators, decided that the perpetrators of these most foul deeds would be punished, and punished to the maximum."

Again Senator Ark hesitated, as he herded his thoughts together. "As first light of the Sun God graced the heavens this day, most of Byzefu's so-called priests have been banished from the Great Assembly for a time knowing no end."

Scans of disbelief involuntary escaped from Jove and Alex.

Mio glanced across at the Senator, but before she could make comment, the Senator continued. "All in good time, Guard Commander Mio, all in good time. Again, at the urging of all Senators, the new King did succumb to these robust urgings, and in great sadness ordered the immediate putting to death of Byzefu, Hur, and Huela.

The three Guard Commanders were struck to shock and silence. Mio was the first to break the numbness of anguish and bewilderment.

"Senator Ark, when will this grim task of execution be undertaken?"

"I am sorry, Guard Commander Mio, you will have to increase your scan strength. The last failed to register."

"My apologies, Senator Ark, but I am shocked by the news you have just delivered, and undoubtedly my fellow Guard Commanders are also shocked."

"Commanders, I fully understand that the gravity of what has happened has upset you all, and if the truth is known, upset is probably not the right word. But rest assured, I do understand."

The Guard Commanders could only nod in agreement, as they waited for the Senator to continue.

"The execution of the condemned three is set down to take place as we speak." Senator Ark watched, as the three Commanders took in his chilled words of kismet. Jove seemed to be the only one struggling to come to terms with the news. The Senator made a mental note to sometime, in the near future, revisit Jove's training regime.

"Guard Commanders, while this news I have just imparted to you is draped with great sadness and sorrow, there is a shard of joy that was passed to me just prior to this call together."

Mio wondered out loud, "Whatever could there be that would, at this time, lift our spirits?"

"Guard Commander Mio, this news affects you. Legion Commander Zen survived the attack, and at this time is recuperating nicely."

"Can I see him please, Senator. Where is he?"

The Senator refused to let this latest interruption from Mio go without a strong rebuke.

"No, you cannot see the Legion Commander. Whilst he only just survived the attack, he is still not well enough to see anybody. In fact, it may be some time before the nursing matrons let him out of their care, let alone out of their sight. And let me give you one final warning, Guard Commander Mio, this is the last time I will tolerate one of your uncalled-for and unacceptable interruptions. Do you understand me? Let me make this very, very clear, Guard Commander Mio. You are testing my patience to the very limit."

Mio felt the full force of Senator Ark's stern scans of admonishment, and promised herself to never be in a position of upsetting this Senator in the future.

"Guard Commanders, all of you are now instructed to accompany me and join with the other Senators and Guard Commanders to help prepare for the new King's first address to the Great Assembly. For this is decreed by, Ira, The Magnificent One, King of all Dolphins."

"So mote it be," was the immediate call of response from the three Guard Commanders.

The Final Days

20

A chill of fear permeated the waters that surrounded the area of confinement in which the three prisoners, who circulated in slow silence, found themselves – each now in their own way coming to terms with their fate. The new King, under advice from his Senators, had rejected each of their individual calls for compassion and clemency. King Ira called his Senators together to clarify the sequence of events that would shortly commence. He was much sickened by the course that had been plotted and dictated by a creed that spanned all known time.

"Senator Ark, present yourself before the here gathered Senators."

"As so directed, my King, as so I obey." Senator Ark felt the sadness that emanated from the King.

"Senator Ark, has a suitable place of execution been found, and has that place been prepared in accordance with the ancient writings that our Most Learned One has referred to us all?"

"It has, my King. Not five asmar from here is a ravine that, in itself, is many asmar deep. After due inspection by Senators Opek and myself, we are, without doubt certain that this location would fill all requirements adequately."

"Thank you, Senator Ark. Please resume your place in the Senate."

The King waited until the Senator had retired to his position before issuing his next call.

"Senator Oly, present yourself before the here gathered Senators."

"As so directed, my King, as so I obey."

213

"Senator Oly, who has been selected to carry out these executions?"

"My King, after much soul searching and in consultation with the Most Learned One, it has been decided that Scout Commanders Idyll and Zarlie would be best suited."

"Your choice surprises me somewhat, Senator." The interruption from the King brought the Senator to silence, and as ritual dictated, any continuance was at the behest of the King.

"Senator Oly, Scout Commander Zarlie I don't have a problem with, but Scout Commander Idyll, as records show, does have a tendency to be – hmmmmm. The words I think best to describe the Scout Commander are momentarily lost to me. Tell me Senator, have the Scout Commanders been made aware that after they have carried out these very unpleasant tasks, they have the given right to be released from all future duties for a time knowing no end?"

"My King, firstly, the words that may be lost to you at this moment that best describe Scout Commander Idyll, if I may be so bold as to say – could they be 'playful', or even 'impish'?"

The King nodded his agreement, as Senator Oly continued.

"Scout Commander Idyll has shown, of late, that he has matured in both stature and dedication to the creed. He is also, without a doubt, one of the strongest with ranking in the Great Assembly. Again, after consultation with the Most Learned One, we feel our decision is the right one with respect to these two appointees, and we trust their ability to carry out their allotted tasks."

"Thank you, Senator Oly. Please resume your place in the Senate."

"As so directed, my King, as so I obey."

"Before you leave, Senator Oly, I have one final question for you. Are you absolutely sure that the Scout Commanders fully understand what is expected of them, and that both have the mental ability to carry out these grisly tasks?"

"My King, I have no doubt whatsoever that both Scout Commanders have the physical ability, along with the mental fortitude, to carry out the orders of the King and his Senators."

"Thank you, Senator Oly."

A strange silence settled over the King's call together as each Senator was momentarily lost deep in their very own private world of thoughts.

"What has been decided as to the disposal of the bodies?"

The King's scan broke the spell of silence. Senator Ark rose up and acknowledged to the King that he wanted to reply to his last question.

"Senator Ark, present yourself before me again."

The Senator moved back in front of the King, acknowledging him as he did so.

"My King, as there is no requirement for any form of burial, or even prayers for those condemned, it has been thought best that the condemned be left to those creatures that rule the deepest part of the ravine."

The words of Senator Ark brought home the cold realities of the path the new King and his loyal Senators had chosen.

"Thank you, Senator. Let us not dwell on the subject of the disposal any longer. Now, please return to your position in the Senate."

"Thank you. As my King has ordered, as so I will obey."

Again the King waited for Senator Ark to take up his allotted position back in the Senate.

"Most Learned One, present yourself before the here gathered Senators."

"As so directed, my King, as so I obey."

"Most Learned One, please tell how goes the extraction of knowledge from Byzefu?"

"My King, I have spent a great deal of time in the company of our former Most Learned One who, for reasons known only to him, underwent a great change on the death of the last King. When he surfaced from his great sorrow, he was not the Most Learned One we all had known, but an evil apparition of his former self named Byzefu. I have asked of him, or to be more truthful I have begged of him, to let me into the great storehouse of knowledge that he has amassed. In the beginning, his attitude was one of belligerence, hate, and defiance of all things related to our creed. During my last visits to the compound that locks in The Byzefu, I had noticed a definite softening of his demeanour. With this softening and encouragement, I have managed to persuade him to allow me to recover a great many things."

Before the Most Learned One could continue, the King interrupted.

"As time is running out for The Byzefu, I cannot help but reflect on his past. He was a great friend to the previous King. He brought down the prayers for the visit of our God Poseidon to the Great Assembly – along with a great many more highlights and accolades that have garnished his life."

The Senators momentarily reminisced about the past deeds of the once highly esteemed and former Most Learned One.

"Most Learned One, how does Hur fare at this time?" The King's call ended the brief moments of melancholy remembrance of a time long past."

"My King, he fares very badly. He has, for want of a better phrase, turned into a sobbing wreck of his former self."

"Most Learned One, has anything been done to calm Hur?"

"Yes, my King. Hur has been brought to a state of tranquillity and acceptance of his fate by way of soothing and calming scans that I have delivered personally."

"Then tell me, Most Learned One, is the so called Priest Huela still defiant and without remorse. Is he still refusing to denounce the leadership of The Byzefu, or his actions against those of Great Assembly?"

"My King, it is with great regret I report the belligerence of Huela remains unabated, and if anything, grows relentlessly. His disdain for Legion Commander Zen has taken on a frightening and unnatural magnitude. My King, it is as if Huela is consumed to the point of having no control, by his hate for one of the most respected members of the Great Assembly."

"Thank you, Most Learned One. Now, please return to your position in the Senate."

"Thank you. As my King has ordered, as so I will obey."

"Most Learned One, all gathered Senators, this day we are to undertake tasks that I have no doubt strike a heavy chord within you all. We, who are so loved by our great God Poseidon, have since time in memoriam always preached the sanctity of life, and that life is precious to all. Now, we have to take it – not once, but three times."

The King let his short solemn sermon drift over those Senators gathered before him, taking a moment to let them all reflect on the magnitude of the day's events that were about to unfold.

"Senator Ark, call forward the appointed Guard Commanders and have them readied to escorted Hur to his place of execution."

"As my King has ordered, as so I will obey."

The call of the King brought with it a cloak of chill to the waters, one that was felt in the very hearts of each and every gathered Regent of the Deep.

"Most Learned One, you go now to Hur, and use all the powers you have at your disposal to ensure he remains as calm and sedate as you can make him."

"As my King has ordered, as so I will obey."

"Senator Oly, go forth and call in Scout Commander Idyll and Scout Commander Zarlie, and escort them to the place of execution."

"As my King has ordered, as so I will obey."

"Senator Opek, you, along with fellow Senators Ramcy and Nova, will accompany me to this place of execution, and there we shall bear witness to these deeds of distaste and sorrow. These deeds that we are about to witness shall, for all time, be seared into the great hall of all our memories."

"Our King has ordered, and so we must obey."

A strange calmness did cover the oceans; the four God Winds that swept the Heavens had retreated, as if distancing themselves from the pending executions, only daring to watch from afar. A great stillness and peace ruled the Heavens and Earth.

In the distance, the very faint chatter of the Great Assembly was now barely audible; most of the members were completely oblivious to the fate of these three well-known, condemned Regents of the Deep.

"Senators Opek, Ramcy, and Nova, as we are now positioned in the area of execution, I must now ask of you all – are you willing and prepared to witness the execution of Hur, Huela, and the former Most

Learned One now known as The Byzefu?"

The King's scan to his accompanying witnesses brought the three Senators to reply in unison.

"As my King has ordered, as so I will obey."

The King felt the scans of steely resolve from his Senators as he scanned out his first order of death.

"Senator Ark, bring forth the first prisoner, Hur, and let him be executed."

"As my King has ordered, as so I will obey."

Somewhere, high in the sky above the arena of execution, a lonely seabird cried, its eerie squawk resonating down amongst those gathering in the arena of death. Again the seabird's cry rang out, as if it was singing an anthem of serenade to the soon to be dying, casting more sombre emotions on all those assembled at the arena of death.

The silence of waiting was broken by the approaching sounds of the Most Wise One, as he chanted his mantra of prayers to the Gods begging them to forgive the waywardness of Hur. Hur's sedate state of mind pleased the King as he watched from the ocean's surface as the procession moved slowly into the execution arena. The four Guard Commanders that flanked Hur were thankful that the warning from Senator Ark – that Hur could become unpredictable – was proving to be wrong. As the escort party approached the ravine's edge, the Most Learned One drew to a halt, and then turned around to face Hur.

"Hur, protocol dictates that no prayers be offered to you before you are sent from this place of your dwelling."

Hur could only just nod his agreement, barely able to focus, let alone understand fully what was shortly to befall him.

"Hur, even I cannot break a tradition that goes back to our

beginnings, so now I must leave you to face your unknown alone."

Again Hur could only just manage a nod, as he tried to focus on the Most Learned One. Lifting his head to look toward the ocean's surface, Hur could vaguely see a number of darkened silhouettes circling overhead. What Hur did not see was the leader of this group of darkened silhouettes nod, to complete the first sentence of death.

Hur felt the gentle upsurge of cold water, as he and his escorts slowly moved out over the ravine – his state of mind now back in that playground of a long-time past – The Shallows.

"Home, home."

Hur's scans were now barely audible. His escorts, on signal, peeled away leaving him to drift further out over the darkened ravine, alone.

Scout Commander Idyll was the first to strike. On receiving the nod and scan from the King, he, along with Scout Commander Zarlie, breached the surface next to Senator Ark, then dived deep into the ravine down past where light dared penetrate.

Then, in unison, both Commanders turned sharply and headed back towards the surface, their muscular bodies powering them both at great speed – up, up towards the drifting Hur. Scout Commander Idyll's first and only strike hit Hur just back from his heart, instantly rupturing it and flooding his lungs with blood that immediately belched from his mouth and nostrils as growing clouds of red.

The next executed blow was from Scout Commander Zarlie, perfectly timed to connect as Hur rolled over in recoil from the impact of the first strike. Her strike found its mark at the centre top of Hur's head, hitting with such force that Hur's brain was compressed and instantaneously forced out through one of his now burst eye sockets.

Both Scout Commanders circulated slowly over Hur's twitching body as they watched it slowly sink into the abyss of the ravine, streaming a smoke-like wisp of red cloud. Then it was gone.

"Senator Ark, bring forth the second prisoner, Huela, and let him be executed."

"As my King has ordered, as so I will obey."

"Hur has gone to his death with a little dignity, albeit induced dignity. The same, I hope I will be able to say about Huela. This former self-proclaimed priest has, during his time in confinement, repeatedly tried to escape with whatever means he had at his disposal." The King's statement was to nobody in particular, so silence was the only response.

"You have no right to hold me! I am beholden only to The Great Byzefu! You are nothing more than slaves to those who have no right to call themselves Senators. As for the new King – he has done nothing more than steal the crown from the only, and rightfully true leader, The Great Byzefu."

A string of abusive rants poured forth from the disgraced priest as he was escorted, in tight formation, by the guards to the edge of the ravine. He cursed and condemned the Senators, and then it was the turn of the King to feel the bitter vitriol of Huela's wrath.

Finally, the Great God Poseidon fell to Huela's cursing. Again, and again, the condemned priest threw himself at the ever-tightening ultrasonic bands his escorts surrounded him with – all in a last desperate effort to escape his fate.

"Keep Huela confined! Keep him moving forward." The call of

Senator Ark to the struggling Guards seemed only to strengthen the resolve of Huela in his frantic efforts to escape his approaching doom.

"You have no right to hold me against my will. I do not, and will not, accept the false laws that you – you the so-called King – have taken on and imprisoned me under. There is but one God, and that God is called The Great Byzefu. Do you hear me? I demand that I be set free – free from this place – free from the false so-called God, Poseidon. As for you, King, may you rot and suffer at the hands of Hades."

At the very last moment, Huela twisted as if he had anticipated the attack, and in so doing, Scout Commander Idyll's strike missed its target, hitting the jaw of Huela, which shattered with the force of the impact. Instantly, Scout Commander Zarlie's strike hit Huela. With the first strike of Scout Commander Idyll missing its mark, so it was that Zarlie's strike was also off-target, hitting Huela mid-body. The strike knocked the Priest sideways, doing nothing more than further infuriating the now wounded Huela.

"You call yourself a King of the highest order? Well, this shows you just how ineffective your reign is going to be, when your servants are as inept as you are. Byzefu! All power to Byzefu!"

Before Huela could get into another litany of verbal abuse, Scout Commander Idyll struck. His second hit did not miss its target, nor did Scout Commander Zarlie miss her new target. Both Scout Commanders hit each side of Huela, in line with his heart; both hits striking simultaneously.

Senator Ark could only stare in mesmerised amazement at the

aftermath of the brutal execution. The two Scout Commanders joined the Senator on the ocean's surface, and together they watched in silence as Huela started to sink from sight, down into the dark ravine. The force of the double strike had burst open Huela's body cavity, causing a string of his entrails to trail out behind him as he too slowly disappeared into the darkened depths of the abyss, to join the departed Hur.

"Senator Ark, bring forth the third prisoner, Byzefu, and let him be executed."

"As my King has ordered, as so I will obey."

Again, a lone seabird cried. Its haunting sounds would forever be a catalyst to recall the memories of those who witnessed these events. The King breached the surface, his Senators in harmony with him.

"Senators, keep your belief in our creed strong, for the final act in this whole sordid chapter is shortly coming to its conclusion."

"I speak for all of us, my King, when I say the sooner this end comes to pass, the sooner we can all begin to put behind us what we have witnessed here."

The King could only nod his agreement to Senator Opek. So it was that silence became the sole prelude to the final act in this drama of death.

"Can I ask you, Senator Ark, who has been appointed to be my executor?"

The King heard the scan from Byzefu, and it struck a sad note deep within him.

"Now you know, Byzefu, I cannot tell you that. I have accorded to you your last request, and instructed all who have been in contact with you, to address you as Byzefu. I am sorry, but you know full well, that is as far as protocol allows me to go."

Senator Ark watched Byzefu as he was escorted closer to the ravine's edge. This once highly respected Regent of the Deep, now succumbed to age and a warped mind, was nothing more than a pathetic old man of the oceans. Byzefu turned again to Senator Ark, and for the first time, the Senator noticed the evil that emanated from this old man's eyes.

Senator Ark saw the eyes of Byzefu burning like fire, as they sought to look into his very soul for one last time. Then, as quickly as the Senator felt the eyes of fire scorch him, the flames were gone, and only the eyes of a tired, condemned old man stared blankly back at him.

"Senator Ark, I shall not die here at this time, for death this day shall but herald my new beginnings."

"Byzefu, what must be done at this time will be done. I, along with those allocated these tasks, will make it as quick and as painless as we can for you, out of respect for your past deeds of good."

"Don't you dare patronise me, Senator Ark. Just who do you think you are addressing? Let me assure you that I am not like your weak King. I am The Great Byzefu! Do you understand me, Senator Ark? I am The Great Byzefu!"

Again Senator Ark saw the fire of the devil flare to life in the old man's eyes; this time he felt the full terror of The Byzefu.

"I am The Great Byzefu! I am The Great Byzefu! I will return; I am The Great Byze……"

The perfect strike, by Scout Commander Idyll, cut short The Byzefu's rant.

It was the second and final strike, delivered by Scout Commander

Zarlie that brought an end to this deadly ritual. The two executing Scout Commanders joined Senator Ark in silence, and together they watched the third and final body slowly disappear into the blackness of the ravine of death.

Suddenly, out of the stillness, the oceans were torn asunder with a ferocity that sought nothing more than to vent its fury on all and sundry. Fire and steam belched up from the blackened bowels of the abyss, accompanied by a great deafening roar as if in defiance of the oceans that surrounded them. This great roar reverberated throughout the water and even into the air above – and fear now stalked this place of death. Again and again the great fury-infused ocean thrashed at the Regents of Deep with an unforgiving ferocity. It was as if the ocean itself sought to take its revenge upon those who had participated in the happening of this day. As the ocean's supremacy multiplied, so grew the searing heat of the flames as they surged from the abyss, immune to their watery covering, in total defiance to all known things. And then, from this blackened abyss of hell, rose up the God Hades, and the seas fell still, the fires retreated, and the lion's roar fell to silence.

"You, who have taken part in this day of shame – you are all cursed to always crawl on your bellies; to forever feast on those crawling insects that live on the sea bed floor."

The sudden appearance of the God Hades shocked all the Regents of the Deep to fear and retreat. Hades then raised his arms, and from the bowels of the abyss rose up the three executed prisoners, their wounds still bleeding clouds of red.

"You who have sought to destroy these my humble servants... You will all live to regret these deeds in which you participated!

225

"Today shall be remembered for all time to come as the day of the resurrection. And cursed shall be those who take and use this day for any purpose other than to sing the praises for what I have undertaken this day. For only these resurrections shall be deemed as true, and so they shall be heralded in praise."

Then the God Hades was gone. As the oceans returned to total calm, and the fires that roared up and burnt from this watery grave were extinguished, silence and peace did then surround all those that dwelt therein.

The King was the first to break the silence when he called to those gathered to close in.

"This day we have carried out those tasks that were necessitated by those who sought to leave and cast asunder our creed and teachings. What we all have witnessed here this day, we must now put into the reservoir of memories. The day has shown that all of us have nothing to fear from the God Hades, nor from any of those who have aligned themselves with him or his teachings. For they have no power to harm us – no power to will us – no power to instil a living fear in us – no power to transform us in his image or in his ways.

"This God has no power over us because of the strong faith we have in our creed. Our love and belief in our God, Poseidon, and the teaching he has passed down from a time knowing no beginning, will have no end. Never let fear be the great adversary. Never let hate be the great adversary.

"Never let the unknown be the great adversary, for we are all strong in our faith, and this instilled faith will always carry us through any, and all great adversities."

226

The King felt the apprehension of the unknown begin to dissipate as his words had their desired effect on these, his faithful regents.

"Senator Ark."

"Yes, my King."

"Lead us all back to the Great Assembly; for this day, your King wishes to address the members gathered there, and speak of these events we all have both undertaken and witnessed."

"As my King has ordered, as so I will obey."

The Sand People

21

As the God Hades ascended to the Heavens, he carried with him the resurrected dead that the Regents of the Deep had executed and then abandoned to the abyss with callous disregard for the welfare of their lost and now wandering souls. To camouflage his deception from his fellow Gods, Hades rebirthed the three condemned dead into his own menagerie of evil.

Firstly, the reincarnation of Byzefu spawned a Beast so evil even its master shuddered at the very sight of it. When this was done, Hades decided the time was right for the two other condemned dead to reappear and complete their transformations, so they too became visible in the form of two double-headed serpents.

The Great Gods of the Heavens spent their days and nights attending to the many tasks within their kingdoms watching over the comings and goings. They were also charged with the protection of these kingdoms, and so fought many great battles with those who dared to stray into their Heavenly domain.

The God Hades and his newly created entities of evil completely divorced themselves from any of these tasks, and ridiculed the other Gods as being weak and pathetically feeble. And while these Gods did attend to their tasks with diligence and care, Hades and the Beast sought out the company of Dionysus the God of Wine and Frenzy. Fuelled with the ambrosia of the vine, Hades called upon Flora, the Goddess of Prostitution, and she too fell to the charms of the ambrosia.

Then it was that Eros, the God of Erotic Sex, Love, and Passion joined in the frenzied debauchery.

With each day that passed, the Beast grew in confidence, and the time came when he began to challenge the very God that had saved him from joining those lost souls that wandered somewhere between life and death, unseen by those around them, their mournful cries unheard. By day, the Beast slept; by night, he prowled the chambers of the many beautiful nymphs. With his voracious appetite, he raped and deflowered these young virgins with great depravity and ruthless violence, much to the concern of the ruling Gods.

The debauchery eventually brought about a great war in the heavens between the Beast and the God Hades, and so it was that the Beast, the once great Byzefu, was finally defeated and condemned to be expelled. As there was no longer a place for him in the heavens, just as there was no place for him in the oceans, the very same one who had longed to be called The Great Byzefu, and now labelled The Beast, was thrown down to Earth – and those two who had followed him into the heavenly domain were also cast out as evil serpents.

This evil one, The Beast, on the condition that he remain on Mother Earth for all time and promise never to try to return to the heavens, was also given authority by Hades to do whatever he wanted to do. He was even allowed to speak great blasphemies against the Gods of the Regents of the Deep. With this new freedom, The Beast was free to speak terrible words of blasphemy against the Great God Poseidon and his fellow Gods, and slander their names and their heavenly dwellings. And all those who dwelt therein felt the stinging detestation of his tongue.

Thus this exiled one, The Beast, was allowed to wage war against all the people who walked on Earth – and to conquer them. He was given absolute authority to rule over every tribe and every people of every tongue. And all the people who belonged to this world were forced, by torture and by fear, to worship the newly arrived and aptly named one, The Beast – and his two double-headed serpents.

One such tribe, whose own names they could not write, had their very beginnings at a time when the God Hades himself had first been banished from the Great Kingdom in the Heavens and forced to live on Earth.

At that time, now long past, the God Hades wandered Mother Earth alone, having lost the great spoils of his possessions to the other more powerful Gods. Cast out from his heavenly home, he sought solace on Mother Earth where he could plot the downfall of all those who had deprived him of what he felt was his rightly deserved inheritance. Hades did decide to make his home in one of the many caves that overlooked the great ocean. In an effort to create company, he had swept up the soiled waste that feral animals had cast about the cave as they sought sanctuary from the burning heat of the sun at its fiery pinnacle. Then, Hades gathered up handfuls of this stench-laden waste and blew life into each and every handful, and from each handful of the waste grew many people.

All were cast in his image and spread throughout the land of sand. As the new people grew in numbers, so did the heat of the sun, and to protect themselves further from this unrelenting heat, they did grow beards, darken their skin, and cover their bodies from head to toe in flowing robes. These sand people grew rapidly in number and they did, without thought and regard, deplete the already sparse lands of vegetation.

With no foliage to hold the land firm, the God Winds did shift the sands from place to place at their will. As the God Winds did so, these sands did fall into and block the waterways until water, other than that hidden deep beneath these shifting sands, was no more. So it was that the water was evaporated from easy access, and all these robed ones were unable to cleanse themselves and the odour of their very beginnings was vested back into their keeping.

The God Hades ruled these people he had created for twenty passes. It was then that the Great God Zeus had second thoughts, and he did forgive Hades for all his transgressions against him. With these transgressions now a thing of the past and forgotten by his fellow Gods, thus was opened a path for this formerly disgraced God to return and be reinstated to his rightful place in the heavens.

And thus it came to be that when Hades expelled from heaven The Beast and the two two-headed serpents, they did take up residence in the land of the Sand People in caves high over the oceans, and all Gods were appeased.

On his first day on Mother Earth, The Beast did send out three facsimiles of the sand dwellers astride beasts of burden, and through these inhuman images he summoned all who lived in the land to appear before him. Those who failed to present themselves were struck down by the bite of the serpents that appeared in many places at once. It was then that The Beast appeared before the gathered Sand People, and rejoiced at the sight of the multitudes that knelt before him. He spoke to them saying:

"I am your new God. I was sent here by the great God Hades to rule over you; those of you who are non-believers, I will strike down and cast into the fires of his hell."

The Beast listened to their cries of anointment, and thus this evil heavenly outcast installed himself as the new Deity.

The Beast then called upon his serpents to bring forth a lamb, and this lamb was given to The Beast. The Beast gathered up the lamb, lifted it toward the Heavens, and then ever so slowly, lowered the lamb to his breast. Looking out over the Sand People, who remained prostrate on the ground, he called on them to observe. As they raised their eyes to their new ruler, The Beast savagely bit down on the throat of the now relaxed lamb and ripped it out. So the lamb was cruelly slaughtered, and The Beast revelled in the blood that drenched him.

"Let this now become your ritual. Go from this place and build altars, then take lambs and have them sacrificed to me, your new God. Then sing your praises to me, your only God."

As time went on, The Beast sought to gain political power and spiritual authority over every person that walked upon these sparse lands of sand.

To accomplish this, it was with cunning deception that he changed his demeanour and tact and began his rise to power as a very influential, and when required, a very charismatic, political and religious ambassador.

The Sand People who had witnessed The Beast's brutality, or felt the brutality of those who had aligned themselves with him, lived in constant fear. When, eventually, his deception was exposed, The Beast flew into a terrible rage, and the Sand People were subject to unspeakable tribulation. During this period, their world endured a time of unprecedented trauma.

Following this, The Beast in an effort to seek even greater revenge, proceeded to make war on the offspring of women. Their female children were subjected to a great cruelty as The Beast ordered that their very genitals be barbarically mutilated.

The cries of the young children were heard even in the Heavens, and the Great God of all Gods, Zeus, called Hades to account for these foul deeds he had permitted The Beast to carry out without fear of punishment or retribution. The God Zeus then demanded that Hades put an end to the suffering of the children, and that the perpetrators be punished and forever banished from Mother Earth.

However, this godly command by Zeus went unheeded by Hades, for he was far too engrossed in his own self-satisfying debauchery to pay heed to The Beast, let alone try to tame him. Hades' flippant refusal of God Zeus's command launched an extra-terrestrial conflict which reverberated throughout the Heavens.

With his overwhelming power and authority, Zeus then did again banish Hades from the Heavenly Kingdom for a time knowing no end. As the now disgraced God departed, he was stripped of his Heavenly God status, and all that was good within him was drained from his very being.

And so, Hades arrived at the cave that housed the Beast and the two-headed serpents and they all did cower in fear and become subservient in the presence of their God and master.

So it was that the Sand People's ruling evil was replaced by a bigger, stronger, and more evil one, namely Hades.

Then Hades ordered The Beast to bring forth the two two-headed serpents upon whom he then bestowed greater powers of depravity –

and to keep them in check, he ordered they become compliant to the will of The Beast. Hades further ordered that from that day forward The Beast would be known as The Beast from the Sea

Hades then further ordered all the inhabitants that walked Mother Earth to worship and bow down to The Beast from the Sea whom he, Hades himself had rescued from the ravine of death and restored back to life.

The Beast from the Sea, encouraged by the urging of Hades, forced the Sand People to make images in his own likeness that showed how his grotesquely deformed body was the result of the sword – and yet he lived. The second instruments of Hades' corrupt evil, the two two-headed serpents, were called upon to instil fear into all the Sand People. Those who failed to sacrifice on their altars did feel their wrath, as did those who failed to sing the praises of the God Hades. All were put to the sword so ruthlessly wielded.

So it was that total evil now ruled the land of sand; and the people that dwelt therein were forced to agree with all that the evil rulers forced upon them. Then it was that the ambrosia corrupted all, and the debauchery that Hades had encouraged upon them completed their spiral into total fraudulence – and so it was that Hades and his followers became as one.

As Hades slept off the rigors of another night of depravity, the two serpents stood guard over the cave, silencing even the seabirds that dared break the morning's silence with their screeches. It was one of the two-headed serpents who first noticed the black mass that drew close to pass by the cliffs, and the now awakened Beast of the Sea watched from the high cliff face cave, as the Great Assembly passed below.

A diatribe of vitriolic profanities permeated the air as his long pent up hostility exploded, and he promised ultimate revenge on those Regents of the Deep that had dared venture into this, his domain

The Second Chance

22

Zen, Legion Commander in the seventh decree, for the second time in his life approached the Great Council of Elders, and spoke of his love and his desire for a union with a member of the Assembly. And, for the second time, the Great Council of Elders did pass down their blessings.

"Let me be the first to congratulate you, Legion Commander. No doubt your father, our King, will be pleased, and I would assume that he will want to officiate at the nuptials."

"Thank you for your kind wishes, Senator Opek. I feel it would be an honour to have my father conduct the ceremony, not only because he is my father, but I do believe it will be his first ceremony of union."

The Legion Commander and the Senator headed out to where the long, low swells rolled and peace ruled the oceans.

"You know, Zen, it's been two passes since those fateful days of the trials and executions, and it is so good to see all have moved on." After a brief pause, the Senator went on.

"To be perfectly truthful, it has indeed been a very long time since our Great Assembly has functioned so well, all of which we in The Senate, attribute solely to your father, our King."

"Thank you, Opek."

The two old friends, once out of range of the Assembly, let the formalities of their respective positions fall by the wayside.

"I can only guess at the joy you have bought to your father with your good news, Zen."

"That is yet to be seen. You see, Opek, I have yet to break the news to him, but I am confident he will accept it with all goodwill and best wishes, as has been done by the Great Council of Elders."

"Yes, there is no doubt that he will, for I do know he has great affection for Mio. He has confided in me more than once that he felt the time was right for you to move on, and that direction he hoped was with Mio. Now there, that has given you a little insight into your fathers thinking – well, it would be more of a big insight into his thinking, my dear friend, and to again be truthful, I don't know if I should have confided your father's confidence to you."

"Opek, let me assure you, your confiding in me shall always be ours, and only our secret."

Then, the two friends set about enjoying the beautiful day, riding the swells that had grown in strength with the rising of the evening winds. Both Regents enjoyed solitary time surfing the now large swells, enjoying the invigorating massage provided by the thumping waves. Opek was the first to break the seduction of solitude they were both enjoying.

"Zen, Zen, it's time we head back to the Assembly."

It took some time for Opek's repeated calls to break through Zen's self-imposed barrier of mental isolation, and finally register in the slightly hypnotic state that Zen had induced for himself.

"Tell me, Opek, why does the Sun God travel so fast when one is having fun, or at the very least, enjoying being alive?"

"My friend, if we all knew the answer to that question, I am of the notion that nothing would ever get done. Don't you tend to agree?"

Before Zen could answer, Opek went on. "Speaking of things that need doing, I still have much to do this day, and you my friend have a father to break some good news to. So come on, let's be heading back. After all, we don't want the Senator for Guards and Scouts to start organising a search party to come out looking, do we?"

"As always, you have given me very little leeway to argue that point, and so I have to agree with you."

The two Regents of the Deep moved in unison out and away from the land's edge, both suddenly realising how close they had come to the dangerous jagged rocks that lay hidden just beneath the sky-blue waters. As the two turned and headed to deeper water, Zen glanced up at the towering cliff face that seemed to reach forever to the skies. Zen thought he saw something move high up on one of the ledges, and for some unknown reason a cold shiver raced down his spine.

"Opek, I thought I saw something move high on one of the ledges. Did you notice anything?"

"Strange you should say that. No, I didn't see anything, mainly because I wasn't looking; but for a moment, I actually thought I heard some distant screams. I guess we have spent too much time here enjoying ourselves, and maybe my relaxed imagination just got the better of me."

"Yes, I do suppose you are right, but somehow hmmmm – yes, I suppose you are right, Opek."

"Senator Opek, Legion Commander Zen!"

The incoming scan from Senate Runner Zuke brought the two returning Regents to a halt.

"Now, what brings you out so far from the Senate, old timer?"

With the full formalities of rank restored between Senator Opek and Legion Commander Zen, it was left to the Senator to enquire as to the Senate Runner's call.

"Greetings to you, Senator, as well as to you Legion Commander. Firstly, to you Senator Opek, the Senate is having a call together as directed by the King. The King has given instructions that all Senators are to attend. Secondly, to you Legion Commander Zen, the King would like you to call on him immediately upon your return to the Assembly."

"Thank you, Senate Runner Zuke."

"My pleasure, Senator Opek."

"I also thank you, Senate Runner Zuke."

"Again, also my pleasure, Legion Commander Zen."

As the Senate Runner retreated, Opek turned to his friend. "I would like to thank you for your company this day Zen. It is a long time since I enjoyed a day as much as I have this one; in truth, I cannot remember when I have so enjoyed riding the swells alone, yet in such esteemed company."

"Again, also my pleasure, Senator Opek." Zen laced his reply with a little mirth, as he scanned to the disappearing Senator, and then he too headed back to the Senate and his meeting with the King.

"The King will see you now, Legion Commander Zen."

"Thank you, Senate Runner Zuke."

"Father, great to see you again. I have some news for you, and I hope you accept it as good news."

Zen moved in close to his father, feeling the warmth he projected.

"Zen, more fittingly, my son, it is good to see you again also. I just wonder if this good news concerns Mio, and your approach to the Great Council of Elders for union?"

"Oh, Father! I am so sorry for not coming to you first. I just got a little carried away. For a start, I did not think Mio would agree to a union, and at that time you were so involved in other business of the Senate that… "

"Come, come, my son! While I am just a little disappointed to hear of this news from my Senators, I am overjoyed to know that you are now ready to move on. So my congratulations and best wishes are no doubt, the order of the day."

"Thanks Father, and I, or should I say we, that being Mio and I, would be honoured if it was you who officiated at our union."

"That would indeed be a pleasure, Zen, but we will discuss this at a later date, as now I am required to attend the call together of the Senate. So, if you will excuse me, Legion Commander Zen, I am not prepared to keep my Senators waiting."

The quick return to formality by the King was, in all due respect, expected and accepted by Zen.

— Ψ —

The union between Guard Commander Mio and Legion Commander Zen started with a day and night of celebration that filled all those in the Great Assembly with a great pride. All the past trials and tribulation the Assembly had passed through were, at this time, far back in their memories.

And thus began a period of happy times for all in the Great Assembly. The warm waters were abundant with food, and any threat of danger to their well-being was, to all intents and purposes, non-existent. Life was good. Mio at last had what she had so long yearned for, and the Legion Commander seemed to have settled into his life of union with a calm purpose.

As day became night and night became day, and then all was repeated again and again, many of the Assembly were also beginning to wonder if this might be the place their great God, the God Poseidon, had spoken of at great length.

It was during one of their times alone that Mio first raised her concerns to Zen about a constant feeling of tiredness she was experiencing.

"Senator Oly, Senator Oly!" The call from Zen pulled the Senator out of a promising nap.

"Legion Commander, now to what do I owe this unexpected pleasure?"

"Now, come on Senator, a self-promised nap, or to talk a little business with a Legion Commander? Now that is an easy decision to make. But I promise you, I will only delay you for a few a moments."

"Come up beside me, Legion Commander. That's better. Now tell me, what brings you out here seeking this audience."

"It's Mio, Senator. As each day passes she shows more signs of exhaustion, and this is becoming a growing concern for me."

"Have you spoken to her about your concerns?"

"Yes I have, but you know Mio maybe as well as I do, and she would never say or do anything that could be even faintly construed as complaining."

"Yes, maybe I do, Legion Commander, but what is it you seek of me?"

"Senator Oly, what I would like is that you, as the Senator for the nursery and the infirmary, use your influence and have her removed from her duties as Guard Commander to the Senate and have her assigned to the nursery where her duties would be less stressful."

"I would be only too happy to do as you want Zen, and recommend to the Senate that in the interest of Mio's health she be transferred to either the nursery or the infirmary. As I am one of the more senior Senators, you can take it as done, Legion Commander."

'Thank you, Senator. This day you have lifted a little of the burden from me."

"Now, if you will excuse me, a short nap awaits me. But before you go, Legion Commander, why did you not bring your request directly to the Senate? After all, you do have unimpeded access to the Senate as well as the full freedom of speech... and then, as a dig at you, you do have unfettered access to your father – after all, he is the King."

"The reasons I sought you out, Senator, are very simple. It is not a good look for a person in my position to speak to the Senate of my needs. Also, I think if you look hard enough, somewhere in our teaching, it is only permitted for me to make a personal request in cases of extreme urgency, and by the grace of God, at this point in time, Mio's case is not one of dire urgency."

"You know something, Legion Commander, that is one thing I did not know. And that just goes to prove, Senators do not always know everything. In truth, none of us know everything, and I hereby order you not to tell a soul what I have just said. Now, be gone Legion Commander – my nap is long overdue."

"Video et taceo, video et taceo, my Senator"

Zen, now excused, returned to his tasks, still smiling at the jovial jousting with the Senator. The self-promised nap was now a distant dream for the Senator, as the last words of Zen, video et taceo, just would not leave him.

As each day passed, it seemed that Mio grew wearier, struggling to finish even the simplest of tasks allocated to her by the matrons. It was during her second semester in the nursery that the pain grew too unbearable for her to continue.

"Legion Commander, Legion Commander Zen! You must come quickly. It is Guard Commander Mio! She has fallen ill."

The panic in the incoming scan from the young nursing matron immediately drew the Legion Commander away from the lecture he was giving to the new guard recruits.

"Over here, Matron, I am over here."

"Thank the Gods I have found you. Mio needs you. Senior Matron has sent me to need you... Mio and the Senior Matron...."

"Calm down, Matron, now calm down. In the state you have got yourself into, you are making no sense whatsoever to me. Now, take a few deep breaths and let's start over again." Zen moved in closer to the young matron as she slowly collected her composure.

"Thank you, Legion Commander Zen."

The young matron, now back in full control of her emotions, addressed the Legion Commander with the formality his rank and position demanded of her.

"Legion Commander Zen, the Senior Matron of the nursery has asked that you join her immediately." The young matron took another deep breath, and then on a scan of urging from Zen continued: "Guard Commander Mio has fallen ill, and at this time has been transferred to the infirmary under the watch of the Senior Matron."

"Thank you, Matron. You are now excused."

As the young matron moved off, Zen could only smile on hearing her self-reprimand for the way she handled her very first encounter with him. The young matron's accord, or more precisely the lack of it, struck a note of dismay in him. To see the way this young lady was completely at a loss for words, and overawed while she was in his presence was something that did not sit well with him. It was something he had to address, but not now; it was Mio that now fully occupied his mind.

The Senior Matron heard the Legion Commander's scan calling to her as he moved into the area of the nursery.

"Over here, Legion Commander Zen, I am over here. If you can wait a moment, I will just pass over the care of this one very lively little man, and I will be right with you."

Zen watched in awe as the many helpers in the nursery tackled the tasks of keeping track of all the new-borns. He watched with some amusement as the little ones raced here, there, and everywhere, always with a keeper in hot pursuit. To the Legion Commander, it was nothing more than organised chaos, and all were just players, with the new-borns always at the centre of the stage.

"Legion Commander, I am glad you have come so quickly."

The call from the Senior Matron dragged Zen's mesmerised attention away from the young. "Senior Matron, I came as quickly as I could."

The old Senior Matron could sense a growing alarm with a drizzle of panic developing in the Legion Commander which she sought to quickly alleviate.

"Legion Commander, before you visit Mio let us go somewhere we can talk; a little away from this hustle and bustle, or as I read from you, away from this organised chaos."

When clear of the nursery, the Senior Matron breached next to Zen.

"Legion Commander, of late the wellbeing of Mio has been of great concern to me and the other Senior Matrons. Has she said or done anything that might have alerted you to the possibility that she may be unwell, or at the very least shown you any symptoms or signs that may have led you to believe that all was not right with her?"

Zen cast his mind back to their union, trawling through all the events from that time until the present.

"Yes, there have been a number of times I have thought Mio was not herself. But they were only minor things and I don't think they will be of any importance."

"Legion Commander, what is important, or what is not important, I ask that you let me be the judge of that. Now, with all due respect, I ask you again, is there anything that you can recall that may shed some light on what is at the heart of Mio's ailment or problem? And before you ask – no, Mio is not with child."

Zen was taken aback at the forthrightness of the Senior Matron, but it was something all in the Assembly had come to accept from the matrons of the nursery.

"There are a number of things I can recall that have of late changed in Mio. The first of these has been her not wanting to eat. It is well known Mio has never been one to take a backward move when it has come to food."

"Is that the only thing you can think of?" True to form, the Senior Matron gave Zen little leeway for thought with her quick interruption.

'Yes, Senior Matron, there are other things."

"Well, out with them!" The quick responses from the keeper of the nursery was starting to rub the Legion Commander the wrong way.

"Yes, Senior Matron, there are other things. Not only has there been a loss of appetite, but for Mio, the thrill of the chase has also lost its appeal."

Zen was thankful that this time the only interruption from the Senior Matron was a nod and a hmmhmm.

"Other than that, she seemed to always have a constant feeling of tiredness. Apart from those things, there is nothing else that comes to mind, Senior Matron."

"You have told me more than enough. I think now would be a good time for you to visit Mio. Follow me please, Legion Commander."

Zen fell in behind the Senior Matron, following her in silence back to the infirmary.

"How are you feeling, my Mio?"

Zen's call as he broached the water next to Mio woke her from her slumber.

"Tired, worn out. You name it – I seem to be suffering from them all at the moment, but more importantly, how is the only Legion Commander in my life doing?"

"Well, hopefully I am the only Legion Commander in your life, but unless you know something I don't, I am the only Legion Commander in the Assembly."

Zen was thankful that his Mio had not lost her sense of humour.

"Mio!" The incoming call from the Senior Matron broke the special bond that Zen and Mio were sharing.

"I am here, Senior Matron."

"Mio, why do you keep calling her Senior Matron? After all, you both do work together?"

"Zen, now you of all regents should not have to ask that question – it's called protocol. Just maybe you are going soft in our union."

Before Zen could answer, the Senior Matron breached between them.

"Legion Commander, I am glad you are still here as what I have to say concerns you both. Mio, you will recall that very old retired Matron I had visit you at this day's beginning, she is one of the very few in the Assembly who has been gifted with the ability, by way of her highly developed scan capabilities, to search your body internally."

Both Mio and Zen were taken aback by the revelation; Zen's mind quickly recalled the discussion with Senator Opek.

"None of us know everything."

"This Matron reports she has detected a rather large lump just back from your heart, and just under your rib frame."

The news temporarily stunned Zen and Mio to silence.

The Senior Matron was the first to speak as she looked over at Zen and Mio and saw the fear of the unknown that was welling up in them.

"I understand your fear, Mio. The old Matron cannot say what has caused this lump to appear, or what it consists of, but what she can say is that it may be possible to rid you of it."

For the time it took the Sun God to grace the sky twenty-six times,

Mio was subjected to the deep penetrating scans of the old Matron and three others whose names eluded Mio at this time. These scans gave Mio a feeling of intense, internal burning that at times bordered on the unbearable, and yet the unbearable Mio endured in total silence, and never once complained.

Her determination to preserve her dignity had become a hallmark of her suffering endurance and continued to be a main topic of conversation throughout the Great Assembly. Mio, being Mio, never once complained, her faith was cemented firmly in place.

Throughout all this time, Zen never left her side, and each and every pain she felt he felt also. Together, they fought this growth that grew by the day. As each day passed, the scans were intensified, causing more and more deep bruising – bruising that manifested itself in large areas of flesh dying and falling from Mio's body. Large weeping holes and deformities covered her once sleek body, yet Mio never complained, believing it was never ever a fait accompli.

Then, it was on the twenty-sixth day that the old Matron informed Mio there was nothing more that could be done. Her fate was now in the hands of the Gods.

On the twenty-seventh day, a large lump of dead flesh dislodged itself from Mio's side, and with this rejection of the dead flesh, so it was that Mio was cleansed of the growth.

And so it was that Mio's Gods smiled on their beloved one, and ever so slowly her wounds began to heal over. Deep open sores washed clean by the salt water healed; the once large holes of weeping flesh turned to scabs which in time turned to scars; and then, in the fullness of time, Mio's health was fully restored, much to the joy of all in the Great Assembly.

The Long Chapter

23

"Legion Commander Zen, Legion Commander Zen."

The incoming calls of the new Senate Runner interrupted Zen's enjoyment of the late day's warmth as he rode the long swells. The newly appointed young Senate Runner was all formality in her approach.

"Legion Commander Zen, I come bearing a message." Taking up a position three dikmar to the right of Zen, the new runner then awaited the pleasure of her superior.

"Approach, Senate Runner."

"So ordered, Legion Commander Zen."

The young runner moved in, acknowledging the Legion Commander, and took up a position parallel with and one dikmar to the right of the Legion Commander. As Zen looked across at the young runner, keen and full of vigour, it brought back memories of his own promotion to his first duties as a Senate Runner. Zen remembered it as if it was the last day just gone – he was together with his Lute – so young, and even way back then, in love.

"Legion Commander Zen, are you alright?"

"I am sorry. Yes, yes, I am fine. You say you have a message for me?"

Must not let my mind wander like that, Zen thought, again his mind recalling Lute.

"The new Senator requests your presence."

"And just what new Senator may that be, my young lady?"

"Senator Joli, Legion Commander Zen." Having delivered her

message, the young scout again awaited the pleasure of the Legion Commander.

"Thank you, Senate Runner, and by the way, I failed to catch your name."

Zen watched as the young Senate Runner fidgeted, now realising that she had failed to properly identify herself to the Legion Commander when she had sent in her first call.

"Senate Runner Ruby, Legion Commander Zen."

"Senate Runner Ruby, tell me is it a mere coincidence that you have been attached to the new Lady Senator Joli, or did she request that you join her staff?"

"I am not sure, Legion Commander Zen. All I did was indicate my desire that if it was seen fit by my trainers and teachers, I would like to start any ladder of promotion in the area of the Senate."

"Thank you, Senate Runner Ruby. You may now take your leave, and please inform the Lady Senator that I am on my way."

"Thank you, Legion Commander Zen. As ordered, as so I must obey."

Just as the runner turned to move away, Zen had second thoughts.

"Before you leave, Senate Runner Ruby, please come in close next to me. That's better."

With a little hesitation, the new runner broached next to the Legion Commander.

"In the future, if you are to approach me, be it for whatever reason, come into about where you are currently now on my call, and most importantly, relax. I can assure you I do not bite, and as you are new to the tasks of being a Senate Runner, so once was I. That is the way of a new Senate Runner, and if the truth be known, I was probably more nervous than you are right now." Zen felt a relaxation in the young runner.

"One other thing, Legion Commander is all that is needed when addressing me. Now, you had better be heading back, as it is never a good idea to keep Senators waiting – even Lady Senators like that one of yours."

"Thank you, Legion Commander Zen, I mean Legion Commander. Thank you very much."

Zen watch as the young, vibrant runner skipped over the oceans, heading back to the Senate

"Zen, Zen!"

The incoming call from Mio lifted Zen's spirits.

"Now, my dear Mio, what brings you out this side of the Assembly?"

"I was relieved of my nursery duties early, and so I thought maybe we could spend a little time together alone. And, I must add, it is far too long since we have spent time alone."

"As much as your invitation is most welcome, and you know there is nothing else I would rather do then spend time with you Mio, I am afraid that Lady Senator Joli has requested a semi-urgent call together with me." Zen felt the disappointment rising in Mio. "I'll tell you what I will do, Mio. If I can get the Senator to put off this call together, I will collect you, and the rest of the day will be ours. Now, come on! Put that sad face away, and accompany me back as far as the Senate."

"Thank you for your quick response, Legion Commander."

"My pleasure, Senator Joli. Now, to what do I owe the pleasure of your company?"

Zen felt the new Lady Senator's warmth as he broached next to her. He did not know a lot about the Senator. She had been elected on the second vote. He did know she had risen to prominence very quickly; first from the school of teachers, then to the last King's group of personal helpers, and then the large leap into the Senate.

"The pleasure is mine, Legion Commander. And I must apologise for dragging you away from Mio. It was Mio I saw you approach with, wasn't it?"

Had Zen not felt her warmth and seen the cheeky twinkle in her eyes, he may have taken offence at the Senator's throw-away remark.

"Yes Senator, it was Mio. And if I get through here in enough time, Mio and I are going to spend what's left of the day together."

"Again, I apologise. But as you are fully aware, Senate business never ends, and always takes priority. All that aside, let us get down to the reasons I have asked you here. This may or may not come as a surprise to you, but it has been agreed by unanimous decision of the Senate that immediate preparations be undertaken for the Great Assembly to move on from here."

"Well, Senator, my father did raise the subject with me some time ago, just before Mio become unwell. But I had no idea that it had gone beyond our brief discussion of the matter."

"Well, yes, it has gone beyond just discussions. With the full blessing of the King, a long-range patrol was sent out under the command of Scout Commander Idyll to start assessing the best route. All this was done while you were preoccupied with concern for Mio, so do not feel you were kept in the dark, Legion Commander. It was on the direct orders of the King that the planning was to be kept from you."

The two Regents broke through the ocean surface in unison and deep thought.

"What was entailed in the reports these scouts submitted, Senator? Anything out of the ordinary?"

"No, no. There was really nothing of substance out of the ordinary."

"You don't sound too convincing, Senator. Was there any doubt of the validity of the Scout Commander's report?"

The only thing, if it was a thing that the Scout Commander commented on, was that he, along with most of the others on the patrol, felt like they were being constantly shadowed."

"Shadowed, Senator? Did you say shadowed? Did the Scout Commander elaborate further on this shadowing?"

"What the Scout Commander said Legion Commander was, and I quote – it felt like we were always being watched, and there was always a cold uneasy feeling attached to this being watched – unquote."

"Senator, I know Scout Commander Idyll extremely well. In fact, he is without a doubt, one of the Assembly's finest Scout Commanders, and he is destined for honours much higher than just Scout Commander. We must always keep what he reported to the fore, for we have been, ever since we left the safety of The Shallows, in uncharted and unknown oceans."

The Senator felt a cold chill run up her spine; what the Legion Commander said made a lot of sense, for they were indeed in the realm of the unknown.

The two Regents let silence momentarily have its say, while they both rode the warm ocean swells.

An incoming scan from old Zuke interrupted the silence of their thoughts.

"Approach, Senate Runner."

"Greetings, and thank you, Senator Joli. And greetings to you also, Legion Commander. I come with a message from the King."

"From the King? And why do you carry such a large smile, Zuke? What secrets do you hide that cast a glow of pride in you?"

Senator Joli thought the interruption of Zuke's call by the Legion Commander a little, but not totally, unbecoming.

"The King, and a wiser King I have never met, has decided in his wisdom to relieve me of all my Senate duties, and to promote me to the position of sole King's Runner."

"Well, let me to be the first to congratulate you, Zuke. At long last your contributions to the Senate have been recognised."

"Thank you Zen, my friend. Coming from you, your good wishes are more than high praise. Now, before I forget, and it would not be very good for me to forget, the first message of the King… I remember once I wa..."

"The King's Message, Zuke, the message."

"Sorry for my dithering, Legion Commander. The King orders that you and Senator Joli present yourselves before him; this to be done by day's end."

"Thank you, King's Runner Zuke. Please inform my father we are on our way."

The smile of pride was so bright in the old sea dog that it seemed to light up the ocean.

"Well, Legion Commander, I think it best we not keep the King waiting."

"Let us just take it very slowly, Senator, for we would not want to steal old Zuke's thunder by reaching the King ahead of him."

"A very good idea, Legion Commander. And as we make our way there, you can tell me a little of this old man of the oceans, Zuke.

The trip back to meet the King took a little longer than expected, but it was just as well. Old Zuke scarcely made it ahead of them, with only time enough to report to the King before attending to the incoming announcement calls from Senator Joli and the Legion Commander.

"Escort my visitors in please, Zuke."

"As my King has ordered, as so I will obey."

"Welcome Senator Joli, and welcome also to you my son. Sorry, I just cannot get out of the habit – I should be addressing you as Legion Commander Zen, seeing as this is a formal call together."

"Thank you, my King." The call was in unison from the two Regents as they approached him.

The King waited until the two visitors broached alongside him before continuing.

"Senator Joli, now that the Senate has had time to further discuss the plans to resume our journey, what has been decided to bring this to a realization?"

"My King, all the planning is now complete and only awaits your final review and approval. Firstly, but before I go into detail, I must remind the King that these plans have not yet been conveyed to the Legion Commander here."

"I think he understands why." The King turned to his son for confirmation, and Zen nodded back his agreement.

"Please continue, Senator Joli."

"Thank you, my King. It has been thought that the best way forward

256

this time would be that we divide the Assembly into only two groups rather than into a multitude of smaller groups as we did when we first left The Shallows... "

The Senator waited for any reaction, and with none forthcoming, she continued: "These two groups shall be divided as such: the first to comprise of the King and his staff, with the addition of a sprinkling of Senators, along with an assortment of Scouts and Guards to protect them if required."

Again the Senator waited for a response, and again, with none forthcoming, she proceeded.

"The remaining Assembly members shall make up the second group under the leadership of Legion Commander Zen."

For the first time in his life, Zen was speechless.

Senator Joli waited for any comments. The first to speak was the King.

"Senator, I am still at a loss as to why the Senate has decided to divide the Assembly into two groups. Why not three or four groups? In truth, I am not yet fully convinced as to why we should not set out as one group. Legion Commander, what are your views?"

Zen was still coming to terms with being named by the Senate to lead a large part of the Assembly, and failed to hear his father's call.

"Zen, what do you think? Zen! Zen, are you still with us?"

"Sorry, Father. What did you ask?"

"What are your views on the Senate's plan?"

"I can understand the reasoning for the division of the Assembly – it is purely a safety thing. By dividing, the leader insures that in the case of misfortune not all are lost. We only have to remember back to the Bay of Death – one can only imagine the devastation to the

Assembly had all members been in the Bay at the same time."

The King and Senator Joli could only nod in agreement.

"So, I agree in principle with the Senate's plans, but without knowing more of the final details, I really cannot offer much in the way of advice. Maybe the Senator has further to add?"

"Well Senator, as the Legion Commander has asked, have you anything further to add?"

"Yes I have my King, and with your permission I will go on."

"That you have, Senator."

"It is planned that the second group, under the leadership of Legion Commander Zen, will depart first, still following the original course set when we left The Shallows – to follow the Sun. They will follow the track set by Scout Commander Idyll to a calm bay that the scouting party have fully investigated, and found to lack in nothing. This bay should be reached, even by the aged and the very young, within the time it takes the God Sun to cross the Heavens eleven times. Once all have reached the new bay, the Legion Commander shall dispatch scouts, who will then return to collect and escort those remaining here, including you our King, to rejoin the Assembly."

"Legion Commander, have you any comment on what you have heard from the Senator?"

"Yes my King. Senator Joli, the only question I have at this time is, has the division of Senators, Guards, and Scout Commanders been decided yet?"

"Yes, Legion Commander, all duties have been allocated, and again all that is required now is the final approval of the King. The King's group will include myself and Senator Ramcy. Guard Commander

Mio has asked to be returned to Senate duties, and as her request has been approved, so she will head the guards and scouts that remain."

"The Senior Matron from the infirmary, the very same one that supervised Guard Commander Mio's recovery, along with the King's personal runner Zuke, and the remainder of the staff attached to those I have just named will make up the group."

"Well Senator Joli, Legion Commander, it seems all is in order. And I, for one, cannot see any reason why I should delay giving this plan my seal of approval. That is unless you, Legion Commander, can see cause why my approval should be withheld. Well, Legion Commander, can you think of any reason?"

"No, my King. It seems that the Senator has done her job well."

"Finally, Senator Joli, when is it planned that the first group leave for this new bay?"

"My King, as soon as possible."

—— Ψ ——

High on the cliff face, the God Hades and his Beast watched as the Great Assembly slowly moved across the ocean. Turning to his serpents that had slithered out from the cave, Hades gathered them up then flung them out over the cliff edge, ordering them again to follow these, the Regents of the Deep

With all the farewells completed, the majority of the Great Assembly had now resumed the search for that place the God Poseidon had promised to them. The young raced ahead, and the aged and infirm lagged behind; the chatty ones still chattered; and the food scouts, as per normal, went about their tasks of seeking out food sources.

259

"My King, Senator Joli seeks an audience with you."

"Thanks, Zuke. Did she say what the nature of her request was?"

"No, my King. She is very relaxed, so I would imagine that it is nothing of great importance."

"Thank you, Zuke. Please tell her I will see her now."

"As my King has ordered, as so I will obey."

"Senator Joli, it is good to see you again. To what do I owe this privilege?"

"My King, on the recommendation of Guard Commander Mio, Senator Ramcy, and myself, we think it would be in the best interest of all for you and your few staff to keep within the boundaries of the remaining group."

"Is there a threat of danger to me, Senator Joli?"

"Not at this time, nor in the foreseeable future. There is nothing that can be conceived of in any way as threatening to you, my King. The recommendations are more in line with general housekeeping."

"I thank you for your concern, Senator. And yes, I think I will take up the recommendation of the Guard Commander. Maybe it would be best if we did move in and combine more closely with the remaining group. Being a King with a greatly reduced entourage, it all really gets a little lonely without the daily duties of a full Assembly to attend to. So, my Senator, yes, I will join you all. Firstly, I will have my runner Zuke call in those few staff still left with me, and we all shall join you by day's end."

"Thank you, my King. I will inform the others of your decision."

"Thank you, Senator Joli. You are now excused."

Day drew back the veil of darkness, exposing a crystal clear blue heaven. The Beast from the Sea, at the behest of the god Hades, went out among the robed population and demanded that at this day's end they all kneel before Hades.

So it was, as the day ended, the god Hades looked out over a crowd of five thousand who had gathered and now knelt before him. He heaped praise upon them, and then let them go ahead and do whatever shameful things their hearts desired.

As a result, they did vile and degrading things with each other's bodies. Instead of believing what they did was wrong, they deliberately chose to place their faith in the god Hades, and believe his lies. Thus they worshipped the laws this god had himself laid down, and the robed ones praised him forever.

Even the women turned against the natural ways of sex, and indulged with their own kind in bold fornication. And the men burned with lust for each other, doing shameful things with other men, thus they were endeared to the god Hades.

"Scout Commander Mio."

The incoming call from Senator Jodi's runner, Ruby, brought Mio out of her sun-warmth-induced nap.

"Yes, Ruby, you can approach."

"My Senator and Senator Ramcy are shortly to hold a call together, and they have requested that you be present at that time."

"Thank you, Ruby. Have the Senators given any indication as to the substance of this call together?"

"No, Guard Commander. At this time, I have not the slightest indication of the reasons for the call together."

"Thank you, Ruby. Report back, and tell the Senators I am on my way."

Mio watched as the young Senate Runner disappeared, a little peeved that her enjoyable nap had been interrupted. Then, with a stretch and a few deep breaths, she managed to shake off the last remnants of the influence of Morpheus, the God of dreams, and returned to the group.

"My god, Hades."

Hades turned to face the Beast from the Sea. Even after all this time, the sight of the hideous one he had resurrected from the abyss still revolted him.

"What is it, Beast? What happening causes you to dare venture into my lair?"

"The multitudes that you commanded to be here have grown restless, for they are without food, and now wish to return to their homes."

"Tell these heathens that their god, Hades, will provide. Have them all assemble on the beaches and prepare bonfires, and at night's darkest, I will appear before them, and they then shall feast."

"Senators," Mio scanned in as she approached the two Senators.

"Guard Commander Mio, it is always a great pleasure to have you in our company. You keep well, we hope. Not missing Zen too much?"

Of course, I am missing my Zen, she felt like shouting at them, but training and strict protocol kept any thoughts in this vein well and truly in abeyance. Mio nodded to both the Senators, and then to the others who had been requested to attend. Even after her short dash in to the call together with the Senators, the drowsy effects of her nap still clung to the edges of her senses.

All the Regents surfed the swell for some time before any of them spoke. Then, it was Senator Joli who first broke the peaceful silence.

"The main group of the Assembly will by this time, or it would be better if I said should by this time, have reached their destination. So, it is expected that returning scouts will have left, or shortly will leave to escort the rest of us to them."

The Senator waited for comment. With only nods of agreement, she continued.

"The King has agreed with the suggestion of Senator Ramcy that as it is expected our stay here will end shortly, we should spend what is left of our remaining time with a little relaxation and enjoyment. Senator Ramcy, I sense you have something to add here."

"No, Senator Jodi. You are covering the subject most admirably."

"The King has recommended that instead of the scouts bringing in the food to us, just maybe we all go to the food – meaning a hunt. If we all agree, this could take place at day's end."

As day drew to a close, the two serpents appeared before the God Hades, and they spoke of the progress of the Assembly – and of the plans of the second group of Regents that still enjoyed the pleasures of the warm waters out from the cliffs.

"Thank you, Serpents. Now go and bring the Beast to me."

Whilst the serpents carried out his orders, Hades sought to wreak his revenge on those who failed to bow before him, thinking how best he could bring great damnation as his justice upon those who had dared to oppose him.

"You summoned our appearance before you, Mighty Hades?"

Hades looked at the three: the Beast from the Sea and the two two-headed serpents – his totally obedient and totally subservient servants – as he formalised plans not only to wreak total havoc on the ungrateful robed ones, but to use the opportunity to rid himself of the Beast from the Sea that had grown overly strong in mind and body.

"Yes, I sent for you. I want you to tell the robed ones that we will no longer require them to bring their livestock to the beach for slaughter."

"What is it then that you will feed these hungry people?"

In fury, the god Hades rose up and attacked the Beast from the Sea for no other reason than that he had dared to question his word. The god Hades attacked with a ferocity that shook the ground, and his lungs filled the air with blood-chilling screams. The Beast from the Sea fought back, for he had grown stronger and no longer feared Hades, but the Beast from the Sea was defeated, and then cowered down and was punished at great length by Hades.

"Is the King ready, Runner Zuke?"

Old Zuke had to really trawl deep in his memory to recall the last time he had actually taken part in a hunt. It was way back when he was a young food scout himself, and that was far too long ago to even try to recall.

"Zuke, Runner Zuke, are you with me, Zuke?"

"Yes, I am with you, Senator Ramcy, and yes, the King is ready. I will go and inform him that you all await his pleasure."

"Thank you, Zuke."

"That's alright, Senator. Always in a hurry; never the time for civil conversation; rush, rush. What is always the hurry? The waters are warm; always in a hurry."

The Senators could only smile as they listened to the rambling rants of the old runner as he wandered off to report to the King.

It was with total consensus that Mio was elected to lead the Regents on what was expected to be their last night. Two scouts had scanned in that they were herding a large school of fish towards them. Mio scanned out her plan of attack to all, and all acknowledged her call. The next scan was from the two scouts.

They were all heading down from below the cliffs, and so directly into Mio's cunning plan to trap them. Even old Zuke had found a new vigour creep into his tired old body, managing to keep up, and fully prepared to enter the fray when signalled.

Hades raised his arms to silence the five thousand, who then fell to the ground and prostrated themselves before him. After a brief moment, Hades called them to rise up and hear his message.

"Tonight, I promised to bring nourishment to you all, and as promised, so this will be done. My serpents have prepared that which needed preparing, to insure that these promises I have made are not false promises but promises that will shortly come to fruition. I will now let my serpents carry out these tasks of gathering in the food."

All eyes turned to the serpents, as they watched and waited.

Then Hades called out to his serpents, "Now!" and the trap was sprung.

—— Ψ ——

Then Guard Commander Mio scanned out to the Regents, "Now!" and the trap was sprung.

Suddenly, from the seabed rose up large nets that the evil serpents had cleverly hidden, well camouflaged in the abundance of swaying plants that flourished in the warm waters. Without warning, all the Regents found themselves being dragged with great haste towards the shore.

Hand over hand, as fast as they could, the robed ones dragged the nets in, and with each pull of the ropes they did sing the praises of Hades for this their good fortune. The screaming savages, on the urgings of Hades, stripped naked and rushed into the water. Drawing their ambiya daggers, they then inflicted indescribable indignities on the now helpless Regents of the Deep.

The first Regent to feel this barbaric wrath was old Zuke, who died trying to protect his King. Then, as quickly as snow disappears on the burning desert sands, so it was at that speed that the Regents of the Deep did have their lives brutally extinguished. It was by the deeds

266

of Hades that the only Regent left alive was the King, and his life was placed in the hands of the Beast from the Sea.

The Beast from the Sea looked down at the King, as he was washed over by the spilt blood of his beloved followers. A brief flicker of recognition showed in The Beast from the Sea's eyes, as he raised the shebriya dagger high in the air, and then without warning or sound, plunged it deep into the head of Ira the Magnificent One, King of all Dolphins. And he lived no more.

And again, man's hands were polluted and stained by the blood of the Regents of the Deep

The God Poseidon was devastated at the second tragedy that had befallen these members of his so beloved Regents of the Deep. He was inconsolable, and so it fell to the Great God of all Gods, Zeus, to bring justice, and to rain down upon those beings the vengeance of all Gods.

Those robed ones, who now had taken to wearing strips of cloth wrapped around and around their heads as a tribute to the evil one, Hades, had been called up from the fires of hell and had helped to execute his plan.

As they feasted and rejoiced in the aftermath of their deeds, Hades ordained the continuance of whatever shameful things their hearts desired.

Zeus then called for the God Mercury to go and find Cerberus, the Dog of the Underworld, and bring him forth. This done, he then

ordered Mercury to go forth and find all of the Keres Sisters, and present them also before him.

Once these tasks were complete, Mercury was sent high in the Heavens to observe the deeds that the God Zeus planned. Mercury was further instructed that once these deeds were completed, he would speedily tell all throughout the Heavens of what he had witnessed.

Then it was that Cerberus, who was now multiplied, was sent down to Mother Earth to round up all the robed ones so they could face their day of judgement; and so it was that these dogs of the underworld, with their eyes of fire and jaws dripping with poisonous salver, did go forth and complete these tasks at the behest of Zeus.

Next, Zeus called before him the Keres Sisters. These were the female spirits of violent and cruel deaths, including deaths in battle, by accident, murder, or ravaging disease.

These Keres were cravers of blood, and feasted upon it after ripping a soul free from its mortally wounded body and sending it on its way to the fires of hell. Thousands of Keres haunted all battlefields fighting amongst themselves like vultures over the dying. The Keres had no power over the lives of men, but in their hunger for blood they would seek and accomplish death beyond the bounds of fate. Zeus and the other Gods, however, had the power to stop them in their course, or speed them on.

Once the Dogs of the Underworld had completed their tasks, the Keres Sisters were called forth to vent the anger of the Gods; and so, they rejoiced and bathed in the blood that poured from the dead and dying robed ones.

When Hades did see the wrath of Zeus, he and his evil henchmen tried to hide from this enraged God, but they were sought out, and were found hiding in the caves that looked over the place of the Regents' death. Then, when trapped like wild animals in a lair, Hades and the Beast fought back. But again, they all were defeated. Zeus then cast them along with the two double-headed serpents into the eternal fires of the condemned, and in so doing, he did strip the name of Hades from the beaten God, and did decree that never again would that name, Hades, be spoken of in the great heavens. Zeus then further proclaimed that those – the defeated ones now thrown into the fires of hell – from this day forward would only be permitted to walk upon Mother Earth while the God Sun slept.

Then, the God Mercury did tell all of what the Great God Zeus had accomplished, and as all the deeds of retribution were completed, all Gods and Spirits returned to the Heavens.

269

The Call

24

egion Commander Zen moved over the slowly rolling oceans in solitude, slowly turning back through the misty pages of his memory, searching for answers and guidance from Kings passed and from the memories of what had been reported by the returning scouts who had arrived at the cliff face in time to witness the brutal slaughter of the remaining Regents.

The vivid reminders of his father and what he stood for, Zen saw reflected everywhere. His love of the Assembly, his love of the long swells, and his brutal killing that Zen was still struggling to come to terms with.

He again saw a young Lute, with her ever-ready, audacious smile, flaunting her flashing eyes and streamlined body in flirtatious passes, dodging as she did so well, in and out of the reefs. She was that beautiful youngster again – the carefree and unfettered ruler of that playground, The Shallows, they had all once shared, now a long time lost.

He again saw the place where the warm waters brought forth the brightly painted corals, decorated and beautified by the brilliantly coloured fish. He was again swimming free on his first command – and then he remembered clearly that sad day he had gone forth into the Bay of Death.

He brought back memories of moonlight reflecting off the white skin of all the dead Assembly members – and how they still seemed to be alive as they rolled backwards and forwards in the ever-moving waters.

His memory was then flooded with the great sorrow of finding Lute

– and how this was somewhat eased by the caring and support of those members of his scouts who had helped in his time of great distress as he placed his cherished Lute in her final resting-place.

Then, again he recalled when he and Lute were as one in that place of magnificent beauty and grace – a special place they had called their own. It was while in this place that they had planned their future together during their days of unification. Those long-gone times he would forever hold in reverence, buried in the most sanctified hall of memories deep within him for all his time yet to come.

Zen again felt the affectionate quivers from Lute that communicated her warm feeling towards him, as she swam gracefully back into his past.

From the bosom of his memory they cascaded: Teacher Tai, who proved that being blind from birth was no hindrance to living a full and rewarding life.

Then there were the memories of Hur – never on time, always more important things to do. And be those things right or wrong, Zen at this time felt not to hold in judgement.

Hur's mother, Dy – always ready to fiercely protect her son regardless of the cost to the others around her.

But again it was Lute who kept drifting back into his mind, carefully nursing along baby Cyan, both now free of the appalling pain and suffering inflicted upon them by the cruel hands of the Jomonese barbarians.

Haunting memories of Cyan, viciously ripped from life at such an age of innocence... the enjoyable times they had shared together as he taught her to dive and twist around the reefs, to chase the fish as they were herded towards them... and the flashing eyes she had inherited from her mother. As Cyan slowly faded back into his past, his tears again mixed with the cold waters of the oceans.

He thought tenderly of Mio, who had come to him in his hour of need to comfort him, to help to take away the pain of his lost family. Mio, who had reminded him that life had to go on, had offered him wise council and unselfish love. His dear, dear Mio, who offered all and asked for little, had comforted him in the great pain that forever ripped at his heart over the loss of his cherished daughter, Cyan.

The loving, wise words once offered up to him by Mio floated to the fore of his hall of memories.

"Don't live a life of regret, only look back in fondness. The Assembly, like life, must always go on. The new world still awaits us all, out there somewhere."

The recollections of the Time Weaver and his nymph – the old man with the snow-white hair and beard, and the nymph's not so trusty steed now drifted into his memories.

The things he had seen in his dreams while held in the cave of the Time Weaver, at the time had felt so real. Now, his memories let him again, momentarily, feel the scorching heat... all things were now better understood.

After a time, Zen mentally closed his book of memories and recollections and prepared to move on.

As had been written and cast to the Heavens by the Great God Poseidon, the path Zen chose was a path embraced and extolled by all in the Great Assembly. For their time had come to continue the search for what the God Poseidon had spoken of and had promised to them, his gentle and greatly loved Regents of the Deep.

—— Ψ ——

And so it came to pass that on the thirty-sixth day of the fifteenth pass since leaving The Shallows, the Assembly waited for the new King to order the departure from this, their temporary home in the cold, wind-chilled bay.

"Legion Commander Idyll, is all ready to depart?"

"It is, my King."

"So, let us now depart this place, Legion Commander. Let us resume our quest."

"As so you, Zen, The Magnificent One, King of all Dolphins, have ordered, as so I must obey."

"For as it had been written in the thirteen houses of the zodiac of the heavens, a new flame shall flicker to life from cold embers past."

And so it was, the third of the Great God Poseidon's heavenly writings had come to pass.

—— Ψ ——

To be continued.....

The Writings of Poseidon

1st "For as it had been written in the thirteen houses of the zodiac of the heavens, the yellow-gold waters of satisfaction turned red in hostility and brought the great tears of rain that turned into fires of remorse."

2nd "For as it had been written in the thirteen houses of the zodiac of the heavens, the fires of torment did sear time; so the elevating of two to the mantle of one had surely begun."

3rd "For as it had been written in the thirteen houses of the zodiac of the heavens, a new flame shall flicker to life from the cold embers past."

4th Not yet fully deciphered and totally understood.

5th Not yet fully deciphered and totally understood.

6th Not yet fully deciphered and totally understood.

7th Not yet fully deciphered and totally understood.

8th Not yet fully deciphered and totally understood.

9th Not yet fully deciphered and totally understood.

10th Not yet fully deciphered and totally understood.

11th Not yet fully deciphered and totally understood.

12th Not yet fully deciphered and totally understood.

13th "For as it had been written in the thirteenth and hidden house of the zodiac of the heavens, so the beginning of the new shall become the end; and so it follows, the end becomes the beginning."

Glossary

Lock   Measurement of a scan, equivalent to one degree

Pass   500 days

Lukmar   1 Metre

Dikmar   10 Metres

Sigmar   100 Metres

Asmar   1000 Metres

Book available as a Kindle book on Amazon

Visit the **Regents of the Deep** website to watch for
announcement of Book Two.

www.regentsofthedeep.com